No other kisses but his . . .

At Ellen's door Michael lifted her chin, and looked at her for a long moment. Then he leaned over and touched her lips with his. In that moment, she realized that no other kisses but his could ever mean anything to her. Something almost like electricity tingled in her lips and down her entire body. She couldn't breathe but she didn't want to. She only wanted to hold him tight and keep that trembling excitement coursing through her forever. But almost at once, he had pulled away and was smiling down at her. "Merry Christmas, Ellen, and I hope the rest of your freshman year is great."

Other Point paperbacks you will enjoy:

The Last Great Summer
by Carol Stanley

Acts of Love
by Maureen Daly

First a Dream
by Maureen Daly

The Party's Over
by Caroline B. Cooney

point

WINTER DREAMS, CHRISTMAS LOVE

Mary Francis Shura

SCHOLASTIC INC.
New York Toronto London Auckland Sydney

ISBN 0-590-44672-X

12 11 10 9 8 7 6 5 4 3 2 1 2 3 4 5 6 7/9

Printed in the U.S.A. 01

First Scholastic printing, October 1992

Winter Dreams, Christmas Love

Chapter 1

On her fourteenth birthday Ellen Marlowe got a dark blue cashmere sweater that matched her eyes, the newest album by her favorite group, a book on fashion design, and a strange wistful longing that made her want to cry.

Everything but the longing had come wrapped in bright paper and tied with ribbons. The yearning just came out of nowhere to settle in on her like the summer twilights that grew steadily deeper when she went out to run or bike alone because her friends were off at camp or vacationing.

Maybe it was natural to have strange feelings when you were taking a big step like starting high school. Ellen's friend Cricket Jacobson said right out that she was scared because it was going to be so different. Ellen knew it would be different, too. Come on, she had never been fourteen before and the difference between thirteen and fourteen was a lot more than one birthday candle.

But it wasn't the kind of change you could see. The night of her birthday she tried on her new sweater in her room. The girl in the mirror looked the same, tall with a huge mop of shoulder-length honey blonde curls that would fall over in her face whatever she did with them. Although her eyes were the color of the sweater, they seemed darker, shaded by her black lashes. She didn't look much different to herself than she had at twelve or thirteen.

Was she ready to go to school with thousands of high school kids instead of just the hundreds she'd known in junior high? Pep rallies would be bigger and football games important. Schoolwork would be harder and good grades tougher to make. Those things didn't scare her. She only had to hit the books harder. She did wonder where to squeeze in her running practice. That hour a day was the only way she'd ever manage to run a marathon.

But what bothered her the most was the social part. High school meant parties and dances, with her friends falling in love, holding hands with their boyfriends in the hall, and having their very own songs. She'd never felt that way about any boy. What if she just kept on being best friends with guys, the way she had always been with Luke Ingram? What if she never met anyone she could really truly love? But surely she'd feel better when her friends got back so she had someone to talk to.

In late August they came, Cricket from visiting her father in Wyoming, Luke from his grandparents' home in Florida, and Maggie Martin from skating camp and a holiday in Door County.

Chicago was always hot in the summer, Ellen's

suburban village was even hotter. She hated starting school in August when it was over ninety degrees. School shouldn't start until fall! But that letter from the principal about book buying day was too clear to ignore. STUDENTS MUST REPORT AT TIME INDICATED.

That Tuesday, Ellen and Cricket reported to the cafeteria at ten-thirty. The next hour and a half lasted forever. They stood in line only to go stand in another line. She was dying of thirst when she and Cricket finally staggered back out to their bikes, loaded with books and schedules, activity cards and combination locks, and some mysterious packet she couldn't even identify.

Cricket looked curiously at Ellen's stuff. "What's that envelope there on the top of your schedule?"

Ellen shrugged. "Don't you have one?"

Cricket grinned, showing her braces. "Wow! I bet you got a mash note from the principal already."

"Oh, sure," Ellen said, dumping her books to open the envelope. "What's this?" she wailed. "I have to report to the office on Friday, for something they call an orientation tour."

"That's crazy. We did that last winter," Cricket said, peering over her shoulder. "In February, don't you remember? They hauled us to Jefferson in a bus. Then some upper-class monitor who had made it into the honor society showed you the whole place room by room. Mine tried to scare me to death by reciting the rules and what would happen if I broke them."

Ellen groaned. "February! No wonder I don't remember. That's when I missed a lot of school with the flu. But I don't need any guided tour of Jefferson. I've been here a million times with my brother, Brad. I'll just tell them I know where everything is and don't want to miss classes the very first week!"

"How much can you miss on the third day of school?" Cricket asked. "Anyway, you'll be excused. An hour's walk around the building with a snooty upperclassman can't ruin your life."

Ellen almost forgot about the orientation tour during those first few days of school. Except for getting lost once and having trouble working her combination lock, Wednesday wasn't bad at all. Thursday went even better. By Friday, Ellen knew she could deal with Jefferson High. She might even learn to like it.

For one thing, the heat wave had passed over so she could run in the early morning without drowning in sweat. Even better, she had friends in all her classes. Cricket was in three of them, Maggie in two, Barb Sanchez in one, and Luke Ingram had almost her exact same schedule in honors classes.

Best of all, after Friday and that silly orientation, she had three whole fun days off for Labor Day. She and Cricket and Maggie Martin would go shopping on Saturday. On Monday, Luke Ingram was giving a cookout and swimming party.

She actually felt lighthearted going into the auditorium at second period. About twenty other kids were scattered around the back of the huge room, looking around nervously.

At fifty-five minutes after eight, the principal came in. In a deep resonant voice that throbbed with self-importance, he talked about the splendid opportunities that Jefferson High offered them. He challenged them to make the most of this bounty, and explained the purpose of the orientation. Then, as if realizing that he was burning up the tour time, he had them stand as he called their names.

Ellen was barely on her feet before she heard her name spoken behind her. Something went thump in her stomach. This voice was deep and firm and most certainly masculine. Why had she presumed that her tour monitor would be a girl?

When she turned, all she saw at first was his smile. It looked mischievous, but genuine, too. But his smile didn't stop with his mouth. His dark eyes danced with amusement as he spoke again. "I didn't startle you, did I?"

He had startled her all right and shattered her self-confidence at the same time. Something about the way he looked at her made her feel about ten years old. She flushed with annoyance. What kind of an upper-class guy would get a kick out of sneaking up and scaring a new freshman half to death?

Then he held his hand out to her as if he were running for mayor or something. But she couldn't ignore it without being rude.

Her books slid as she tried to switch them to her other arm. Flushing with embarrassment, she struggled to hang onto them.

He straightened the books in her arms as he said, "I'm sorry. I had an unfair advantage on you. I'm Michael Tyler. You are Brad Marlowe's little sister, aren't you?"

Since she hated being embarrassed, she just looked at him. Being born before her didn't give him any right to patronize her. Brad's "little sister," for crying out loud. At her silent nod, he stepped into the aisle. "Come on," he said. "Let's get our little show on the road before we get caught in the crush."

Ellen had been the tallest girl in her class ever since fourth grade. Still she felt short standing beside Michael. He was even taller than Brad, who called her Big Runt as opposed to their ten-year-old sister, Robin, whom he called Little Runt.

"I've got a great idea," he said when they reached the hall. "You wait here. I'll dump your stuff in the office so we don't have to fool with it. We only need the school map anyway."

She watched him cross the hall with a storm of conflicting emotions. He might be bossy and a little insulting, but he was still the best-looking guy she'd ever seen. Ever. But just being her monitor didn't give him a license to play Bigshot Upperclassman lording it over Brad Marlowe's "little sister."

He wasn't going to get away with it. She'd see to that.

Chapter 2

Even as Ellen simmered resentfully watching Michael cross the hall, she knew she was halfway angry at herself. Why had she let him make her feel so inadequate in just those few minutes? She hadn't felt that helpless since kindergarten. She hated it. What's more, she hated him for making her feel that way. Yet he was appealing. She liked his voice, his quick warm smile, and the way he handled his body smoothly like an athlete.

Maybe she was scared because he *was* so attractive. Maybe he really was a level guy in spite of his charm. His smile had seemed sincere. She shivered, vaguely afraid without knowing why. As Cricket had said, an hour could hardly ruin her life.

Michael Tyler wasn't scary to anyone else. In fact, everyone moving along to class seemed to know and like him. Boys slapped his shoulder and the girls smiled as he crossed the hall to her.

He made it to her side as the warning bell sounded and the hall began to clear. "Now, that's better, isn't it?" he asked.

When she only nodded again, he frowned. "Okay," he said. "I have a problem. Even though Brad was a year ahead of me, we got to know each other. Brad bragged about your brains. I know you're a bike racer and runner because I read the sports page. How about words? Like, do you ever *speak*?"

She laughed without meaning to. That was fair. She hadn't said a word. But then again, he hadn't given her any chances.

"A laugh is at least a start," he said with an air of triumph. "Nonverbal communication at its best."

There he went again, being irritating and superior.

"I can talk," she said, not caring that she sounded cold and aloof. "I don't think it's strange to be struck dumb when somebody takes over like you did. And you *did* startle me."

He blinked. "That sounds like I owe you an apology," he said. "I apologize." He studied her in a way that made her painfully self-conscious. She had to struggle not to turn away. Was he seeing the Ellen she saw when she looked in her mirror, or was he only seeing Brad Marlowe's kid sister as a tall blonde girl who had told him off practically as soon as they had met?

"I'll try not to let it happen again," he said with a mocking humility. There he went, making fun of her again. He unfolded a school map, then frowned at her. "You must know this place pretty well already from coming here with Brad before he graduated."

"I do," she nodded. "I think this drill is a waste of time."

"My time or yours?" he asked, still looking at her. Before she could reply, a sudden smile tugged at the corner of his mouth. He deepened his voice to that self-important tone the principal had used. "I assure you, Ms. Marlowe, it's not a waste of my time. I choose to view this orientation tour as a glorious opportunity that I can waste only at my future peril."

When she laughed right out, he did, too. Then he turned very businesslike. He poked the map with one finger. "You are here."

"Just like a shopping mall," she said quietly.

He glanced up and chuckled. "All right, Ellen Marlowe. I can see this isn't going to be your generic-terrified-freshman guided tour. Let's ditch the routine. If we start at the top floor and work down, we could have some extra time before next period."

The third period started at nine fifty-five. Between the principal's speech and their little argument, a lot of time was already gone. Michael seemed conscious of this. He talked for the next fifteen or twenty minutes in a rapid patter. He walked quickly, pointing out academic classrooms, art department, music practice rooms, the computer center, gymnasium, basketball and wrestling courts, the science rooms and their labs, swimming pool, library, and administrative and counseling offices.

When he showed no sign of catching his breath, Ellen finally broke in. "What about drama and theater?" she asked.

He frowned and shook his head. "How did you hit on the only thing I know nothing about? There's a drama course that's an English elective, but it's only for sophomores and above."

"I've been to a lot of plays here with Brad," Ellen protested. "Isn't there a drama club, or something like that?"

"You've got me," he admitted. "I do know there's something called the drama group but I don't think it's a club. They do about five plays a year, one that tours other schools in the area. I'm sorry that's all I know. You like acting?"

She shook her head. "I like the design part, scenery and costumes."

"Now there's a switch," he said, obviously surprised. "I thought all pretty girls wanted to be actresses."

Ellen stared at him. Was he really going out of his way to be patronizing? Maybe Brad had spoiled her by always treating her like an equal, but Michael Tyler wasn't going to get away with anything.

"Do all handsome guys want to be actors?" she asked, looking him right in the eye.

He blinked again and laughed. "I see I'm going to have to toe the line with you."

He checked the time. "We have eighteen and a half minutes. Let's go outside so you can ask me any questions you have."

He led her to a bench in the thin shade of a dusty tree beside the tennis courts. He had to raise his voice over the shouts of the coach and the plop of balls beyond the fence. From the band room came scattered bits of instrumental music that made Ellen want to get up and march.

"Besides being Brad's beautiful athletic baby sister with brains and an interest in design, tell me about *you*."

She rose to her feet and looked down at him. "Look, Michael," she said, keeping her voice level. "I know you're an ancient and honored upperclassman with distinguished credits and all that stupid stuff. That doesn't give you the right to look down on me. Brad and I have a younger sister. She's only ten but we don't ever insult her with that 'baby sister' business."

Michael was instantly on his feet, too. He struck his forehead with the palm of his hand. "Two apologies in less than an hour," he said. "I'm really making a mess of this. Believe me, Ellen, I'm not out to insult you. Please sit down."

She looked at him a moment, then perched on the edge of the bench. "Why talk about me? I thought I was supposed to ask the questions."

He checked his watch. "Okay," he said genially, "Your time is up. I'll ask the questions. You have to answer each one in less than a minute or we'll run out of time. Favorite color?"

"Blue," she said quickly.

"A very dark shade, I hope," he said. "Like your

eyes. And before you fly off again, the truth is never insulting. Pets?"

"A cat named Tawny," she said. This was actually fun. And it was challenging to see how fast she could come back with answers.

"Favorite foods?"

"Apples and carrots and almost anything white."

He laughed. "Now that's confusing. What do you mean by white? White bread, white meat of chicken, cream?"

She shook her head. "More like pasta, potatoes, rice, and milk. The same thing every athlete eats."

"Are you serious about running and biking, or just lucky?"

That was a borderline insulting question. "Nobody wins on luck alone," she said. It was none of his business that she ran even when she didn't feel like it and only missed a day of biking because of the weather. Or that she was Brad's practice opponent at tennis.

"That was a revealing statement. If you don't depend on luck, you work out," he said. "So when do you read?"

At her surprised look, he grinned at her. "Hey, nobody makes grades like yours by luck any more than they win races. Every good student I've ever known is also a reader."

Later she tried to remember the rest of his questions. They had come friendly and fast and he had listened intently. But he was distracting. His eyebrows were heavy and a little curly and almost met above the ridge of his nose. Although his eyes were mostly intent on hers, she didn't feel like looking away as she usually did when boys watched her straight on like that. He was tan without having that toasted look, and strong without all those awful bulging muscles or a thick neck like a weight lifter.

He checked his watch again and made a frustrated sound. "In one minute we have to go get your books. Final question. What do you collect?" He was reaching for her hand to pull her up.

"Paperweights." When he stared at her strangely, she explained. "You know, those round glass ones with figures or scenes in the middle. When you shake them, the snow flies."

"You're kidding," he said, taking both of her hands. Then he laughed. "What a trip! I was crazy about those when I was a kid. I'd forgotten all about them. Then you must like winter, too."

"My favorite season," she said. "You forgot to ask that."

"Can I help that we ran out of time? I like it best, too," he said, starting for the door. "Chicago and the lake are great in winter, but this village is out and away the greatest. All those huge old trees, the houses with their dormer windows and odd-angled roofs. And Salt Creek with the woods muffled with snow along its banks, like block after block of Christmas cards."

They were inside at the office before she realized it. He handed her things to her and smiled. "Thanks for a good hour. You are one cool kid, Ellen."

Suddenly she asked, "Why did you ask me all those questions?"

He looked at her as if he was genuinely puzzled by the question. Then he grinned and raised his shoulders in an elaborate shrug. "Hey, I was interested," he said. "What other possible reason would I have?"

Suddenly a bell rang. No bell had ever sounded louder, but at least it saved her from having to answer. "We'll both be late unless we rush, Ellen," he said. "Have a good year." As she turned away, he called after her. "Not just a *good* freshman year, Ellen, a wonderful one!"

He was almost instantly lost in the crowd. She felt strange, as if she had just returned from some distant place and was totally disconnected from her own world. She let the crowd carry her along without even thinking. Her head was so full of his voice that the noisy hall might as well have been silent.

She never would have made it to class if Luke Ingram hadn't run by, skidded to a stop, and caught her by her shoulders.

"Stop!" he cried. "You're going the wrong way!" He spun her around and hustled her along with one hand at her back. "This isn't like you, Ellen. You and your perfect attendance record. You could spoil it for yourself the first week of high school!"

Chapter 3

Nothing registered on Ellen the rest of that morning. Even when she tried to concentrate on a teacher's words, Michael Tyler's voice echoed in her mind. Her emotions swung back and forth endlessly. She had hated Michael when he treated her like a child, but she had a wonderful feeling when he quit playing "upperclassman."

Brad's "little sister," indeed.

Being with Michael plunged her into a dream that only the noise of the cafeteria woke her from.

Maggie was behind Ellen in the cafeteria line. Although they had been friends for years, Ellen almost hadn't recognized her the first day of school. Maggie had dyed her hair an astonishing color somewhere between purple and black.

"Aubergine," Maggie explained, cupping her hand around a mass of curls. "It's a brand-new color."

"Only for hair," Ellen told her, grinning. "It's always been a popular color for eggplants."

"That's disgusting," Maggie told her, shaking her

head so that her earrings swayed against her neck. "Anyway, I can wash it right out whenever I get tired of it."

Ellen had to admit that no matter what Maggie did to herself, she always looked cute. With her dark brown eyes and heart-shaped face, she even looked wonderful wearing a tiny silver fork in her left ear with a matching spoon in her right one.

Her loud mouth was something else. That day Maggie was in her hysterical mood. She shoved Ellen along and talked too loud even though Luke kept saying, "Cool it, Maggie! Tone it down."

Cricket, behind Maggie, was lost to the world. She shuffled along automatically, reading the year's first edition of the school paper, *The Monticello*, and mumbling, "Wow. Oh, wow."

Halfway to the food counter, Ellen said, "This place is a madhouse!"

"Yeah," Maggie agreed. "Isn't it wonderful?"

Ellen stared at her. "Wonderful? You have some burning desire to replace those earrings with hearing aids?"

Luke frowned at her. "Are you all right, Ellen?"

"I'm fine, but how can anyone eat with all this noise?"

"Fast," he told her.

"This is a closed campus," Maggie said. "I already checked because they sell fried chicken just down the block and we aren't allowed to go down there and buy any."

"The handbook says you can't even take food outside," Cricket added, looking up. "No picnics, no leaving the grounds."

She and Michael hadn't had to leave the school grounds to find privacy. How had they managed that? Had it been the intense way his eyes had seldom left hers and the way he had listened — really listened when she talked? Just remembering made the noisy clatter of the room hateful. She wasn't hungry anyway. She only wanted to keep remembering that time with Michael, to replay it in her mind like a piece of music that made her happy and sad at the same time.

She turned to Luke. "I'm skipping lunch. I'm going to go read on one of those benches by the courts until the bell rings."

"Guess who just had her school tour!" Maggie said. "What a smashing idea. I'll come later. Adam could be out on the court."

"Adam?" Luke asked.

"She's starting at the first letter, planning to work her way through the whole alphabet," Cricket said, not looking up.

"Lay off," Maggie told her, giggling so wildly that kids at other tables looked around at her. "His name is an accident. But he's a dream, an absolute dream of a guy."

Ellen felt her face redden. Maggie had always been loud and show-offy, but somehow it mattered more here at Jefferson. Didn't Maggie realize that she was making a fool of herself in public? Michael might feel the same way about public scenes that she did. When they were outside, he had asked her to sit down before they drew a crowd. What if he was hearing all of Maggie's silliness with Ellen right there as a part of it?

Suddenly Ellen had to escape. "See you later," she said.

Luke grinned. "It's a little frantic for me, too. I'll be out in a couple of hamburgers from now. With fries, of course."

Ellen went out the same side door she and Michael had used. Seeing the tennis benches filled gave her a stab of pain, as if she had been robbed of the place that belonged to her and Michael. The parking lot ran along the walk. Some older guys leaned against the cars talking and laughing. They fell silent when she walked by. A couple of them whistled.

One of them stepped into the path with Ellen. "Hey," he said. "You're Brad Marlowe's kid sister."

There it was again. Kid sister. But this tall, grinning redhead made it sound like a compliment. She smiled as she looked up. "Well, anyway, Brad's my brother," she said. "And you?"

"Bud Leonard," he said. "I played football with Brad. If any of these hoodlums here try to give you a hard time, just yell."

When Luke came out, Ellen joined him. "Thanks, Bud," she called back. "Are the others coming?" she asked Luke.

"I doubt it," Luke said. "Cricket's in there memorizing the athletic schedule." He paused, looking around for a place to sit down. "Maggie is drunk with new prospects. She's probably down to the letter *C* by now. There," he said, starting toward a bench farther up. "Those guys are getting up to leave."

Maggie always said that Luke was ordinary-looking. Maybe his eyes only looked huge because of his glasses but they also were beautiful, a rich unusual color halfway between hazel and gold. Was there such a thing as cinnamon-colored eyes? He was skinny in spite of a huge appetite. He probably had already wolfed down two hamburgers and fries along with dessert.

A hard-hitting game of singles tennis exploded beyond the parking lot as Ellen stared silently into the street.

"Are you okay?" Luke asked, looking over at her intently.

She ducked her head because she could feel a rush of heat to her cheeks at his question. "Why wouldn't I be?" she asked.

"That's what I'm trying to figure out," he said. "You were sleepwalking in the hall before third period and you didn't open your mouth until we hit that cafeteria. Hey," he interrupted himself. "Did some conceited upperclassman give you a hard time during your orientation? I forgot about that tour."

"It was all right," she said.

"Just all right?" he asked. "Who was your monitor? They're always juniors or above and members of the honor society."

"Maybe," she said. "Anyway a junior."

"What was her name? My sister, Adrienne, is a junior this year. Maybe I know this person."

So she had been right. She should have had a girl monitor. "It was a guy, not a girl," she told him.

Luke sat quietly a moment, staring at her through his giant glasses. Then he leaned close and whispered in a confidential tone. "If the identity of your monitor is classified information, I have documents that establish my top security clearance."

She gave up. "Oh, don't be silly," she said. "His name was Michael Tyler. Now are you happy?"

Strangely, he said nothing, but stared off across the drive.

"See?" she said. "You wormed that out of me for no good reason at all. You don't even know who he is."

"The question is whether you know who he is," he came back.

She shrugged. "All I really know is that he knows my brother." That wasn't quite true, but she said no more.

"Everybody in this school knows your brother except a few nonreading freshmen aliens who transferred in from distant planets in the galaxy."

"If you think I'm going to ask you about Michael Tyler, you're wrong, Luke Ingram. He was my monitor for orientation and that's the end of that."

Luke stood up. "That's the best news I've heard in a long time, Ellen," he said, his voice suddenly serious. "Michael Tyler knew Brad because they were on student council together. Michael was president of the sophomore class last year, dean's list with all straight A's. He broke a half-dozen speed records for the swim team. We are talking Big Man on Campus without holding back any capital letters. He didn't tell you any of that?"

When Ellen shook her head, he went on. "Then what did you two talk about?"

She rose and picked up her books. "Luke, I don't know where you're coming from. He showed me around school and asked me a lot of questions, that's all."

Luke kicked the gravel beside the bench. "I bet he did. I just bet he did. And you came out sleepwalking with your head all twisted around. Come on, Ellen! Don't do it."

Maybe she and Luke had been good friends too long. Could he read her mind? How did he know she had thought of nothing but Michael since meeting him?

"Do what, Luke?" she asked, trying to sound unconcerned.

"Get a monster crush on Michael Tyler," he said angrily. "There's absolutely nothing wrong with that guy. In fact, he's great, going on monumental. But, Ellen, you've never been the cliché type. Falling for Michael Tyler would only put you in line with a cast of thousands. I should know. My sister, Adrienne, has been a Michael Tyler worshipper since they were freshmen. I still live in constant fear of destruction by fire caused by that torch she carries around for him."

She dropped her eyes. Luke wouldn't believe it if she told him how angry Michael had made her, both at him and at herself. He wouldn't understand that she was only terribly confused that such an appealing guy could also be completely infuriating.

Luke took her arm. "Okay, Ellen, let's take a run at hypnosis. We'll use your own words. Look deep in my eyes and repeat after me: *He was my monitor for orientation and that's the end of that. He was my monitor for orientation and that's the end of that.*"

"Just do me one favor, Luke," she said quietly. "Promise we'll never talk about this again."

He groaned and hesitated. Finally he shrugged and nodded. "Only if you promise you won't forget what I told you," he said. Neither of them spoke again on the way back into the building.

Chapter 4

Ellen's strange mental haze didn't fade. No matter what she tried to think about, Michael Tyler managed to shove her thoughts aside. She went to bed wondering what he did with his Friday nights. Did he have a steady girlfriend or did he run around with a crowd of guys like Brad always had? Most of all, had he thought about her the way she'd thought about him? The next morning she wakened with tears in her eyes for no reason. Had she had a bad dream? If not, why did she feel so sad?

She ran five miles, and then two more, in the fresh morning air. It helped. She was humming when she came out of the shower and heard the phone ringing. A wild burst of hope exploded in her chest. He *had* thought about her and was calling. The hope died swiftly when her ten-year-old sister, Robin, rapped on the bathroom door.

"Cricket's on her way over here!" she called in to Ellen. "I'll go meet her out in front." Ellen sighed as Robin clattered down the stairs, sounding like an awkward pony. What had given her the crazy idea that Michael would call anyway?

She pulled on shorts and a shirt and went to look out of the window while she brushed her hair. She could see the porch steps through the green of the maple tree. Robin was sitting there with her chin in her hands and her elbows propped on her knees, waiting for Cricket to arrive.

Ellen shook her head in amazement as she went downstairs with Tawny leaping from step to step behind her. What a mutual thing her little sister and her best friend had always had. Robin was only waiting to chase down the drive the minute she saw Cricket. She also knew that her little sister would trade Ellen herself in for Cricket in a minute if she could get away with it.

But then Cricket would gladly kidnap Robin if she could. As long as Ellen had known her, Cricket had wanted a younger brother or sister. She had only finally given up that dream when her parents got their divorce.

The thought stopped her inside the door. Did Michael have brothers or sisters?

When Ellen got outside, Robin was hanging onto Cricket's bike and talking a mile a minute. Except for Cricket's height, she and Robin could have been the same age. Robin even tried to look like Cricket, both in jeans and T-shirts with their hair pulled back. And neither of them ever quit talking about horses.

When they started off on their bikes, Robin

waved them good-bye until they were out of sight of the house. Then Cricket braked her bike and turned to Ellen. "You'll never ever guess what wonderful thing is happening," she said, her face filled with happiness. "My dad and Lynn are getting married this weekend. They were planning to have the wedding at Thanksgiving if I could come back there to be in it. Since Mom won't let me go, they're getting married right away. I couldn't wait to tell you. I'm not supposed to be over here."

"Why not?" Ellen asked. She was *always* at Ellen's house.

"I'm being punished for having a tantrum and screaming at my mother. I only got out of the house because I have overdue library books. But I just had to tell you my wonderful news."

Ellen shook her head, confused. "That's great, Cricket, but why a tantrum when you're so happy?"

"When my mother refused to let me go to Dad's wedding, I blew up. She claims she's just sticking to the custody rules, but I know better. She tells me what a bad influence Dad is on me. She says I'll never be well-mannered until I quit trying to please him." Cricket stopped and blinked hard to hold back tears. "But, Ellen, I was going to be maid of honor and we were going to a rodeo. Now I'll never be anybody's maid of honor. And they don't even have rodeos at Christmastime when I get to go out there."

Cricket's voice dropped to a hoarse whisper and

Ellen hugged her. "Be happy that you'll have Lynn from now on," she said. "And you can't be under house arrest all that long."

"Forever," Cricket said sullenly. "Forever and always and until Monday because I'd already promised to go to Luke's party."

Ellen smiled. Cricket always described things at least three ways. "That's hardly forever or always," she reminded Cricket. "Monday's only two days away."

"It seems like forever," Cricket grumbled. "I was going to the mall with you and Maggie. She was so crazy at school that we didn't talk. I haven't really seen her since she got home."

"We'll miss you," Ellen said. "I'll even eat a slice of pizza in your honor."

"Now *that's* friendship," Cricket said, making a face. Then she smiled. "But it is wonderful about Lynn, isn't it?"

"Perfectly wonderful," Ellen agreed. Cricket had come home from her summer with her father raving about his friend Lynn. "She's a tomboy like me, only older," Cricket had explained.

And Cricket certainly was a tomboy. She never gave her appearance a second thought. Ellen wasn't sure she even owned a skirt. But she looked great anyway with her strawberry blonde flyaway hair held back with anything handy. Her eyelashes were pale and her freckled nose tilted up at the end. When she smiled, her pointed face wadded up until her eyes completely disappeared.

According to Cricket, Lynn was crazy about horses and all sports. The three of them had gone trail riding, and camped out, and cooked food over outdoor fires — just Cricket's kind of life. Lynn sounded exactly right for both Cricket and her dad.

Ellen stared after Cricket. How could three good friends be so different? Cricket was still a little kid inside, crazy about horses and rodeos and ball games. She couldn't imagine Cricket hurting the way she had since meeting Michael Tyler. She *couldn't* be in love with him or even have a crush. She didn't know him well enough. But meeting him *had* changed her, bringing back that longing that made her cry on her birthday.

Maggie would never let anything like that hurt her. She was into ice skating, astrology, and boys, lots of boys. She could fall in love in five minutes and back out in two without feeling a pang! She had probably claimed to be in love a dozen times just this past summer. While Cricket was in Wyoming, Maggie had been at a camp that trained figure skaters for competition. Then she had gone on vacation in Door County with her family.

Ellen smiled as she started home, remembering Maggie's phone call. "I can't wait to see you," Maggie had said, her voice up and down excitement. "You'll never *guess* what happened!"

"You met the man of your dreams," Ellen suggested.

"That's mean of you," Maggie said. "But you're right! I'll have pictures by Saturday. His name is

Sven. Isn't that the most thrilling name you've ever heard in your life?"

"It's different," Ellen conceded, understanding Maggie better than she ever had. Michael was hardly a "different" name but just thinking it gave Ellen a little shiver.

"When you see his pictures, you'll see why I'm so excited!" Maggie told her.

They met at the pizza parlor in the mall. The minute they got their orders and sat down, Maggie fished out pictures. "What about Adam?" Ellen asked as Maggie laid them out triumphantly.

"Don't be stuffy," Maggie said, glaring at her. "Just look at the pictures. He's Swedish. Isn't that glamorous?"

Sven turned out to be a really ordinary-looking boy. He was clowning in the water with a beach ball on his head that was the same shade of blue as his swim trunks. "He has eyes that color, too," Maggie said.

Ellen couldn't keep from comparing the boy in the snapshot with Michael Tyler. Sven looked nice enough in a kiddish way but years younger than Michael. Sven's blondness looked washed out next to Michael's vivid coloring and the dark brilliance of his eyes. Even Sven's smile looked ordinary, nothing like Michael's slow grin that made deep dimples in his cheeks.

Maggie was still chattering. "And Sven was born

under the sign of Leo . . . that's a very strong-minded and forceful sign!"

Ellen hadn't even thought about astrology since Maggie left. She wondered what sign Michael was.

"Obviously those pictures don't do Sven justice," Maggie said, putting them away, a little miffed. Then she looked up, appearing hopeful. "What are the plans for the weekend?"

"Luke's having a party on Labor Day," Ellen told her.

Maggie groaned. "There goes Monday. I'll be bored to death while you and Cricket are there. Why does a boy as dull as Luke Ingram have to be the one with that great house on the lake? Why can't some attractive kid live out there and throw those parties? I can't figure out what you see in that boy, anyway. He's not the least bit good-looking and he's boring besides."

Ellen stared at her. What made Maggie talk that way when she knew how much Ellen liked Luke? It made her mad. She was sure Maggie wouldn't be that tough on Luke if he ever invited *her* to his parties. But Luke had told Ellen more than once that he could hardly stand being around Maggie's craziness.

Maggie didn't understand about being just friends the way Ellen had been with Luke since they were in third grade. She had to be "in love."

Ellen stirred in her seat. She hated hearing anyone say rotten things about her friends. "Nobody with a sense of humor like Luke's could be boring," she told Maggie.

Maggie twisted her mouth down, "Boys who look like Luke better have a sense of humor."

Ellen glared at her. That was too much! "Come on, Maggie," she said. "You just pick on Luke because he tries to avoid you."

Maggie's eyes widened. "You mean he doesn't like me?"

"Close," Ellen said, wishing she hadn't said anything.

"Is that why he never invites me to his parties?" Maggie asked, leaning toward Ellen with a puzzled look.

"Maybe," Ellen said.

Maggie's cheeks flamed with color. She had been annoyed with Ellen for not raving about Sven, but *this* had made her furious. "What possible reason could that twerp have not to like me?"

Ellen caught her breath angrily. Confidence was fine but this was pure conceit! "Maggie," Ellen said, leaning toward her and looking right into her eyes. "If you want the truth, I'll give it to you. The way you act embarrasses Luke. It sometimes embarrasses me, too. Some of us don't like it when everybody in a room stares at us because of your squealing and carrying on."

"Well," Maggie said huffily. "That's *perfectly* ridiculous."

"That's your opinion. Some people think it's ridiculous when girls wear silverware in their ears, dye their hair purple, and can't talk about anything but astrology, ice skating, and their latest mad love affair."

"If that's how Luke thinks, he's narrow-minded," Maggie said, sitting up very straight and pouting. "I've a right to run my own life the way I want to."

Ellen nodded. "And so does Luke. He doesn't have to try to explain you to his parents unless he feels like it."

Before Maggie could get her mouth shut, Ellen stood up. "I need to go look for ankle socks. Want to come along?"

To Ellen's surprise, Maggie did. She also decided not to buy eggplant-colored ankle socks in case she got tired of her hair before school started again the following Tuesday.

Chapter 5

Ellen could hardly believe she had actually looked forward to Labor Day weekend. But that was before she'd met Michael Tyler. Now she only wanted to be back at school where she might see him instead of just thinking about him.

It was too hot to run and there was nothing else to do. Even her parents were no help. They took Robin out horseback riding and invited her along. Spending a blazing hot afternoon on an equally hot horse was something she could do without. There wasn't even anyone to bike with. Luke was helping his mother get the party ready, and Maggie had gone skating at the indoor ice rink two towns away. Cricket was still under house arrest for throwing that tantrum.

Anyway, none of them knew Michael Tyler. The only two people she could ask about him were Brad and Luke. Brad was at the university, and she had forced Luke into that stupid promise.

Boring. Boring. Boring.

She was sure that Michael Tyler *wasn't* being

bored to death. Did he have some really *wonderful* girlfriend that he was doing *wonderful* things with? His family might even be one of those who went away to a second home over long weekends.

Was it possible that she kept thinking about Michael because she knew so little about him? Maybe when she really got to know him he would be just another guy, only more insulting with all that "little sister" stuff.

Just to keep busy she went through her clothes and straightened her closet. Even that made her think of Michael. She kept her collection of paperweights at the far right end of her closet shelf, each globe in its separate box. When she had told him about her collection he really seemed excited.

"You're kidding," he had said, stopping dead and taking both of her hands in his. "What a trip!" he had said. "I was crazy about those things when I was a kid. I had forgotten they even existed."

Maggie couldn't understand why Ellen didn't put her collection out on display. "They belong to winter and snow," Ellen had told her. "I put them out when the first snow falls and pack them away when spring comes." Of course, Maggie had thought that was weird.

Ellen stood on tiptoe to read what she had written on the ends of the boxes. Which one would Michael like the best? She chose the one marked VILLAGE and took the box down. Just lifting the box from the shelf had made the snow begin to swirl. The tiny dormered houses with brightly painted wreaths on all the doors were quickly covered with snow, looking as welcoming as a Christmas card. When the snow settled, Ellen put it away with a wistful sigh and went back to sorting out her clothes.

By three o'clock she had finished her closet and all the drawers in her dresser. She curled up with Tawny to try to read, but the book that had started so well became boring in Chapter Three. She kept having to read pages over a second time because she was thinking about Michael instead of the words.

At three-thirty she decided she could at least find out where he lived. She went downstairs and looked in the telephone book. Two Tylers were listed, one on Park Street and the other in the next village. Michael's family had to be the one on Park or he would be in a different high school district.

At four o'clock, as she opened the garage to wheel out her bike, her parents came home with Robin smelling like a horse but grinning from ear-to-ear.

"Don't be gone long," her mother called. "The Willoughbys are coming for supper. Dad's going to barbecue ribs about six o'clock."

"I'll be back," she promised.

Now she could actually look forward to the evening. She liked the Willoughbys. She had grown up calling them Aunt Silvie and Uncle Alex. They had been close friends of her parents since they had all gone to Northwestern University together. Their only son was married and gone. When he was in high school they started having a big Christmas party for him every year. Even after he left home, his parents kept giving the party for high school kids every year. Brad said the Willoughby parties spoiled you for any other way to start Christmas.

It was cool wheeling along the quiet streets under the deep shade of the giant trees. She started toward Park Street, then changed her mind. What if Michael was home and saw her? What *difference* did it make where he lived anyway?

The ice cream store across from the railway station was crowded with little kids and their parents. She had really gone in to have a chocolate chip sugar cone with almonds but by the time she got waited on, she took raspberry sherbert in a cup instead. Michael had said she was slender. That was so much nicer a word than skinny, which was what her grandmother said she was.

In the end, she biked down Park even though it meant taking a chance. The Tyler house was red-brick and looked huge from the street. Although the lawn was freshly trimmed and a long bed of bright dark red chrysanthemums lined the walk and the driveway, the house itself looked empty and bleak.

Looking at the house didn't really help her at all. It was just another of Michael's worlds that was unknown to her. She couldn't even *guess* which of the upstairs rooms was his. Would it look like Brad's, with pennants all along the top of the wall and snapshots of his friends stuck into the edge of the mirror so you could hardly see into it? What kind of music would be on the cassettes stacked by his stereo? She tried to imagine him throwing baskets on the outdoor hoop or coming down the front steps, but she couldn't see him at all.

But, she could see him studying her face in the auditorium, and feel his hand on her back as he hurried her out into the hall. And laughing with him on that bench out by the tennis courts until he pulled her to her feet with both hands.

The impulse was crazy but she didn't care. She turned and rode over to the high school. The building looked as deserted and bleak as the Tyler house had. In spite of the DON'T LITTER signs posted all over, trash blew around the parking lot in the late afternoon breeze. She sat on the warm concrete bench and tried to hear his voice again in her head. She could remember his words, practically every word he had said, but his voice had fallen silent in her mind.

"So this is what a crush feels like," she whispered out loud to herself, just to break the silence. The minute the words were out, she knew.

She didn't have any crush on Michael Tyler — she loved him.

Everyone had heard about love at first sight but nobody really believed in it. So how could this have happened to her? How could one single hour make her so obsessed with a boy she hardly knew. She'd seen a lot of movies, read a lot of romances. She had thought love was supposed to be stars in your eyes and joy that made you feel like dancing.

She didn't feel like dancing. Her chest ached and she felt cold. She clasped her arms across her chest and held her breath to keep from crying. If love hurt this much, she didn't want any part of it. When tears started to trail down her face she made herself get up and start for home.

The thought of how Michael would laugh to know that Brad's baby sister, a stupid little kid, was crying her eyes out over him made her pedal home faster than she would have thought possible.

She made sure she got the tear streaks washed off her face before anyone saw them. Everyone had too much to talk about to notice how quiet she was. Robin chattered about the horse she had ridden and her parents and the Willoughbys visited happily the way they always did. Even though Ellen kept nodding and saying all the right things, she felt far away, as if she were in some kind of shock.

She loved Michael Tyler. She couldn't even say she was in love *with* him because that sounded as if it took two people.

She couldn't go on like this. Would she quit thinking about him all the time if she could talk to someone about him? But who?

Maggie would be impossible. Her best record was keeping a secret for five seconds and that only with her mouth taped shut.

What if she told Cricket? She had never deliberately kept an important secret from Cricket and she never had been sorry. But the way she felt about

Michael was different, private and painful. How could she explain her feelings to Cricket, anyway? Cricket wouldn't understand any more than Robin would.

When the Willoughbys left, Robin yawned off to bed. Ellen carried Tawny up to her room, turned off her lamp, and sat on her window seat in the dark. Fireflies winked in the grass below and Ellen could hear her mother and father talking on the porch. She couldn't hear their words — only the low contented hum of their voices with her mother's occasional soft laughter.

They loved each other so much that sometimes it made Ellen want to cry. She went to sleep hating herself. What kind of a fourteen-year-old girl would be jealous of her own parents because they had each other and she had no one?

According to Luke, the Ingram house had been part of a working farm before Chicago spread out and ate its way into the countryside. Luke's grandfather sold off most of the land but kept the house and the spring-fed lake for boating and fishing and ice skating.

Luke's parents had added the outdoor pool with its big deck area, a built-in barbecue grill, and lots of lounging furniture. The house itself was big and cool with deep porches and a greenhouse stuck on one end where Luke's mother grew orchids and poinsettias for Christmas.

Luke's parents planned their parties for both

Luke and Adrienne. Mostly the crowds stayed pretty much apart, with Luke's friends cutting up in the pool while Adrienne's older friends stretched out on lounge chairs and talked or danced.

Ellen felt that she was apart from both groups. She stayed by the pool with Cricket and the others but didn't have her heart in all the horseplay. How could she keep seeing everything through Michael's eyes when she knew so little about him? Why did she keep thinking what an exciting party it would be if he were there with her? But he wouldn't be. He would be with Adrienne and her friends, ignoring the kids like they were.

She was getting a can of soda from the big ice-filled tub when Adrienne left her friends to come over. "What do you hear from Brad?" Adrienne asked. "You must really miss him."

"We do," Ellen told her. "He's called a couple of times already and he seems to like it fine." She smiled. "Mostly he complains about the food."

When Adrienne laughed, she was beautiful. She had a thin face like Luke's and the same color hair except that hers was curly. It fitted her head like a slightly rumpled cap with wispy ducktails around her ears and down the back. Her eyes were as expressive as Luke's but a more conventional shade of brown.

"Luke tells me that you got Michael Tyler as an orientation monitor," Adrienne said.

Ellen felt a cold bath of terror. But no, Luke wouldn't have been disloyal enough to say anything about the way she had acted. He absolutely couldn't have.

Adrienne took a can of soda and flipped the tab. "That Michael is a really remarkable guy," she said without looking at Ellen. "Everybody likes him. He was a lifeguard at Dad's golf club pool last summer. Dad says he's the best ever."

Ellen relaxed and smiled at Adrienne.

"I've had a crush on that guy for years," Adrienne went on, smiling into Ellen's eyes. "Me and half the other girls in school, of course."

"He must have a steady girlfriend," Ellen said, carefully trying to keep her tone light.

Adrienne shrugged. "Come and go, you know how guys are. He's big in swimming, which takes time, and he and his dad spend lots of time together. They're really close. They eat out a lot together, stuff like that. I guess you knew that his mother died a few years back. Mr. Tyler is an engineer who travels a lot, but Michael holds down the fort. What can I say? Michael's just a great guy. Didn't you like him?"

"Right off," Ellen said. Then she laughed. "As well as I could like anybody who treated me like a kid."

Adrienne laughed. "Consider yourself lucky that he pulled such a dumb act on you. Most girls fall flat on their faces for Michael. And never quite get up again."

Adrienne drifted away just as she had come. Right then the party was almost over as far as Ellen was concerned. No matter what was happening, she only thought about Michael. Ellen was glad when her mother picked her and Cricket up at twilight.

"Back to the old grind tomorrow," her mother said as she let Cricket out.

Ellen said nothing. It couldn't come soon enough for her. Going back to school meant that she would probably see Michael again, if only in passing. Not until she was getting ready to go to bed, did she discover another change in herself that she didn't like.

For the first time she found herself agonizing over what to wear. How many times had she kidded Maggie for making such a production of dressing for school? She tried on everything she owned, looking at herself as she thought Michael would see her.

The key word was still *kid.*

Chapter 6

These first few days of school Ellen watched for Michael constantly. On Wednesday she saw him from a distance, going down the stairs with his back to her. Her heart hammered ridiculously from just that glimpse of him. How would she be if they had met face-to-face? Would he be able to tell from her face how she felt about him? Would she have blushed and stammered and made a perfect fool of herself? She decided she didn't want to see him after all, not ever again. But she couldn't keep herself from looking for him anyway. She told herself that she would manage her feelings better now that classes had started in earnest and she would have a fixed routine.

All of her schedule was okay, but she liked her honors English class the best. On Thursday Ellen passed Barb Sanchez and Tom Winter just outside the door to English. Before junior high, Barb had been one of Ellen's little crowd along with Luke, Maggie, and Cricket. In the seventh grade, that changed. Barb began spending all her time with

Tom Winter. They biked to and from school together, ate lunch together, and Tom walked Barb to her classes. Ellen had thought this was pretty weird. It seemed too soon for them to be so involved. She finally got used to them. As Luke said, "I'm not sure I would recognize Barb anymore if her right hand wasn't glued to Tom's left one."

Ellen set her books in the empty seat beside her to save it for Barb, who always got into classes at the last minute to keep from missing any time with Tom. When she appeared at the door, every boy in the class turned to stare. Once when Ellen told Brad that Barb was the prettiest girl in her class, he had laughed.

"Sanchez isn't beautiful, she's awesome."

Barb looked around, color staining her cheeks. When Ellen signaled her to come over, Barb ducked her head and whispered, "Thanks," her eyes shining under her dark lashes.

Ellen grinned. What would Brad say about Barb today? She always wore vibrant colors that accented her coloring. She had pulled her thick black curls back with a brilliantly colored red and purple scarf with splashing gold. Her skin was the rich olive shade that other girls lay out sunbathing to get.

Ellen had never envied Barb and Tom's longstanding crush. Suddenly it hurt. How fabulous it would be to have a boy you loved as much as she loved Michael be in love with you, too. Maybe even so crazy about you that he risked the late bell at every change of classes the way Tom did.

Only when their teacher, Mr. Burns, strode into the room and rapped on the desk did the boys quit staring at Barb to look at the front of the room.

"Now that we're settled in, let's get to know each other," Mr. Burns suggested. "As I call your name, stand up, or slouch to your feet, whichever is your style."

The class was almost evenly split between boys and girls. This made sense because everybody had to take freshman English to graduate. Ellen watched the other students rise. Linda was the tall one with the shining fall of straight, almost white hair. The chubby girl whose voice was rich with laughter was Meg. Ellen recognized two of the boys from seeing them around her own junior high, but she had never had classes with them.

Hank Ober was the tall, slender boy whom the girls looked at with as much interest as the boys did at Barb. He smiled at everyone when he got up to say his name. Something about his dark good looks reminded Ellen of Brad, which made her smile back at him.

Mr. Burns first explained what they would study. Grammar and William Shakespeare got the most groans with poetry coming in a strong third. After assigning a hefty hunk of homework, the class was finally dismissed. Hank Ober caught up with Ellen going out into the hall. "Ellen, isn't it?" he asked.

When she nodded, he fell into step beside her. "Someone said you were interested in drama. They just put a notice on the bulletin board about the

Jefferson drama group. Auditions for the freshman play are next week."

"Thanks for telling me. I might have missed it," she said. "You like acting?"

He nodded. "Only for starters. I really want to direct. How about you?"

"I'm not into acting even as a starter," she told him. "I want to work on the sets and maybe costumes."

"That surprises me," he said. "You aren't shy, are you?"

"Not really," she said. Then she grinned, "But I'm not that crazy about the spotlight either."

"It takes all kinds," he said, smiling at her. "Anyway, with any luck, we'll still get to work together."

Maggie had turned a corner and seen them talking before Hank walked away. She bumped into two or three people running to catch up with Ellen. Naturally they turned around to glare at her, but she was staring after Hank. "*Who* was *that*?" she squealed loud enough to be heard clear down the hall. "What a fabulous, knockout guy."

Ellen kept walking, trying to ignore the way other kids were nudging each other and grinning as Maggie went on. All this time Maggie was tugging at Ellen's arm. If Michael Tyler came along and saw Maggie putting on this boy-crazy show, Ellen knew she would die. Curl up in a ball and literally die from embarrassment!

"Come on, Ellen," Maggie cried. "Put me out of my misery. Tell me who that wonderful hunk is.

He's the most incredible guy I've ever seen in my whole entire life."

"For maybe the last ten minutes," Ellen said unhappily. Then she whispered, "Maggie, please don't make such a scene. I can't stand having everyone stare at us."

Maggie stopped a minute as Ellen walked on. Then she ran in swift steps to catch up, her face pink with annoyance. "What makes you such a miserable spoilsport, Ellen Marlowe? It's all in fun, don't you know that?"

"I just *hate* being stared at," Ellen said softly. Then, sorry she'd been so snappish, Ellen looked over at her. That was a mistake, too. Maggie had washed the eggplant color out of her hair and replaced it with a deep burnt orange, rather like the coating on a taffy apple. Instead of the silverware jewelry, she had something hanging from her ears that looked like curled tropical fish. Their splashy colors matched the giant top she was wearing over fitted gold tights. The top was too long to be a shirt but too short to be a miniskirt. Maggie had beautiful long skater's legs, but gold tights were too much! And all the guys were turning to stare when they saw her.

"If that look means you disapprove of my tights, forget it," Maggie said. "This afternoon I go straight from school to a skating lesson without time to change."

She tried to sound insulted but Ellen heard the pride and excitement behind her words. She was glad enough to change the subject anyway. "Skating lessons?" she asked. "Something new?"

Maggie giggled. "Can you believe it? Mom got a letter from the skating camp director. He thinks I have 'Olympic potential.' They cost a bundle but I get to take figure lessons with a coach twice a week after school all year."

When Ellen told Maggie how wonderful that was, Maggie hugged her. "I shouldn't have been surprised. I'm a Scorpio, you know, and the sun joined Mercury in my sign in August while they were making out those reports."

When Ellen grinned, Maggie glared at her. "There you go again, laughing at me. I'll have you know that I looked up your horoscope, too, smarty. You were supposed to make a life change right at the end of August, too. I think it happened. I also think I liked you better before."

Chapter 7

Maggie's remark about a life change haunted Ellen. Did falling in love count? She knew it had changed her in small ways.

She had loved to run since she was tiny. As soon as they would accept her (at twelve) she had joined a running club. Any day she didn't get out to run had seemed a lost day. Suddenly she found herself covering the miles thinking about Michael rather than pushing herself against time.

She'd always loved to be with her friends. Now she really liked being alone better. She'd always loved bright days, the sunnier the better. Now she welcomed misty evenings when she could walk the shining streets of her neighborhood in a drizzle of rain. The more she was alone, the more time she had to think about Michael. And only the darkest weather fitted her mood when a whole day passed without her seeing him. But juniors didn't hang out in the same places that freshmen "kids" did, she thought bitterly.

From the first she had dreaded seeing Michael with another girl. She had figured it was coming even before Adrienne talked about his girlfriends. She had been through Maggie's weeping and wailing with jealousy and thought it was an act. Now she wasn't sure. While she knew she wouldn't ever scream and pound on things like Maggie did, she knew she'd feel awful. She just hadn't realized how dismally awful it would be until it happened.

At all-school assembly the freshman class had filed in on the left near the back. Ellen sat down between Luke and Maggie. When she looked around, she saw Michael a few rows down in the center section. That painful thumping in her chest started the way it always did. She tightened her hands around her books and told herself she wasn't going to look his way again.

She didn't need to look anyway. She had memorized everything about him, the shape of his head and the way his dark hair waved a little above his collar. Because Michael's back was to her, she didn't realize at first that he was with the dark-haired girl at his side. Then he looked at her and put his arm along the back of her seat. The girl turned and smiled at him, a quick laughing sort of smile, which looked warm and loving even from that distance.

Maggie had always said really mean things about girls she was jealous of. Ellen wasn't going to do that, but she did want to believe Michael's girl was ugly. If not ugly, at least plain. She would even settle for ordinary-looking.

No luck. The girl's straight black hair, cut short and sleek, shone even in that light. She had a model's kind of smile that showed gleaming teeth and brought a dimple to her left cheek.

Ellen dropped her eyes and blinked hard. How could she hate a girl she hadn't ever even seen before? And why did she keep looking at her when every time she did it hurt worse?

Michael must have said something very funny because the girl threw her head back and laughed. Then she swayed against him, bumping his shoulder playfully, with her eyes still on his face.

When Ellen drew a deep painful breath and looked down at her hands, she felt Luke's eyes on her. He looked away when she glanced at him, but she knew he'd been watching her. To her relief, the auditorium lights winked for silence, and then dimmed. Ellen breathed a sigh of relief. Now she *couldn't* watch Michael and his girlfriend. Maybe she could even forget about them if the movie was good enough.

Right away, the loud whispering began. A fair-haired boy in the row behind Ellen was leaning forward to talk to Maggie. Their heads stayed together as Maggie giggled and said something back.

Soft music played on the sound track behind the actors' words. Ellen and Luke both leaned forward to try to hear above the chatter of Maggie and her friend. Before long people up and down the row were whispering "Sssh!" and "Shut up!" to them. Maggie and the boy just laughed and went on talking.

The adult monitor appeared from nowhere. "All right," a man's voice said, "Whoever's making that disturbance, step out into the aisle."

Nobody moved. Luke stared up. Maggie was wide-eyed with put-on innocence. Ellen felt herself sink with embarrassment. Someone behind them in the darkness yelled, *"Freshmen, wouldn't you know?"* Of course a lot of people laughed.

"One more chance," the male voice behind said. "The talkers come on out or this whole section goes."

When Maggie only shrugged and looked around, the man lost his temper. "All right, you in the first six seats, out!"

Luke groaned and some of the others started a chorus of low protest, but they rose and moved out anyway. Ellen didn't exactly look at Michael but she could see his row of seats as she stepped out into the aisle. He and his girl were both looking around and laughing, but so was everybody in that giant room except Ellen and the other kids out in the aisle. Was it possible to die of embarrassment? Walking to the auditorium door, Ellen was sure it was.

Then they were out in the hall, being herded into an empty study room. The lecture went on forever, covering everything from common civility to punishment procedures at Jefferson. Only when they had been left to sit out the rest of the assembly period, did anyone make a sound.

Maggie giggled. "Well, at least they didn't get Gordon," she said, smiling at Ellen.

"Shut up!" one of the boys said. "If I had it to do again, I'd rat on you."

"Spoilsport," she told him crossly, looking at Ellen again for support. Ellen stared straight ahead, not meeting her eyes. She felt physically sick to her stomach at being on display like that with Michael watching. She could still hear the words somebody had yelled before the monitor came, *"Freshmen, wouldn't you know?"* And she could still see Michael, laughing.

When the bell rang, Ellen rose and began to walk away quickly. Luke caught up with her, "Come on, Ellie," he said. "You'll live. That's just your typical Maggie Martin in action."

"It's different here," she told him, her voice feeling strangled in her throat.

"Maybe the difference is who is watching," he said quietly.

She didn't answer but she argued with him in her mind. No matter what Luke said, Maggie was becoming a worse show-off every day. Of course Luke was thinking about Michael Tyler. That was the *most* horrible, but it wasn't *all* of it. She had also felt awful when Maggie threw her boy-crazy act over Hank Ober.

Did Maggie honestly think that *any* attention was worse than none? Couldn't she see that Ellen was embarrassed by her scenes? If Maggie wasn't going to care about anyone's feelings but her own, Ellen would just quit being around her.

Then it was Friday and Ellen was on the way to her last class. She was rushing along, trying to make it before the bell, when someone came up from behind and spoke, she looked around, startled. Michael Tyler grinned at her. "I was glad to see you there in assembly," he said. "I decided I had goofed up your orientation and gotten you lost forever."

She felt her face turn rosy but tried to laugh it off. "No such luck. I haven't missed a class since that one."

"How's it going?" he asked. "Did you luck out on teachers or get some dragons?"

"No fiery breath yet," she told him, wondering that he couldn't hear her heart pounding.

"That's a relief," he said. "It can happen."

"How about you?" she asked, wanting to keep him there.

"Junior year is a mixed bag," he said. "You work like crazy because junior marks make or break you at getting the college you want." He grinned. "On the other hand, juniors can pick their courses. I don't have one I didn't want. Tough about you freshmen. Age does have privileges."

There he went, spoiling everything again. Why was she kidding herself that she'd ever be anything but a kid to him?

Just then Maggie barreled in on them with one

of those wild cries. "Ellen," she said, her voice too loud and too high, "Every time I see you, you're with yet another super guy!"

Michael stopped and looked at her.

"Never mind," Maggie trilled, flirting with him. "I know who you are!" She poked Michael in the chest with her finger and then giggled. "You're the great Mike Tyler."

"Michael," he corrected her, smiling. Then he turned to Ellen. "Take care, Ellen, hear?" As he spoke, he wheeled and walked off down the hall.

Ellen knew her face was flaming. If Michael had ever doubted that she was a kid, he never would again. Who but a kid would have a friend like Maggie?

Maggie stared after him. "Not big on manners, is he?" she asked, obviously offended.

"Look who's talking about manners!" Ellen said hotly, and walked away, too. She left Maggie standing open mouthed in the middle of the hall with students streaming around her, and a stunned look on her face.

Ellen didn't see Maggie again until she and Cricket were getting their bikes. Maggie came up and spoke only to Cricket, glaring at Ellen as she did. "Watch out for your snooty friend there, Cricket," she said. "She will not only try to run your life and teach you manners, but she's into making a public fool of you, too."

Cricket stared at her, then laughed. "Come off it, Maggie," she said. "What's your problem?"

"Marlowe is my problem," Maggie said angrily. "First she tells me that people don't invite me to their parties because they're ashamed to introduce me to their parents. *Then* she can't tell the difference between a little joke and a public scene. *Then* she makes a crack about my manners and walks off in the middle of a conversation."

Cricket caught her lip between her teeth and stared at Maggie. "That doesn't sound like the Ellen I know."

"This is the new Ellen," Maggie said. "The snobby Ellen who treats her old friends like dirt."

Ellen stood very still. Other kids who had come for their bikes were watching and listening. Maggie was making yet another scene. Ellen couldn't stand it. She didn't have to, either. She pulled off her lock, got on her bike, and looked past Maggie to Cricket. "I'm off," she said, trying to keep her voice normal. "Race you home!"

Cricket caught up after three blocks. They didn't talk until they took cold drinks out on Ellen's front porch.

"Want to explain all that?" Cricket asked.

"Not really," Ellen admitted. "But I guess I have to. That Saturday before Labor Day, Maggie asked me why Luke didn't invite her to his parties. I told her what I thought. Then, she threw one of those loud fits when I was with a guy from class. Then you saw her get a bunch of us thrown out of assembly. This afternoon she annoyed me again and I'm fed up."

"Was it a guy again today?" Cricket asked. When Ellen nodded, Cricket asked who it was.

If she only didn't always blush when she even *thought* about Michael, but Ellen felt her cheeks get hot. "Not that it matters, but it was Michael Tyler. It was almost time for the bell. When Michael left, she accused *him* of bad manners."

Cricket frowned and stared straight ahead.

Ellen looked at her, a little puzzled. "It's just so *completely* embarrassing, Cricket. Don't you understand?"

Cricket shook her head and rubbed her boot on the walk. "I really don't. Maggie's been throwing fits around guys for years. What's different now? Is this Michael special?"

"No," Ellen said swiftly. Too swiftly, she realized. She looked away, knowing she wouldn't have felt half that annoyed in front of anyone but him.

Cricket was looking at her, waiting. When Cricket smiled, her eyes almost disappeared. But when she was serious, her green eyes were so large and searching that Ellen felt like a bug with a pin through it.

Before Ellen could think of what to say, Cricket rose. "Thanks for the drink, but I don't get it. Maggie is our friend."

Ellen was instantly beside her. "Come on, Cricket. I'm just fed up with the way she acts out all the time. It's like she thought she was doing a music video or something. At least try to understand."

Cricket lifted her bike and got on without meeting Ellen's eyes. "I am trying," she said. "Believe me."

"Okay, let's not talk about it," Ellen said. "Want to do something tonight?"

Cricket shook her head. "There's a practice game in about a half an hour," she said. Then she smiled. "I'm going down in school history as the girl who got every last penny out of her activity card. I'm not missing a game — not even a practice."

That weekend lasted forever. Not only was it too hot, but Ellen felt too miserable to run. She had only her awful memories to live with. Michael with his arm around that girl, Michael laughing at the freshman clowns in assembly, Michael turning to escape while Maggie was poking him. Of course Maggie didn't call, but neither did Cricket. A couple of times Ellen went to the phone and almost dialed Cricket's number but always held back.

The little bit of guilt she had felt about Maggie was growing. One thing about Cricket, she was always fair. And Ellen *had* always been able to shrug off Maggie's scenes before. If Maggie had embarrassed Ellen in front of anyone in the world but Michael Tyler, would she have been this angry?

She wasn't sure she wanted to know the answer.

Chapter 8

That next Wednesday the freshmen interested in the Jefferson drama group met in the auditorium after school. It was a big group with about as many guys as girls. Hank Ober dropped into the seat beside Ellen. "Here we go," he said, grinning over at her. "I hear neat things about the director, Quigley."

The room fell silent as Mr. Quigley entered the auditorium and walked briskly down the aisle. Once on the stage, he leaned his weight on the podium, looking them over. Then he smiled.

"The new thespians," he said. He was tall and thin with short, dark hair and an interesting, open face. A rolled-up suede touring cap stuck out of his blazer pocket and he was wearing eelskin boots. His voice was as lively as his step. Ellen liked him right off. He held up a sign-in sheet and shook it.

"Look at this, a full page of absolute strangers. Before the year is out, believe me we'll know each other better than we want to. For now, let's talk plans."

He got right down to cases, explaining the group wasn't a club but a theatrical group. "We do five plays each school year. Your freshman play is scheduled in October, just a month away. This is the only time you won't have to compete for parts against upperclassmen. Practice is daily after school, here or in the band room since the November play will also be in production."

When the play scripts were handed out, Ellen shook her head. "You don't want to audition?" Mr. Quigley asked her. "I thought all pretty girls wanted to be actresses," Michael had said.

"I really want to work on the sets."

He looked at her quizzically. "Why?"

She hesitated. "I like to design things."

He grinned. "Are you familiar with computer graphics?"

"I know what they are," she said.

"That's the way play sets are designed these days," he said. "The skills we need for set preparation are pretty physical, carpentry, painting. How are you with a handsaw?"

She laughed. "I'm better with a paintbrush."

"Acting is cleaner work," he told her, shaking his head but putting her name down. "Just so you're warned!"

Ellen hoped that working with the drama group would help her stop brooding about Michael Tyler. Instead, it only changed her schedule, keeping her at school every day until late. But Michael stayed late, too, practicing with the swim team. She found an upper-story balcony where she could slip into the gallery and watch the last of swim practice. Even though the swimmers wore matching suits, she could pick Michael out as he sped from one end of the pool to the other. He swam like a seal, almost as if he were native to the water. No wonder he had set new records.

Time became a problem. If she ran every day, she didn't have enough time for homework and sleep. Even when she quit running, except on weekends, she had hardly any free time. And on top of the pain of her yearning for Michael, she missed her old friends. Maggie passed in the hall without seeing her and even Cricket seemed strained when they were together.

It would have been easier if Cricket was the only one to disapprove of her quarrel with Maggie. But Luke's attitude caught her off guard, too. Late that next week, he caught Ellen at lunch. "What's happened between you and Maggie? Cricket would only say that the two of you had a blowup."

Ellen swallowed hard. She didn't want to go through it all again, especially not with Luke.

"I'm not complaining," he said. "I like how quiet our lunches are. I just don't understand what's up."

"She embarrassed me one too many times in public."

He laughed. "I thought you'd had shots to make you immune to her fits. Cricket didn't say much. Fill me in."

"Please," she said. "I don't want to talk about it."

She felt his eyes on her face but didn't look up. "Okay, if you won't talk, I will," he said genially. "If you ask me, you're being too tough on her. Before blowing up a ship, you're supposed to fire a warning shot across the bow. Did you ever tell her before how she was getting on your nerves?"

Ellen stood up. "Yes, I did let her know she was getting on my nerves, and no, I didn't ask your opinion."

Before she could get away with her tray, he said, "*He was my monitor for orientation, and that's the end of that.*"

She stared at him in disbelief. Cricket had said more than enough. And he was taking advantage of her. What she really wanted to do was bring her lunch tray down hard on his smart-aleck head. Instead, she moved away swiftly before he could see her sudden tears.

The following weeks taught Ellen two important things. The first, that while she was no great shakes with a handsaw, she was a demon with a hammer. The second, and most heartbreaking, that she wasn't the only person watching Michael's swim practice. The girl with the sleek black hair watched, too. The difference was that she waited after the practice and she and Michael went off together arm in arm.

She quit going to the balcony and only saw Michael from a distance in the halls. Since he was usually with his girlfriend, he waved but never stopped to speak. She told herself that it was Maggie's fault.

Although Ellen missed Maggie, Maggie was apparently unconcerned. She laughed and acted out in the halls in her usual flamboyant way. Ellen could tell from her costume which days she was going to skating lessons. She also heard from Barb Sanchez that Maggie, like Cricket, was out in the bleachers every time any of the teams worked out on the field. "She cheers for everybody," Barb said. "I only go because Tom wants me to cheer for him." She flushed proudly. "I guess you've heard he's playing right guard for the junior varsity team."

Suddenly Ellen, just learning how to be jealous, was battered by it. She was fiercely, painfully jealous of the black-haired girl who walked through the halls with Michael. She hurt with envy for the warm closeness that Barb Sanchez and Tom Winter shared. Six weeks had passed and her love for Michael Tyler was as painful and absorbing as it had been at the first. More than anything she wanted to confide in someone, talk about Michael, and have somebody care that she was hurting. But she had cut herself off from all that. If she talked to Luke, he would be impatient with her. He already blamed her trouble with Maggie on her carrying a torch for Michael. Anyway, talking to a boy wasn't the same.

At least she was busy. Along with drama group,

every week brought something new, yearbook pictures, freshman open house, then a week of pep rallies and preparation for the October homecoming parade and game. Everybody was busy and had run off in all directions by the time drama group broke up for the day.

Everybody but Hank Ober. He was always there, and he was easy company. "It's a jungle out there," he warned her as they left the deserted building. "I'll give you safe conduct home. By armored bike, of course."

"You look bushed," he told her another day. "There's nothing like a double chocolate milkshake to give a girl strength to face her evening meal."

Having Hank ride her home was an easy habit to fall into. It wasn't fair to compare him to Michael but she couldn't help doing it. Hank was as handsome and appealing in his own way as Michael was. He was as witty and easy to talk to. The difference was in her, not him. Nothing happened when he caught her hand or smiled into her eyes. She liked Hank. She loved Michael.

When she let herself think about it, she felt guilty about Hank. She knew he cared more for her than she did for him. But she did enjoy having him as a friend. The awful part was that she wouldn't have missed the fact that he didn't make her heart race or her breath come short if she hadn't met Michael.

She had been right about being able to handle the schoolwork. In algebra and French she only had to stay on top of the homework She could have done without biology, but it was too late to second-guess that with midterm coming up the first week of November.

Sometimes she wished Mr. Burns didn't take honors freshman English quite so seriously. He kept three things going at once, reading the first novel, working on grammar, and studying individual poems he assigned. And he was tough, insisting that they write their own interpretations of the poet's meanings, and turn in perfect papers.

Ellen was holding her own in everything but control of her feelings. Even when she finally gave up running even on weekends, she was always tired. Mostly she just wanted to hide in bed and cover her head. Her mother suggested she was doing too much. Ellen knew better. She seldom passed more than a couple of days without seeing Michael and his girlfriend. It was seeing them that deepened her despair. Even when Michael spoke to her, as he sometimes did, his tone was light and teasing, the way a grown-up talks to a child. And his girlfriend just smiled vaguely at her, as if she were some species not worth identifying.

Ellen didn't notice *when* Luke started staying late in the library every evening. Lots of nights she and Hank and Luke were the last kids to go. As twilight came earlier, Luke's mother or Adrienne were waiting with the car when Ellen and Hank left.

The week of the pep rallies, she and Hank biked

home in the half-dark. "Do you know that it's already October?" Hank asked.

"Not really!" she said, teasing him.

"That means we've missed an anniversary," he told her.

"A what?" she asked.

"On the twenty-seventh of September we had known each other a month. How about we celebrate with a movie this Friday night?"

When she hesitated, he spoke up quickly. "Hey! If we don't celebrate now, we won't get another chance until after the play."

"You sound like the play is the end of the world."

"You'd think so if you had the male lead," he said.

"I might at that," she admitted, laughing.

"What about Friday night?" he asked.

The glow of the porch light threw Hank's face half in shadow, accenting the lines of his jaw and shading his eyes. He looked more wistful than hopeful, as if he expected to be turned down. She had one of those quick stabs of guilt that had become a real problem to her. She liked Hank so much, but was she willing to take the next step? He was suggesting a real date. She had dreamed about going on her first "real date" with Michael.

"I'd like to," she said impulsively, smiling at him.

His smile made her glad of her decision. He caught her hands tightly. "Quick! Remind me of the French word for wow."

She laughed and leaned toward him, "*Wow!*" she

said, pronouncing it carefully, "Or in a pinch, *quelle wow.*"

For one terrified moment she was afraid she had invited a kiss she wasn't ready for. The same sensitivity that made him such a super actor, somehow let him know this. He only smiled and whispered. "Of course. Why didn't I think of that? *Quelle wow!*" Then he caught her in a hug and left at a dead run.

She went inside feeling warm from Hank's impulsive hug, but that night she cried. Going to a movie with Hank would be fun, but she didn't want to think of it as a date. How could she go on a date with anyone but the boy she really loved?

And the way Luke was hanging out in the library confused her. She'd never seen him study like that and she'd never seen him as quiet and downcast as he'd been the past weeks. Lots of time she almost asked him what the matter was, but didn't dare, he might put the question right back to her. She didn't need to be told that she was wasting her time loving Michael Tyler.

She knew that already.

Chapter 9

When Ellen said she had a movie date that coming Friday night, her mother asked, "With that nice Hank who bikes you home?"

Ellen stared at her. "Who else?"

Her mother shook her head and laughed. "I don't know what I was thinking. Of course it would be Hank." She went back to making a salad. After a minute, she turned. "How are you kids planning to get there?"

"I hadn't thought about it," Ellen said. "I figured we would ride our bikes."

Her mother nodded. "That makes sense. I'll be sure and have supper over early."

Nothing more was said until a storm passed through on Thursday night. It wasn't just cold, it was icy. Ellen's mother frowned as she peered out at the thermometer on the back porch that Friday morning. "It's too cold for you kids to bike anyplace," she said. "You'll need a ride to the movie and back."

Ellen stared at her. "Ohmigosh. That's right.

And Hank's not old enough to drive."

"I know that," her mother said in a surprisingly satisfied tone.

"Why don't I talk to Hank about it today."

Her mother nodded. "Be sure and tell him that Dad or I would be happy to drive you there and pick you up after."

Ellen shuddered at the thought. She might as well be back in junior high if her parents had to drive them around. No wonder Michael treated her like a kid! She still was!

Hank caught her at the door of the English room looking worried. "It's too cold for us to bike tonight," he said. "My brother offered to drive us. Will that be all right?"

"It's wonderful," she said, inwardly sighing with relief.

"But we do have a problem about getting home," he went on, obviously embarrassed. "Jay can't pick us up after."

That was only half as bad. "My mother offered this morning," she said. "I'll need to call her, that's all."

"Sure she doesn't mind?" he asked, obviously worried.

"She offered," Ellen told him, smiling to reassure him. "She calls you that nice Hank who bikes me home."

"Whew!" he said. "I was sweating that."

She only smiled. That made two of them!

Hank's brother was big, tall and broad with hair

the color of Hank's and bright blue eyes. He might have looked like Hank without the drooping mustache that hid his mouth and chin. He looked amused and kept glancing at them as if he wanted to tease them. To Ellen's relief he didn't say anything until he let them out. "You sure you've got a way home?"

Hank nodded. "Ellen's mom offered."

"Tell her thanks for me, too," Jay said. After saluting them with a grin, he took off, squealing rubber.

The movie was a comedy Ellen had looked forward to seeing. Hank grinned at her as they sat down. "Jay says smart guys take girls to horror movies to scare them into cuddling up."

Ellen laughed. "Brad tried that. He said all it got him was butter stains on his jacket."

Hank groaned and slapped his forehead with his hand. "Butter stains! I've already blown it. How could I forget popcorn? Now you know I'm a beginner at this."

She laughed softly. "No problem, Hank. That makes it two of us. Anyway I just ate dinner."

He chuckled. "It's neat that we're both beginners. But we've got to do it right. Aren't we supposed to hold hands?" He slid his hand over on hers.

Ellen had promised herself that she wouldn't think of Michael while she was out with Hank. She couldn't help it. He had probably taken out dozens of girls, well, quite a few anyway. Maybe it was easier being with somebody who hadn't dated before. But she thought about the crazy way her heart pounded whenever Michael was around. How would she feel if Michael was holding her hand the way Hank was?

It was icy when they walked outside. Ellen gasped and pulled her wool scarf over her face.

"Boy! They sure cut enough scenes out of that movie!" Hank said as they ran toward a nearby Mexican restaurant.

"Did they really?" Ellen asked. "How do you know?"

"We were only in there about twenty minutes. How about we sue and get our money back?"

She giggled and tightened her arm in his. "You think somebody changed all the clocks to make it look like two hours?"

He nodded. "They even changed my watch," he said soberly. "I know the difference between twenty minutes and two hours when I'm holding your hand."

He paused at the restaurant door, almost shouting over the thrumming guitar inside. "I didn't think to ask. It's okay if we eat before calling your mother, isn't it?"

"She said any time before eleven-thirty."

Mostly they talked about the play and school. The hot, spicy food tasted wonderful after coming in from the cold. Hank checked his watch at eleven and groaned. "We've got to call your mom. That's one lady I mean to stay on the right side of."

Ellen's mother must have been sitting at the

phone. She caught it on the first ring and said she was on her way. "Watch for the car," she said. "It's murder to park around that place." They gave her five minutes then went outside to huddle together out in the wind.

"Is it possible that driver license laws are a fiendish plot?" Hank asked.

She peered at him over her scarf. "Against what?"

"Us kids," he said. "A sneaky conspiracy to rob us of good-night kisses until we're old and decrepit and sixteen."

Ellen giggled, realizing with a swift intake of breath that this moment was what she had been dreading all the time.

"That's not funny," he told her, putting his arms around her. She looked at him and felt a sudden rush of feeling. How nice he was, and fun to be with. The only thing wrong with him was that he wasn't Michael.

That wasn't fair and she knew it. She smiled into his eyes. She felt him catch his breath when their lips touched. He pulled her close against him, his mouth warm and firm against her own.

No bells rang. Her heart didn't hammer. But she felt a yearning tenderness toward him as his lips held hers. His arms were tight and sheltering around her. She clung to him, swept away by the astonishing pleasure she felt in this closeness. Then headlights flooded the ornate carved door of the restaurant as Ellen's mother pulled in at the curb.

Ellen felt her breath come short as they ran for the car, his hand holding hers.

"You two slide into the front seat with me," Ellen's mother said. "The polar bears are freezing in Brookfield Zoo tonight."

The warm car felt like heaven. Ellen's mother insisted on taking Hank home. They let him out on a street Ellen didn't recognize, in front of a row of brick apartments.

How little she knew about Hank! He was smart and sensitive to words. Nobody read the difficult poems Mr. Burns chose for honors English class with more feeling than Hank did. When he read some poetry aloud, she had tears in her eyes. But she knew nothing about him. She hadn't even known he had a brother.

Yet she had been so curious about Michael that she had looked up his address and gone to see his house. Even now, she wasn't sure where Hank lived. He had stood and waved until they turned back out onto the street.

"Have a good time?" Ellen's mother asked from the darkness.

"I really did," Ellen said. "The movie was good and Hank is just great. And funny, too."

Ellen felt her mother's gloved hand press her knee. "I was thinking about my first date tonight, honey. I had fun, too, but I was scared to death."

"Was it with Dad?" Ellen asked.

Her mother's quick bubble of laughter caught

Ellen off guard. "For heaven's sakes, no. He was still years away!"

Later, as Ellen carefully folded her dark blue cashmere sweater and laid it on her shelf, she thought about her mother's remark. Maybe she and Michael would get together "years away" like her parents had. The thought was so awful that she plopped down hard on her bed. She didn't want to wait years to be with Michael. She wanted to be with him *now*. She didn't want to have gone on her first date with anyone else not even as nice a guy as Hank. She didn't want her first kiss to have come from anyone but Michael.

She undressed slowly and slid in between the cool, smooth sheets. "This isn't fair to Hank," she whispered into the darkness of her room. Hank loved her. She knew it. She remembered that sense of pleasure as they clung to each other in that doorway. Would she have thought she was in love with Hank if she didn't have this burning obsession with Michael?

She knew the answer to that. She almost wished that she'd never even met Michael Tyler.

Almost, but not quite.

Chapter 10

The freshman play came off that third weekend in October. Mr. Quigley himself called it "a smashing success." Hank and two of the other freshmen actors got rave notices in *The Monticello* review. The reviewer also wrote at length about the sets and took pictures of the set crew as well as the actors. Somehow Hank Ober managed to be in both pictures. Ellen's mother put the write-up of the play and Ellen's picture on the fridge and sent Brad a copy.

The guilty feeling Ellen had after her date with Hank didn't go away. She and Hank still spent a lot of time together but she always had some reason to turn down other dates.

Hank got strange and quiet and finally challenged her. "Okay, Ellen. What did I do on that date that turned you off on me?" The words were light and teasing but his face looked hard and he didn't smile.

They were on her porch. She put a hand on his arm and said, "You didn't turn me off." Mom just thinks I'm too young to date one guy. You know

pitcher. "You know, the Tyler who's an urban engineer, the one whose wife died a few years back? He and that boy live over on Park. I don't know how Bruce manages to raise a child alone as much as he travels."

"He's sure doing all right with the kid's manners," Ellen's father said, leafing through *The Chicago Tribune* sections beside him. Then he grinned at Ellen. "And with his taste, too. 'Typical Marlowe first class.' A nice phrase."

When Ellen rose, her mother frowned at her. "You can't be through! You haven't eaten a thing."

"Late pizza," Ellen explained, turning away to hide the tears welling in her eyes.

"Her father's child," her dad said, frowning at the financial page.

She was barely in her room before the tears came. She simply gave way to them. The thought of Michael looking up her number and making that call made her want to wail and yell and throw things the way Maggie did when she was crossed. Instead, she pulled down her window shade, locked her door, and cried until she didn't have any tears left.

That early storm the night of her date with Hank had just been a warning. After it passed over, the weather became sensible again. Ellen even ran in the morning for two weekends. Then winter got serious in one single furious November night.

Hank and Ellen had biked home from school wearing sweaters. Just a scattering of curled scarlet maple leaves rattled around her feet as she walked her bike into the garage. She had gone to sleep with her windows wide open and her comforter folded at the foot of her bed.

The chattering of the wind in the shutters woke her with a start. The wind whipped around her room, twisting her delicate white curtains in the chilled air like frantic ghosts. Shivering, she flew across the room to shut her windows. The wind pressed her nightshirt tight against her body. Once the storm was locked out, the room became calm. Wrapped in her comforter, she curled in her window seat to watch the wildness.

She had fallen in love with Michael like the storm had come, with a startling suddenness as exciting and terrifying as it was joyful. But this storm would sweep over, batter the skyscrapers in Chicago, jerk at the sailboats in the marinas, then disappear into darkness over Lake Michigan. Her feeling for Michael *wasn't* blowing over. It was a storm that was twisting her all out of shape with no promise of getting better.

The rain began, not with a pattering, but with a great dark rush. She finally went back to bed, and drew her shades tight against the awful turbulence and thought, If she hadn't ever met Michael Tyler, she would probably adore being Hank Ober's girlfriend. They couldn't walk down the halls together without girls staring at him. He was a natural actor, perfectly convincing in roles that were nothing like he himself was. She could go on and on. He was thoughtful and funny. She never felt as warm as when he caught her in one of his big bear hugs. He certainly didn't deserve a girl who just *appreciated* him while she stayed in love with someone else.

She wished that some magic would make her fall just a little bit in love with Hank. Then her longing for Michael would go away just as the storm would. Then she would be her old self again.

Luke called early that next morning, saying he was leaving right away to ride to school with her.

"I don't need to start early," she told him, "But come by if you want to anyway."

He laughed. "Believe me, Ellen, you *do* need to start early. The town is a mess this morning. Tree limbs and power lines down everywhere. We're lucky to have a phone. Anyway, I need to talk to you about something personal."

She hung up the phone with dread. Something personal. That was scary. She had seen Luke watching her, frowning and thoughtful. Sooner or later he was going to make her talk to him about Michael.

But he was right about the storm. They finally worked their way to school, by taking one detour after another. At the bike rack, he stood with his face twisted a minute, then said, "I can't believe I'm saying this, Ellen, but you've got to help me."

She stared at him, caught off guard. She had prepared herself to keep him from talking about

Michael at all costs. What a rotten friend she was! She was actually glad that he wanted to talk about a problem of his own.

"Help you how?" she asked, still a little wary.

"Schoolwork!" He grinned at her. "This interpretation stuff in English has plowed me under. Give me numbers or a formula and I'm flying, but this stuff murders me. Could you possibly help me get a handle on it? I'll make it up to you anyway you say."

When she didn't answer for a moment, he exploded with frustration. "Come on, Ellen. I'm in heavy duty trouble. Mr. Burns called me in. He's giving me a warning progress report instead of a midterm pat on the back. My scores are below a C."

She caught her breath. Luke Ingram — straight A honor student — with a warning note in freshman English?

"What did your folks say?" Ellen asked, wondering what kind of reaction a warning slip would get from her own parents.

"You know how fair they are. They asked me if I could bring that grade up myself. When I told them how hard I've been trying, *living* in the library, they offered to hire me a tutor."

"Ellen," he went on, his voice pleading. "I can't imagine that any old tutor could help me make any more sense of that stuff than I've been able to do by myself. But you've always been able to make me see things in new ways. I told my folks I knew I could bring that grade up if *you* were willing to help me."

"You know I'd be glad to do it, Luke. But it scares me. What if I couldn't help, and you really needed an expert. I'd die if it didn't work."

A couple of kids skidded through the puddles toward them, their tires spraying muddy water. Ellen jumped to one side and they started toward the building. He went on, "Please, Ellen, I am really up against the wall."

She couldn't stand how desperate he sounded. She knew how smart Luke was and how important his grade average was to him. But if she tried and failed, he'd be in even worse trouble. That was the only reason she hesitated. He was the best friend anyone ever had. And although he was the only person who knew what she was going through over Michael, he hadn't said a word even when all that trouble came with Maggie.

"Ellen," he said, very quietly. He didn't say her name as a question or a plea, but just a friend waiting for a decision.

"Luke, you know I'd do anything for you that I could," she told him all in a rush. "I was only hesitating because it scares me. I can try but I can't promise anything. Poetry isn't clear-cut the way math and science are. You have to put yourself in the writer's place and try to feel what the poet felt and was saying."

"See?" he said, his face bright again. "Already that makes more sense than anything I've tried.

You will help, won't you? Ellen. Name your price."

She grinned at him. "You are one brave guy!"

"The word is *desperate*," he corrected her.

That afternoon, instead of going with Hank to watch the rehearsal of the November play, Ellen met Luke in the library. She knew how smart he was. It shouldn't be too hard. Still, she wasn't prepared for how differently his mind worked from hers.

The assigned poem was one of A. E. Houseman's, and wasn't easy to understand. By the time the light finally dawned on Luke, the librarian was closing up shop. But Luke was exultant. "I think that poem is also about two crazy people," he said as they gathered up their books. "The lover for doing what he did and the poet for writing about it. But to a couple of crazy men that might make sense."

Ellen only smiled at him. Then she must be crazy, too. The hopeless passion in Houseman's "The True Lover" made her cry inside for Michael every time she read the poem through.

Chapter 11

That night when Ellen and Luke left the library together, Hank Ober was waiting out in the hall. He didn't smile at all but only spoke quickly in a strange angry way.

"I want to talk to you a minute, Ellen," he said. "Alone," he added, looking at Luke.

"No problem," Luke said, widening his eyes at Ellen. "I need to cut along home anyway. See you tomorrow, Ellen. And thanks."

Ellen hugged her books against her chest, waiting. Hank made a weak attempt at smiling. Offstage he wasn't that great an actor. "This may come off sounding stupid," he told Ellen. "But what's with you and Luke Ingram?"

"With?" she said. "What kind of a question is that?"

"Personal," he blurted out. "I'm sorry. I just don't get it. I know you used to ride home with him like you did later with me. Then tonight you came here with him instead of being at rehearsal with me. Am I out of the picture? Are you Luke Ingram's girlfriend now?"

She stared at him, then laughed.

"If you think it's funny, maybe I got my answer," he said. When he turned to walk away, she put her hand on his arm and made him stop.

"Please, Hank," she said, "I didn't laugh because it's funny. I laughed because I was surprised. I thought you knew that Luke's been my very special friend all my life. We've hung out together since way down in the grades."

Hank frowned, studying her face. "Just friends? Like brother and sister, you mean?"

She shook her head. "Not exactly," she said. "I've got a brother and Luke has a sister. We're just friends with a lot in common. We have fun together."

"Two and a half hours in the library? For fun?" His tone was scathing. Why hadn't she ever thought of Hank's being jealous? She had sure learned the feeling from having blazed with jealousy every time she saw Michael with that girl of his. But she'd never thought about Hank feeling that same way.

She took his hand. "I'm really sorry, Hank," she said softly. "I wasn't thinking and that was stupid of me. Luke came to me this morning with a problem. I was trying to help him."

He waited without smiling.

"Okay," she said, sighing. "I probably should have told you but I didn't want to broadcast Luke's business. He got a progress report in English. I'm trying to help him get that grade up."

Hank studied her face a minute. "As simple as that?"

She nodded. "It doesn't seem simple to Luke," she said.

He studied her face a moment, then smiled that broad, warm smile that lit up his face. He squeezed her hand hard and then pushed the door open for them. "So he's your friend. That makes him the second luckiest guy in school."

"The second?" she asked.

"The luckiest guy gets to call you his girlfriend."

She looked up at him. What a big, handsome, good-natured guy he was, and she liked him so very much. Why was she putting them through this anyway?

Except for Michael, she liked Hank better than any boy she'd ever met. "Girlfriend," she repeated, frowning. "Would that be the guy I had my first date with?"

He stared at her, then stepped outside and did a comedy leap, striking both heels together as he came down.

At Ellen's house, Hank refused to come inside to warm up. "I'm already running late," he explained. Then he smiled. "And for some reason I'm not feeling the cold."

She laughed and opened the door.

Ellen had just gotten her coat off when Luke called. "You want to explain that business with Hank?" he asked instantly.

Ellen giggled. "No matter what I say, you'll believe what you've already decided. But he was jealous of me and you."

"Then I was right," Luke said. "Just in passing, he wouldn't be a half bad guy if he didn't look like a designer jeans ad."

She hung up the phone, smiling. What Luke meant was that Hank Ober was better for her than Michael Tyler. Silly Luke. She knew that. But falling in love wasn't something you *decided* on.

The next week the first-quarter grade reports came out in *The Monticello*. Ellen read the list with a shiver of joy. She and Michael had both made the dean's list. His class rank was almost the same as hers, too. She folded the paper and put it away, a little annoyed with herself. What was so great about belonging to a tiny private club that never met?

When Ellen sat down next to Cricket at lunch, Cricket was openly envious. "Hey," she said to Ellen. "How come you made dean's list and I'm only on honor roll?" She made a face. "Don't answer that, I know. I only pulled a C in world history. He's tough. I shouldn't have signed up for the honors section."

"He *is* tough," Ellen agreed. "I was lucky."

Cricket wasn't listening. She was studying the list again, frowning. "Your friend Hank's on the honor roll but I can't find Luke on either list. I can't believe that."

"Honors English," Ellen explained. "He'll bring

that grade up." As she spoke, she mentally crossed her fingers. She'd never forgive herself if she wasn't the right person to turn Luke around in that course. But the light did seem to be dawning behind those thick glasses. He had even liked a Christopher Marlowe poem and written a good report on it.

"I hope Maggie can do that in algebra," Cricket said. "She got a failing notice. She's so desperate that she did something really stupid. She caught the letter before her folks saw it. They don't know she's having trouble."

Ellen stared at her. "Doesn't she know about parent-teacher conferences in a couple of weeks? They'll find out then, anyway."

Cricket shrugged. "She's hoping to get her grades up by then. Those skating lessons depend on her making good grades."

Ellen groaned. Never mind that Maggie hadn't spoken to her for a month, Ellen knew how scared and unhappy Maggie must be. As much as she carried on about other things, deep down Maggie's figure skating was the most important thing in the world to her. "Math is the hardest subject to catch up on. She needs a good tutor."

"Where would she get the money to pay a tutor without telling her parents?" Cricket asked. "I really hate to say it but we're talking a lost cause here."

The solution was so obvious that Ellen couldn't believe she hadn't thought of it at once. Instead, the answer hit her when she and Luke were working in the library that afternoon. "Maggie got a fail slip in algebra," she told him.

"So? Big deal," he said, without looking up.

"You didn't feel that way when you got your progress report," she reminded him.

"We're different people," he said, finally looking up.

"Now come on, Luke," Ellen said. "Maggie's no dummy."

"She acts like one. While she's been prancing around giving free shows, I've at least been *trying.*"

"That's true enough," Ellen agreed. "But Cricket says that if her folks find out, she'll have to quit skating lessons."

"That would be a public service," he grumbled. "She might even have to wear real clothes on Tuesdays and Thursdays."

Ellen looked at him in silence a moment before reaching over and forcing his pencil down so he would listen. "Luke," she said. "Can't you see that becoming an Olympic skater could be as important to one person as getting into a college of choice would be to another one?"

He stared at her with his mouth open, then he narrowed his eyes. "All right, Ellen. What's the violin music leading up to?"

"Listen, Luke," she said, leaning toward him across the table. "You could catch Maggie up in algebra with your pencil tied behind your back. Her math skills are okay. It's a matter of understanding."

He didn't even let her finish, but held both palms up as if to ward off a blow. "Oh, no. No, you don't. Not on your life. No way will I try to deal with Maggie. And what's it to you anyway? You two aren't even friends anymore."

She sighed. "You forget. She's the one who got mad at me. I've even been sorry I came down so hard on her, but she's the mad one. Maybe it's silly, but I care about her, and I know exactly how important her skating is to her."

"Then let her parents get her a tutor," he said, pressing his book open to the sonnet they had been assigned.

"Her parents don't know she's failing," Ellen told him. "She intercepted the letter from the office."

He whistled softly, then shrugged. "There's your answer right there. It's a federal offense to intercept mail. Let the attorney general take her away and lower the decibel count in Jefferson High."

"Luke," she said softly. "You owe me one."

He stared at her, horrified. "Ellen, how could you do that to me? Why, I'd have to be seen with her in public."

"You managed it pretty well all those years that we ran around together, you and Cricket and I."

"Shared embarrassment is different. This would be one-on-one. People would notice. They might even think I *liked* her. I'd pay a tutor myself before I'd get linked with a girl who acts like a cartoon character."

"What if she toned it down?" Ellen asked.

"Brain surgery costs more than a tutor," he pointed out. "Anyway, you of all people know how she feels about anyone trying to get her to 'tone it down.' "

"You'd only have to put up with her for two weeks," Ellen pointed out. "If she could show real improvement by the parent-teacher conferences right before Thanksgiving break, her parents might ease up on her."

"Shades of Albert Einstein," Luke groaned. "Relatively speaking, two weeks of being seen with Maggie Martin would be a working definition of eternity."

Ellen glared at him. She hadn't made any bad jokes when he came to her with his problem. Didn't he realize that nothing stayed news more than a few weeks in a high school? So if he took some kidding for a couple of weeks, everyone would have forgotten it by Christmas. She had never been disappointed in him before. She hated it. She stood up and gathered her books together.

"Where are you going?" Luke asked.

"Home," she said. "I guess I believed you when you said I could name the price for my helping you."

"But this is blackmail," he said. "Torture. Public humiliation. I expected something less than the death penalty."

Instead of going home, Ellen went to look in on play practice. She had her hand on the auditorium doorknob when she heard Michael call her name.

He was halfway down the stairs and ran down the rest. "Hey," he said. "Dean's list first quarter. Congratulations! Brad told me you were a brain."

"Watch it!" she said. "You were on the junior list. And I wasn't taking SATs during the midterm tests."

"You noticed," he said. "Having the tests didn't help," he admitted. "But I couldn't let my little freshman pal get one up on me, could I? Can I walk you somewhere?"

A minute before she might have said, "Anywhere." But that "little freshman pal" was too much.

"Thanks, no," she said, her voice cooler than she meant it to be. "I'm just going in here."

She slumped in a chair at the back of the room. How could words, spoken in air, leave her feeling as if she had been physically bruised? Just once, couldn't he think of how his words sounded? He might be smart and good-looking and a Big Man on Campus, but he was a lot of other things, too.

But even as she tried to whip herself into anger at him, what she really felt was pain. She couldn't wipe the memory of his voice from her mind or forget the way his smile changed his whole face.

By the time Hank saw her and came to sit beside her, her cheeks were wet with tears. She leaned forward, pretending to concentrate on the rehearsal so he wouldn't notice. Finally she glanced at Hank. His concentration was complete. From the almost imperceptible movement of his lips, she knew he was following the script of the male lead word for word. Only when the play was over did his mind leave the stage and return to her.

"Want a coke?" he said, putting his arm around her. "I'll buy you one."

"I'll take a rain check," Ellen told him. "It's so cold that I need to get on home." On the way out to the bike rack, they talked about the play and how well it was going. When they turned the corner, Hank put his hand on Ellen's arm. "I don't believe this," he murmured.

Ellen looked up to see Luke leaning against her bike, reading out of his open poetry text. "You've got to be bionic," Hank told Luke. "A human being would freeze to death out here."

"Don't kid yourself, I'm solid already," Luke said, grinning weakly at him. "I was waiting for Ellen." He looked at her bleakly. "I give up. I accept the death penalty."

"Wow!" Hank said, looking at Ellen. "I mean that's one high price for friendship."

Hank took Luke's hand and shook it solemnly. "It's been nice knowing you," he said in a mournful tone. "May your last days on earth be peaceful."

Luke clutched his throat and gagged. "They'll be anything and everything but that."

"Never trust a couple of ham actors," Ellen said, unlocking her bike. Now she only had to get Cricket to beat some sense into Maggie Martin. She didn't envy Cricket the job.

Chapter 12

As soon as Hank left, Ellen went to the phone to call Cricket. She had already dialed half of the number when she set the phone back down. Robin, filling out a worksheet at the table, looked up at her. "Lost your number?" she asked brightly.

Ellen shook her head. "Just my nerve," she said.

Her mother looked over curiously. "Problem?" she asked.

Ellen nodded. "I need to talk to Cricket. But I need to do it face-to-face, not over the phone."

Her mother, who was pouring a cup of coffee, turned, looking concerned. "Nothing wrong between you and Cricket, I hope."

"Why would you ask me that?"

Her mother shrugged. "Don't be so defensive. It's pretty obvious that you and Maggie are on the outs after being friends all this time. Your tone just made me wonder."

Ellen sat down across from her. "It's too complicated to explain." Actually, it wasn't as complicated as it was strange. She wanted to spill out the whole story to her mother the way she used to unload her problems when she was Robin's age. But how could she tell it without Michael Tyler creeping into the story, in fact, if not by name? And she was sure there were at least seven things about her idea that her mother wouldn't approve of.

"Can't it wait for school tomorrow?" her mother asked.

Ellen shook her head. "Luke would call it time-sensitive."

Her mother rose. "Put on your thermals if you're going to ride over there. But hurry back, it's already dark."

When Ellen picked up the phone again, Robin recited Cricket's number without even looking up from her work. Cricket sounded breathless, having just come in from watching football practice. "Can't you tell me over the phone?" she asked. "I mean it *is* cold out there."

"Not really," Ellen told her, conscious that although they both seemed to be busy, her mother and Robin weren't missing a word. "It won't take long, promise."

The minute she got inside Cricket's door, Ellen wished she had at least tried to talk to Cricket on the phone. While they hadn't been as close as in the old days, she and Cricket had seen each other quite a bit through the month since her fight with Maggie. Yet Cricket invited her to sit down as if she were a stranger. Then she looked at her in a wary, almost suspicious, way that chilled Ellen worse than the ride over had.

"What's up?" Cricket asked.

Now that she was there, Ellen didn't know where to begin. "I figured out a way to help Maggie," she said, "but I need your help." Although her words tumbled out too fast, before she could catch her breath, Cricket broke in.

"Why?" she asked. "Old time's sake?"

Ellen stared at her. It wasn't like Cricket to be sarcastic but there was no other way to read her tone. This was maddening. What was wrong with her trying to help an old friend?

"If you want to see it that way, okay," Ellen said, not caring if she sounded angry. "It's just that I know how important her skating is, and how she could probably get those grades up."

When Cricket just waited, Ellen stumbled on, explaining that Luke had agreed to tutor Maggie until the conferences came up.

"Why don't you just call Maggie up and tell her that yourself?" Cricket asked.

"You know she's not speaking to me," Ellen protested.

"So you want me to take Luke's offer to Maggie, is that it?"

Ellen nodded, then sighed. "There's more. Luke agreed to work with her if she would 'tone it down.' "

Cricket got up in her usual quick agile way and

went to the window to stare out. "I keep hearing that phrase," Cricket said, "but I'm not sure I know exactly what it means. Is he talking about changing her style? Does he want her to act like somebody she isn't, to please him? Is this his price for helping her?"

"Cricket," Ellen wailed. "You know what he means — the strange-colored hair and all that crazy loud talk."

Cricket bristled with anger from clear across the room. "That's insulting," she said. "First, that you and Luke think you can play God with Maggie in exchange for helping her out. Second, that you think I would stoop to do your dirty work for you."

"Cricket," Ellen pleaded. "I'm only trying to help Maggie. And it wasn't Luke's idea at all, it was mine."

Cricket turned to stare at her. "I guessed that," she said. "I know Luke, but I don't really know you anymore. I do know you're pulling the same kind of garbage on Maggie that my mother tries to pull on me when she tries to make me over into the frilly little wimp that she wants instead of the girl I really am."

"I only want to help her," Ellen cried, fighting tears.

"My mother's exact words," Cricket said. "If you had any guts, you'd go straight to Maggie with this yourself."

When Cricket kept standing there, staring at her, Ellen got up and put her jacket back on. "Good luck!" Cricket called after her as Ellen let herself out. "I have a feeling that you're going to need it." By the time Ellen got home, the tears were freezing on her cheeks.

After dinner, with the kitchen empty, Ellen called Luke. He wasn't surprised at Cricket's refusal. "I don't even know how to get her to listen!" Ellen wailed. "I wish I hadn't started this."

"That's two of us," he said. "But it *is* a good idea, as loathsome as it is. I know how much you've helped me already. How about I try talking to Maggie myself?"

"Oh, Luke," she cried. "I know I should, but would you?"

"I'll give it a try. The worst she can do is kill me. I can only die once, you know."

Even Hank noticed how nervous Ellen was all the next day. "A guy might think that *you* got the death penalty instead of Luke," he said, studying her face. "What's this all about?"

He listened thoughtfully while she explained. Then he took her hand. "Hey, relax! It'll work or it won't. You tried." Then he frowned. "I can't imagine your letting it bother you so much when she acted out with you in public."

Ellen flushed, remembering the words of the upperclassmen when she filed out of the assembly with Michael and his girlfriend laughing. And that day with Maggie's brightly painted finger poking Michael in the chest. Hank fell silent and kept walking along, not looking at her. When he spoke, she realized that he had been waiting for her to explain. She hadn't and she couldn't, no matter how much he wanted to understand.

"In any case," he said. "This idea of yours will either work out or it won't. And I give you a point and a half for trying."

"A point and a half?" she asked. "That's not much."

"Two points for thinking it up, take away half a point for not facing Maggie yourself."

She stared at him. He had never criticized her before. But she knew he was right about the lost half point. Luke managed the first step just fine, to her immense relief. That night Maggie called. Her voice sounded strange, half angry and all the way confused. "I know I should hate you for setting this deal up with Luke," she said. "I got myself into this, I should have gotten out by myself. But thanks anyway for whatever reason you did it." She paused, but not long enough for Ellen to say anything. "I take it back about your friend Luke," she said. "He's a good guy." Then she hung up the phone.

Maggie didn't "tone it down" right away but as the days passed, she was quieter in the halls and somehow managed to find time to change out of those wild tights on skating lesson days. Ellen was burning up to find out how Luke had managed to get that done. "Come on, tell me your magic method," she asked him.

He shrugged. “Maggie’s basically a good kid who bucks for attention by being weird.” He grinned, flashing his braces at her. “If you tell anyone this, I’ll say you lied, but I went to that great fountainhead of common sense known as Mom. When I told her what was going on, her advice was right on the money.”

“I can’t stand it. What did she say?” Ellen asked.

He shrugged. “She said to compliment Maggie when she looked good to me and ignore her when she didn’t. At first I winced a lot, but Maggie’s basically okay. And she’s catching on in algebra faster than I ever thought she could. And everything else, too.”

Chapter 13

The long-awaited and potentially killing parent-teacher conferences were held on the Tuesday night before Thanksgiving. "How can anyone on the dean's list be so nervous about these conferences?" Ellen's mother asked her as they cruised the crowded parking lot looking for an open space.

Ellen only shrugged. It wasn't her conference she was nervous about. Since Maggie said her terse thanks over the phone two weeks before, she had continued to mellow toward Ellen. She smiled and said hi when they passed in the halls, and brought her tray to eat lunch with Ellen and Cricket and Luke. Ellen was sure Maggie was coming more because of Luke and Cricket than herself, but it was still great to see her close like that again, and hear her funny remarks. Said more quietly, but still funny.

Cricket hadn't mentioned that night she was so angry at Ellen, and probably never would. Cricket's quick temper had always cooled quickly. She didn't hold grudges but she didn't like to hash things over either.

Ellen was edgy all evening, hoping desperately that both Luke's and Maggie's grades had come up enough. She promised herself that no matter what happened she was through minding other people's business. She had been too close to losing both Maggie and Cricket forever to want to risk that again. Luke had asked *her*. That was different.

As she and her parents went from one appointment to the next, Ellen watched for Maggie and Luke. No sign of either one. She did see Hank with his brother, Jay, making the rounds with him. "That can't be Hank's father," Ellen's mother said, waving at Hank down the hall.

"It's his big brother," Ellen explained. "Remember? He drove us to the movie that night."

"I don't know anything about his family," her mother said in a confused way.

"Neither do I," Ellen told her. "He just doesn't talk about them." She felt that funny stab of guilt. She hadn't talked to Michael about his family either, but she had picked up every scrap of information she could about him. Was being endlessly curious about someone part of being in love?

When her parents' last appointment was over at nine-thirty, Ellen wanted to go straight home. "How about we celebrate?" her father asked. "A milkshake or something. It's a half day of school tomorrow, then Thanksgiving."

"Thanks a lot, Dad," Ellen said, "But I'm expecting a call. Maybe even more than one."

Luke called just as they walked in the door. "I made it," he said. "I made it and Maggie made what her teacher called significant progress. I really can't thank you enough, Ellen, and Maggie said to tell you the same."

"I'm just glad it worked," she told him. "What about Maggie's skating lessons?"

"From what she says, she got the dressing-down of the century from her folks, but she can keep on with the lessons if she doesn't get lazy again." He paused. "And Ellen, believe me, once I got into it, I didn't mind helping Maggie. It was even fun. Listen, I've got to run. We've got some serious celebrating to do."

Ellen stared at the phone a long time, wondering about that "we." Could Luke and Maggie have possibly learned to like each other enough to celebrate together? After all, hadn't Luke come all the way from thinking of Maggie as cartoon character to being "a great kid"?

Brad got in too late the night before Thanksgiving for Ellen to see him until the next morning. When he finally made it downstairs for breakfast, she was content just to sit and listen to him talk. He looked wonderful. He seemed bigger than when he left, and older. He grinned at her over the rim of his coffee mug like he was glad to see her, too.

"Don't look at me like that," he told her. "You

brains who make the dean's list don't understand about people who have to live on caffeine to study all night." He complimented her on the pictures from the play. "There are about ten guys in my dorm waiting for you to grow up," he told her.

She dropped her eyes. She knew he was teasing but it wasn't the sort of stuff Brad would make up. She liked hearing that college boys thought she looked okay. And Brad's friends all had to be older than Michael Tyler. The difference was that Michael wasn't ever really looking at her. He was only looking at Brad's "little sister."

She kept hoping she and Brad would get a chance to talk. She had lived with Michael constantly on her mind and in her heart ever since August. Sometimes she'd thought she would just die if she couldn't talk to somebody about her feelings. She had decided that Brad might understand. Maybe he could even say something that would give her some hope.

But she didn't get a minute with him alone. Instead he took off in the car to look up his old buddies until it was dinnertime.

As always, there was too much Thanksgiving dinner but Ellen liked all of it. Robin got the lucky end of the wishbone and cried out, "A horse. That means I get my own horse."

Brad and her parents laughed but Ellen only sighed. It was a good thing she wasn't superstitious enough to believe in things like wishbones. But just in case she had a wish ready, too.

When she and Cricket met at the Oakbrook mall on Friday, every tree and storefront twinkled with lights. Canned Christmas carols boomed from loudspeakers everywhere. The crowds were so thick that they gave up and went to Marshall Field's for hot chocolate and cookies. "I hoped Maggie would come," Ellen said. "Was she skating today?"

Cricket looked confused. "I don't know what she's up to. When I called, she just said thanks but she couldn't make it. But she did say to tell you hi!"

"I'm just glad that mad business is all over," Ellen said, scooping the last of the whipped cream out of her mug. "Luke was a real great guy to coach her like he did."

"Don't kid yourself. I think he had a good time doing it. In fact, if we were talking about anyone but Luke, I'd say he is getting a king-size crush on Maggie," Cricket said.

"You're kidding!" Ellen said, staring at her.

Cricket shook her head and grinned. "That's only half. I think Maggie likes him back. A lot. A whole lot!"

Ellen stared at her. "That's crazy," she said. "Two weeks ago Luke said that being seen with Maggie was a death penalty. Luke doesn't change his mind about anything that fast. And if Maggie liked him, the whole world would know it."

Cricket shrugged. "You know Luke better than I do," she said. "But don't forget how much Maggie has changed."

Ellen shook her head but she kept remembering

Luke's saying that *we* have a lot to celebrate. Who could have made the other half of *we* except Maggie?

Ellen baby-sat with Robin Friday night and watched an old Katharine Hepburn movie that made her cry. Did everyone in the world have to be happy in love but her?

Since Brad had to leave for college right after lunch on Sunday, Ellen's father took them all to the country club for dinner on Saturday night. Ellen had forgotten how much fun it was to dress up and go out for dinner. She wore her favorite dress, the sheer white wool one that made her feel like a princess. When Brad shook his head approvingly as she came down the stairs, she knew she'd made the right choice. Robin changed her clothes three times and ended up wearing the red jumper and blouse she started out in.

When her father first announced the dinner plans, Ellen wondered if Brad wouldn't rather be out with his friends. That night Brad got the best of both worlds. The minute they were seated, friends started coming over to their table to greet Brad, ask him about school, and catch him up on their news.

They were waiting for dessert when Brad looked up with a grin and rose with his hand out. "Michael," he said. "Hey, how are thing's anyway?"

Ellen glanced back to see Michael Tyler standing with one hand on the back of her chair. He smiled down at her as Brad introduced him to the family.

"No need to introduce Ellen and me," Michael said, putting his hand on her shoulder. "We're old buddies by now. I got to teach her the ropes at the start of school. And has she taken over with a flash! I guess you saw that great picture from the freshman play story."

"See it!" Brad laughed. "I had it laminated. Nothing raises your stock in a dorm like having a knockout little sister."

"Never thought of that," Michael said, looking down at Ellen and smiling. "Not that she looks like anybody's little sister tonight." When the waiter brought the desserts, Michael excused himself. "I think we're about to take off," he said. "Great to see you, Brad." As he left, he touched Ellen's shoulder again. "See you soon, Ellen, okay?"

"What did he mean by showing you the ropes?" Ellen's father asked, looking after Michael as he crossed the room.

"He was my monitor for orientation," Ellen told him, wishing her mother would quit looking at her with that funny little line of thought between her eyes. It was bad enough that her heart was thundering so loudly that everyone could probably hear it.

"That's falling into it," Brad said. "That guy's about as nice as they come." He glanced across the room. "Who's the knockout girl with him and his dad and that older woman?"

Ellen would have died before she turned around to look at Michael's group. She expected to see the black-haired girl he was always with at school and didn't need that. As it turned out, she didn't have to look. From where she sat, she saw them leave the dining room. And it wasn't the girl from school! This girl was a knockout, all right, but with thick auburn hair that swung to her shoulders. As Michael held her coat, she smiled up at him as if they shared a thousand secrets. Ellen didn't look across at her mother. She didn't have to. She could feel her mother's thoughtful eyes, watching her daughter's face flame with color.

Brad had promised to meet some friends later and needed the car. Ellen was glad to go home early. She was never going to be able to eat in that dining room again without seeing that girl smiling up into Michael's eyes. But once at home, she was restless. She had been all ready to talk to Brad and the chance never came. More than anything she needed to talk to *someone* about her feelings.

Maybe Maggie knew something Ellen didn't. As soon as Maggie broadcasted her crushes to the whole school, they seemed to go away. Maybe just the fact that she loved Michael secretly made her feelings keep getting deeper and more painful all the time.

Her father made sausages and waffles for Brad's good-bye brunch. While Robin stared off into space eating one waffle after another, Brad chattered on about his late party of the night before, but that didn't keep him from eating. As Ellen's mother lifted the last hot waffle and offered it to Brad, he shook his head. "That one is Dad's," he teased. "I wasn't really hungry this morning."

Ellen's father laughed and held his plate out. "We all realized that, Brad, when you stopped at only seven waffles."

Robin wailed and began to eat faster. "I'm behind," she said. "I'm really way behind."

When Brad's friend picked him up, Ellen almost wanted to cry. The whole weekend was gone and she didn't feel that he had been there at all. Her mother did cry or come close. From the living room Ellen could hear her father's voice in the kitchen going on and on quietly. Her mother sniffled a lot even though she didn't seem to be catching a cold.

Ellen pretended to be reading the novel Mr. Burns had assigned for English. Actually she kept remembering how wonderful Michael had looked in his navy blazer and cream-colored crew sweater. She had felt wonderful about his saying she didn't look like a kid sister until she saw *that* girl. She'd never feel like a princess in her white wool dress again, not after how Michael's girl had looked, so grown-up and sophisticated in a deep brick-red suit. She hadn't even worn a blouse under it but only loops of black beads against her throat.

Cricket called a little after dark, breathless with excitement. Her father had called and talked a long time. "You'll never guess what he told me," Cricket said. "He and Lynn have a wonderful surprise for me when I go out for Christmas. I know what it is but I didn't spoil it for him by guessing."

"You really know?" Ellen asked, hoping that Cricket wasn't building herself up for an awful letdown.

"Of course I know. They've gotten me a horse, I know they have," Cricket told her. "And it's only three weeks until I'll be out there to ride it. Isn't that wonderful?"

Ellen finally got off the phone with that here-we-go-again feeling heavy in her chest. All her life she had watched Cricket decide what she wanted and honestly believe she was going to get it, only to be disappointed.

She sat staring at the phone. Who was she to think that Cricket was foolish to ask for trouble by building up false hopes? She had met Michael Tyler, fallen flat in love with him, and still dreamed that he would feel the same way about her.

Chapter 14

Monday morning, after Thanksgiving, Ellen's windows were white with spidery frost. For one wonderful moment, she thought it was snow. She ran to the window and blew a warm place on the glass so that she could see out. The barren limbs of the maple tree were coated with white and the lawn frozen stiff with frost. No snow!

Robin tapped on her door and stuck her head in. "Mom says not to forget warm underwear. It's ten below," she said. Then a delighted giggle. "I get to wear my new boots."

Ellen groaned and sat back on her bed. She hated thermal underwear. She could only stand it when ice skating on Luke's lake or sleigh riding. When she was dressed, she packed up her books and homework. She tested a ballpoint pen on an empty sheet of notebook paper. When it didn't leave a mark at first, but worked fine the second time, she stuck it in her book bag and turned to close her notebook.

She looked down and gasped in horror. Had she

really done that? Had she really written MT three times on that paper without even thinking about it? She tore the sheet out and left it crumpled on her desk. How many times had she kidded Maggie about writing the initials of her current crush everywhere? Usually Maggie added her own initials underneath and drew a ragged heart around them both. Had she become at least half that silly herself? It was thinking of the snow and winter that made her do it. Winter was Michael's favorite season, too. He had told her so.

Why did she have to remember every word he said to her? She flushed with shame at how wonderful she'd felt during that dinner at the club with his hand on her chair, smiling at her. And all that time his beautiful date was waiting for him just across the room. Every contact with him was joy and pain mixed together, with the pain lasting longer.

Robin came pounding down the hall again and stopped. "I forgot Mom said you'd better call Luke. You have to take the bus because it's too cold to bike." Then she frowned and crossed to Ellen's window. "How did you make that peephole?" she asked, peering through it. "My glass is white I can't see through."

Ellen swung her book bag onto her shoulder and started out. "Blow on the glass and it will melt a place," she told Robin. "It's only frost."

The warm air from the kitchen smelled delicious.

Ellen breathed the sweetness of maple as she dialed Luke's number. He answered on the first ring. "Great minds!" he said. "I was about to call you. Mom's driving us. We're starting out right away."

No wonder the air smelled so good. Instead of the cold cereal that she and Robin usually ate, Ellen's mother set plates of thick golden French toast in front of them. "There," she said, smiling. "That should stick to your ribs until lunch."

It looked wonderful. When Ellen poured her maple syrup, the handle of the pitcher was hot to the touch. "Want me to pour yours, too?" she asked Robin.

"I'm no baby. I can do it," Robin said, reaching for it.

Her mother moved fast and took the pitcher from Ellen. "Oh, no, you don't, young lady," she said, smiling. "I want this breakfast to stick to your ribs, not your sweater."

Robin always ate slowly and didn't usually talk until her food was gone. Instead, she stared off into space with an expression of total ecstasy. But as Ellen set her dishes on the counter, Robin looked up, "What does MT stand for?" she asked.

For that split second Ellen couldn't move. She knew she was blushing and was conscious of her mother watching her face. Before Ellen could catch her breath, her mother spoke in a tone of firm authority. "Mt is the abbreviation for the word *mountain.*"

"But why would you write that three times in a row?" Robin asked, looking up at Ellen.

Ellen was sure her mother knew. Somewhere along the line, something she had said, maybe the phone call after the play, maybe the way she had frozen when Michael came to stand with his hand on the back of her chair at the country club, something had laid her secret open to her perceptive mother's eyes.

Oh, if her mother would please just *not* say anything, not put what she was thinking into words, it might still be all right. When she was ready to go, her mother held her close for a long moment. "Stay warm and be careful, honey," was all she said to Ellen.

Luke's mother arrived within minutes. She smiled as Ellen climbed into the backseat. "We're making another stop," she said. "But don't worry. We have plenty of time."

Luke deliberately didn't let Ellen catch his eye. But that didn't make any difference anyway. Right away Ellen realized the stop was at Maggie Martin's house. Luke was out of the door and up Maggie's walk before she even got out on the porch. Ellen grinned crazily to herself. Then Cricket was *right* about Luke and Maggie liking each other. Luke never came to the door to get *her*. But then, they were only friends! What a trip!

Mrs. Ingram chuckled from the front seat. "Isn't that cute? I thought Luke was never going to be interested in a girl except as a friend." She turned to smile at Ellen. "And what an entertaining girl that Maggie is. Luke asked her over for turkey leftovers Friday and we all enjoyed her. She's promised to bring her skates next time."

Maggie slid in beside Ellen. She was wearing a new parka. The white fur framing her face made her look wonderful. "How are the skating lessons going?" Ellen asked because she just felt like teasing her.

Maggie giggled and looked at Luke with a sickly sweet expression that Ellen was glad Mrs. Ingram couldn't see from the driver's seat. "Absolutely wonderful," Maggie said. "Along with everything else in the whole wide world."

Ellen's schedule between Thanksgiving break and Christmas vacation was breathless. It didn't help that she saw Michael once or twice and was confused. He didn't seem to be hanging out with the dark-haired girl anymore. He was always alone or with a bunch of guys. When he waved or smiled at her, her heart hurt with hope. Maybe enough time had passed that he could see her as a girl instead of a kid.

Auditions for the spring touring play were held the first week of December. Ellen signed up to work on the sets but Hank tried out for a part, expecting nothing. To his delight, and Ellen's, he got the second male lead. "That's all the Christmas present I need, right there," he told Ellen as they celebrated over cokes. Then he paused and drew a deep breath. "Especially since I have news I hate. I haven't told you because I hate it so much." He leaned toward her. "All I want is to stay here with you for Christmas. But I have go spend it in Ohio with my father." He sighed, falling silent.

Ellen reached over and took his hand. "I'm sorry, Hank," she said. "Really sorry."

"Will you miss me?" he asked.

"Of course I'll miss you!" she said as he took both her hands and held them tight. He had to believe her because she was telling the truth. What she didn't say was how much she dreaded the holiday herself. She was ashamed of her reasons. With school out that whole two weeks, she might not see Michael, even from a distance. Two whole weeks!

She and Hank went together to the Christmas choral concert the next Sunday. Michael was there with his father. She sat with Hank holding her hand feeling like the worst awful person in the world. She couldn't look at Hank for fear that he notice the look in her eyes. She couldn't raise them without seeing Michael and having that awful longing cut her breath short.

All that beautiful music and the cold starry night she and Hank walked home through should have given her a little Christmas spirit. Nothing. She only kept seeing Michael turning to talk to his father, then rising to clap at the concert end. She told herself she would feel Christmas when snow came.

Brad came home from college and immediately started working at a store in the Loop. He was either off at work, on the train, or out with his friends. Ellen went with Cricket to pick out presents in malls loud with canned Christmas music. The difficult person on her list was Hank. She'd never bought a present for a boy before, except Luke and her brother. But she knew Hank would have something for her, and this alone made her feel guilty.

She couldn't find anything that seemed right. But even as she looked, she kept seeing things she was sure that Michael would like. She went back three times to look at a framed poster of an Olympic diving contender. The diver even looked a little like Michael, lean with dark hair that was a little wavy.

"That isn't even Hank's sport," Cricket told her, suggesting that she buy him a scarf. When Ellen asked Luke, he said that every guy liked to get computer games. Brad was even less helpful. "Get him a funny calendar," he said. "You know, one of those tear-off ones with a cartoon on every day of the year."

In the end, she went back and looked at Michael's poster one more time, then bought Hank a leather key ring. Fastened to it was a brass medallion with the two-faced mask of drama, the mask of tragedy on one side and comedy on the other. Technically it seemed perfect because of his absorption in the theater, but after she got it home she couldn't even remember whether he carried keys.

Hank and Cricket would both leave as soon as school was out on Friday. Hank walked Ellen home that Thursday night before the last day of school. "Please don't open this until I'm gone," he said. "I'm not sure you're even going to like it."

She was relieved not to open the gift with him watching. The size of it scared her. The tiny box suggested jewelry. She couldn't stand it if he had spent a lot of money.

"Can I open this now?" Hank said as she handed him her wrapped gift.

When she nodded, he unwrapped the box carefully and put the wrappings in his pocket. "Hey," he said, lifting the key ring from the folded tissue paper. He turned it to look at the two masks, looking completely happy. "I love it, Ellen. It's just perfect."

He took her in his arms and kissed her gently a long time. She clung to him, loving their closeness, but feeling an incompleteness that made her hate herself.

She watched him transfer his house key and a bike lock key to the ring. Then he grinned. "This is not only great, but it's something I can always carry around to remind me. Like I wouldn't be thinking of you anyway, Ellen."

When he had to leave, he kissed her again, holding her close a long time. He finally pulled his lips away with a sigh, and smiled at her. She watched him walk off into the darkness with his head down and his hands in his pockets, one holding her gift.

She ran upstairs because she didn't want Robin to ask her why she was crying. Was it for Hank? Or for herself?

Chapter 15

During those busy weeks before Christmas, Ellen received a formal engraved invitation. She never dreamed that a piece of paper could cause so much trouble. Her mother watched her read it. "The Willoughby Christmas dance," Ellen said. "But, Mom . . ."

Her mother smiled. "You're in high school now, remember? And Silvie is so pleased that you'll be coming this year. You know how crazy she's always been about you."

"But, Mom, I don't *want* to go." Ellen cried.

Her mother stared at her. "For heaven's sakes, why not? Remember how Brad always raved about those parties?"

"Boys are different. They can go anywhere alone," Ellen protested. "And I don't even have anyone to go with."

"A lot of the kids have always come alone. But if that bothers you, Silvie would love to ask your friend Hank."

Ellen shook her head. "Hank won't even be here.

He'll be in Ohio with his father. Mom, I really don't want to go."

Her mother frowned, then looked at her intently. "Do you have some reason you're not telling me, Ellen?"

Ellen caught her breath. They were both thinking about Michael Tyler. When Ellen was silent, her mother went on. "I seldom interfere in your life. This time I intend to."

Ellen held her breath for fear her mother would mention Michael. If she called him a crush, she might even die. Instead, her mother's voice turned stern and a little cold. "Your father and I are too close to Silvie and Alex Willoughby to let you hurt their feelings for some childish reason that you won't even discuss. And it would hurt them deeply. I'm not asking you, Ellen, I'm telling you to accept that invitation, go to their dance, and be a delightful guest."

Ellen's mother had never walked away from her like that with such crisp, angry steps. At the door, she turned to face Ellen. "When you're ready to go shopping for a dress, tell me."

It had been stupid to put off looking for that dress until the worst Christmas crowds. It was a wonder that she found anything she liked. It was a miracle that she found the most beautiful dress she had ever seen. The saleswoman called the color ivory but to Ellen it looked like a silk pearl. The style was simple, a straight neckline that caught at her shoulders, and a short, full swirling skirt. Ellen gasped at the price tag.

"Never mind," her mother said. "The dress is classic and silk is good all year around. We'll have to find discount shoes."

Ellen tried the dress on every night before going to bed. Whirling in front of her long mirror, she tried to imagine Michael's reaction to it. He couldn't look at her in *this* dress and think of her as a kid. Anyway, he was probably off for holiday or hadn't even been invited.

The dance was the last Saturday before Christmas. The first snow began to fall a little after noon. It came out of a sunny sky, tiny spangles spinning in the bright air. Robin was so excited she couldn't speak straight. She flew up to Ellen's room. "Now," she said. "Now you've got to put out your snowballs."

"Now," Ellen said, lifting the boxes down. "You can decide where to put them this year." By the time Robin had set the paperweights out, the sky had turned to a cotton color. The snowflakes had grown and were falling so steadily that by three o'clock, passing cars were only moving shadows. By four, every twig of the maple tree was piled high. The shrubs along the porch were giant white mushrooms. The lawn was a silken drift that reflected the colored lights of the Christmas tree inside the living room window.

And Robin's baby-sitter called to cancel.

"Never mind," Ellen's mother said. "We'll stay with Robin and make other arrangements to get you to the party, Ellen."

"Other arrangements!" Ellen wailed, but her mother was already dialing. To her horror, Ellen realized she was talking to Luke's mother.

"But he's taking Maggie," Ellen whispered desperately. Her mother turned her back and went on talking. Ellen flew upstairs and threw herself on her bed. It wasn't fair. It wasn't decent to make her tag along on somebody else's date to the biggest party of the Christmas season. Then her mother was at her door.

"I can't imagine anyone wearing that dress of yours with her eyes all red from crying," her mother said.

Ellen rolled over and sat up. "Mom," she said. "You don't understand. Maggie and Luke are a couple. I can't horn in on them. Why can't Brad take me and pick me up?"

"This snow could stop the trains," her mother said. "Brad'll probably bunk with friends in the city tonight."

"Why Luke?" Ellen cried. "It's so humiliating."

"Three reasons," her mother said, stubbornly cheerful. "He's your good friend, he is happy to do it, and their car has front-wheel drive."

The snowplows were working by five o'clock. At seven, when Luke's mother came by, the snow had stopped. The clear sky was studded with stars. Ellen's father held her coat and smiled into her eyes.

"With you and this village both so beautiful, you could have a night you will remember forever."

The village was a fairyland of frosted trees and gleaming drifts. The Willoughby house was lit like a three-story Christmas tree. Music spilled out the front door and the air inside smelled of balsam and pine. When Ellen took off her coat, her Aunt Silvie smiled widely. "How beautiful you are," she whispered. "I was afraid that this storm would keep you away. Your uncle Alex wants to dance the first dance with you!"

Brad hadn't told the half of it. That the music was live, a four-piece band from Chicago, and that the waiters wore tuxedos. He hadn't told her that the house would be lit with candles in the windows and on all the mantles, with a different decorated Christmas tree in every room.

"Having fun?" Uncle Alex asked as he steered her smoothly around the floor.

"I feel like Cinderella," she said. "In fairyland."

He smiled. "And you look like her, too," he told her.

Bud Leonard asked her to dance next. She didn't have to believe his flattery to enjoy it. She'd danced with tons of people when suddenly Michael was there, smiling at her and holding out his arms to a slow dance. "I finally get my turn," he said, his voice halfway laughing against her hair. "I waited long enough. When this one's over, we'll eat together, okay?"

She had never tried to imagine dancing in Mi

chael's arms, which was just as well. As always with Michael, the joy came with fear built in. Would he feel the ridiculous hammering of her heart under that sheer dress and think she was crazy or sick?

Michael made a big deal of picking out white food for her, tiny diamonds of sandwiches, a serving of pasta salad crunchy with fresh vegetables, and a pair of tiny white cakes in fluted cups with frosting shaped like holly on top. "How's that for a good memory?" he asked.

They ate and talked and then danced again. Ellen saw Luke watching her every time he and Maggie passed them.

"My aunt came from back East to spend Christmas with Dad and me. Her house is my second home since Mom died. In fact, I'm going to stay with her family while Dad does a project in Egypt right after the holidays. I hate being away from home and Jefferson High, but it's only for this one semester."

"But what about school?" she asked. Only one semester! He couldn't mean he was really leaving for all those months!

"Surprise, Ellen," he said, grinning at her. "They have high schools in Connecticut, too. I'll finish this year there and be back at Jefferson in the fall. Want to dance?"

Ellen was glad to be back on the dance floor. They slow danced. That way he couldn't see her face. He was leaving. To be gone for the rest of the school year. She closed her eyes against the waves of pain.

How could she bear not even seeing him all that time? Had she really once wished she wouldn't see him? Only now did she realize how desolate she would feel.

His arms tightened around her. She forced herself to smile brightly at him as he looked down at her. At least she had this time with him, longer than she'd had since that first day. The closeness of the dance was sweeter and more intimate than anything she had dreamed of. She couldn't believe how close she had come to missing the most wonderful night ever.

At the end of the dance, Michael stopped suddenly to steer her through an open door to a sunroom with windowed walls. "Look at that, Ellen. The snow has started again." They were standing with his arm across her shoulder, watching the flakes drift down when Luke came looking for her.

"I'm sorry, Ellen. Mom called. It's snowing like crazy out by our place. She's coming for us while she can make it."

"That's tough, Luke," Michael said. "It's only eleven." He paused. "You're not going to take Ellen with you, are you?"

"She came with Maggie and me," Luke said.

"I can take her home when the party's over."

Luke looked at Ellen, who held her breath. She knew Luke was convinced that Michael was dangerous to her. Luke wasn't easy to intimidate, but Michael was sure working on it. "I think she'd better come with us," Luke said with a good solid try at authority. "We have front-wheel drive and, like I said, it's snowing like crazy again."

"Well," Michael said, touching Luke's shoulder. "If that's the problem, no problem. My car has front-wheel drive, too, and Ellen lives close. How about it, Ellen?"

Ellen couldn't meet Luke's eyes. But Luke didn't know Michael was going away. She only had the holidays left. Let Luke be mad and her mother, too, if she wanted to be. Right then she didn't much care. In fact, she didn't care at all. "I'll stay with Michael," she said. "Please thank your mother for the ride."

Luke glared at her, turned on his heel and left.

"What's the matter with that kid?" Michael asked. "Did he want to see my credentials or something?"

"He's my friend," Ellen said, laughing in spite of herself. "A little protective, but my very good friend."

"That's not all bad." Then he turned to the window. "If this keeps up, we may want to leave soon. Anyway, there's something I want to show my little winter-loving friend."

At midnight, they got their coats, and said their good-byes to the Willoughbys. Michael brought his car to the entrance and helped her in. "Have you ever watched the snow fall on Salt Creek?" he asked as he pulled away.

She shook her head. "Never," she told him. The

intimacy of the car overwhelmed her. It smelled like leather and Michael's after-shave lotion. Muted carols played on his radio as he drove along streets filling up again with snow.

He made a dozen detours to avoid the screeching, grinding snowplows whose colored lights circled and spun in the dazzle of falling snow. "How about this?" he asked, smiling over at Ellen. "A new classic card. Christmas night with snowplows."

Out at the creek, Michael draped a plaid blanket over her hair and shoulders. The view from the bridge was as beautiful as he had said, the water a racing blackness under swift ice floes, with the snowflakes plunging to disappear into that darkness. The white-burdened trees bent gracefully as if they were bowing.

Finally Michael sighed and took her arm to walk back to the car. "That's what I call one special evening, Ellen Marlowe. It would be a shame to waste a snow like this on just anyone. Thank you for being a winter nut like I am."

At her door he lifted her chin, and looked at her for a long moment. Then he leaned over and touched her lips with his. In that moment, she realized that no other kisses but his could ever mean anything to her. Something almost like electricity tingled in her lips and down her entire body. She couldn't breathe but she didn't want to. She only wanted to hold him tight and keep that trembling excitement coursing through her forever. But almost at once, he had pulled away and was smiling down at her. "Merry Christmas, Ellen, and I hope the rest of your freshman year is great."

She leaned against the inside of the door for a moment. She had read of people being weak with joy the way she was now. She closed her eyes, holding her memories as if they could be kept forever, frozen in time like the scenes in one of her snow-filled paperweights.

Finally she hung up her coat, turned off the night-light, and tiptoed up to her room. She didn't want to take off her dress because then the evening was over. He hadn't said "kid" one single time.

This night had been what she had waited and yearned for since that first day. She couldn't stand it that he'd be leaving but it was all different now. He had chosen to dance almost the whole evening with her. And he had kissed her. She lay wide-awake a long time. Her father had said it before it even happened. This night she would remember forever.

Chapter 16

Fortunately Brad had gotten home on an early train after spending the night on a bench in Union Station. Ellen's father was also at the table that next morning when Mrs. Ingram called. Ellen watched her mother's face with a sinking heart, listening to her side of the conversation. "Yes, she's fine," and, "We really can't thank you enough." Her mother finally replaced the phone and looked at Ellen.

"You told us what a wonderful time you had," her mother said in that stiff voice that Ellen feared. "You failed to mention that you didn't come back home with Luke."

Although Ellen didn't trust her voice, neither could she deal with that silence. "The storm was worse out in the country," she said. "When Luke's mom came to get him and Maggie early, a friend offered me a ride later."

Ellen felt like a bug stuck on a pin for an audience of four. "What friend?" her mother asked icily.

"Michael Tyler," Ellen said right out. She might as well face up to it right then and have it over with.

"Hey," Brad said. "No problem. There are guys in that school I don't want near my sister, but Michael's okay."

"That's the boy we met at the club at Thanksgiving," Ellen's father said. "Nice-looking kid, good manners, too."

Ellen's mother sat very still. "Let it be said for the record I want to know who's bringing my daughter home."

Brad said, "Leaving that dance early would be awful. And Michael's strictly straight-arrow."

"Doesn't anyone ever call that boy Mike?" Ellen's dad asked.

"Only once," Brad said. "When I heard him correct a faculty adviser during student council, I knew he meant it. He told a dean that his mother had named him Michael after her own father. Since she disliked the nickname, he didn't ever use it."

The rest of the morning Ellen began listening for Michael to call. She knew he would, she just didn't know when. Each time the phone rang, her heart flipped into her throat. Each time it wasn't Michael, she made some excuse for him in her mind.

Except for her intense listening, she floated through the next few days in a dreamlike haze. The tree was beautiful, the fire burned brightly, even the tired old Christmas carols sounded wonderful. Everyone liked their presents, especially Robin who got a cowboy hat from Cricket and didn't take it off all day.

Ellen set Hank's present under the tree the day

she got it. When Robin handed it to her, Ellen held it a long time. "Aren't you going to open it?" Robin finally asked.

Ellen nodded and undid the ribbon slowly. She had been right. It was jewelry, and it was from Marshall Field's. The silver bracelet inside was beautiful, very supple and delicate in design. It couldn't have been more elegant.

"How lovely, Ellen," her mother said. "Who is it from?"

"Hank," Ellen told her, "He shouldn't have done it." Her mother's face was unreadable. Ellen had tried the bracelet on and taken it back off before she saw the engraving inside. She instantly recognized the line from Elizabeth Barrett Browning. Luke had understood that poem at once but Hank knew it by heart.

"Let me count the ways" was all it said. It was enough. Ellen heard Hank's rich voice saying the line with the one that came before it. *"How do I love thee? Let me count the ways."*

She slid the bracelet swiftly back on her wrist so that no one else could read those words. Christmas died for her that precise moment, buried in guilt.

When Christmas Day was past, Ellen started listening again for Michael to call. That night couldn't have meant so much to her without meaning a lot to him, too. It didn't help that the phone rang all the time with Brad home and her parents' friends calling with greetings. The third time in a single day that Ellen caught the phone only to have to hand it to someone else, she saw her mother watching her with a strange sad expression. After that she only answered it when her mother was out of the room.

With every day that passed without hearing from Michael, Ellen felt herself shrink away. Her mood swung from aching sorrow to a frantic impatience. She and Michael didn't have that much time. He had said he was leaving for Connecticut right after the holidays.

She looked up the Tyler number and tried to think of some sensible reason to call. There wasn't any.

Three days after Christmas a fresh snowstorm moved in. This one didn't let up. The town was literally shut down for the rest of the holidays. Planes were all off schedule at O'Hare. The phone rang constantly but the only calls Ellen got were from Maggie. Since there was no business, Brad wasn't called back to his job downtown. He left for school three days early for fear he couldn't get back if he didn't grab the first ride he got.

Maggie kept calling because she was desolate. Luke couldn't even get into town so they could be together. "We were going to ice skate on his lake," she wailed to Ellen. "I hate snow!" Ellen listened and said sympathetic words. At least Maggie had someone to cry her grief to.

When the New Year's Eve dance at the club was canceled because of road conditions, Ellen's parents threw an impromptu party, asking their friends within walking distance to celebrate with them. Cocooned in her own grief and disappointment, Ellen went through all the motions of being a good daughter with numb persistence. She made fancy sandwiches and a relish tray with dip for her mother's midnight supper. She watched TV and then played games with Robin until the child wore out and fell asleep.

Ellen curled up with Tawny in her bed with a pillow folded around her ears. Even that couldn't shut out the music and laughter that flowed up the stairs from her parents' party. She had just about cried herself to sleep when she heard the bells ringing and distant horns honking.

The new year had come.

The holidays were over and Michael would be gone.

Chapter 17

The New Year came in black and white, black tree trunks against frozen drifts of snow, dark slush swirling along the gutters, and the sun a pale cold disk in a milky sky. With her own life swept as clear of color as the outside world, Ellen felt numb. How could the night that she had wanted to remember forever have turned into the night she'd give anything to forget?

She didn't really want to forget the evening itself, just that Michael hadn't called and was gone. If she could only think of those glittering hours, the ache in her chest would go away.

While she felt she had nothing in the world to look forward to, everybody talked about New Year's resolutions. Even her mother. "This is the year that I go back to school," she announced, her eyes glistening with excitement.

"What grade will they put you in?" Robin asked, staring at her curiously.

Her mother laughed softly. "I won't really be in a grade. I'll just take brush-up courses in accounting. One semester should catch me up enough to get a job."

"Are you tired of taking care of us?" Robin asked.

Her mother hugged her. "Of course not, honey. But you don't need as much care as you used to. Besides that, with Brad already in college, and Ellen not too far from it, your dad and I have some expensive years ahead."

"My New Year's resolution is to get a horse," Robin said.

"That's a wish, not a resolution," her mother told her. "You should decide to change yourself to be better or happier."

"Nothing would make me happier than a horse," Robin said. "And, anyway, I don't want to change. I like me the way I am."

Ellen looked away. While she wasn't that stuck on herself, she had only a wish for the New Year, too. But wanting Michael back and in love with her was as outlandish as Robin's horse.

Usually those last days of holiday were wonderful fun. Luke almost always had a party, either a huge bonfire and cookout with ice skating, or a sleigh ride with supper afterward. Other years Ellen and her friends had prowled the after-Christmas sales or gotten together to try on new Christmas clothes for each other.

This year it was too cold to go outside. Icy drifts turned the sidewalks into wind tunnels. She couldn't possibly run or ride her bike. Her face blazed with the cold just getting from the house to the car.

Maggie spent all her time with Luke and his family or at the indoor skating rink. Barb Sanchez was visiting her grandmother in Arizona. Cricket wasn't due back from Wyoming until the weekend.

But Hank was coming back on the weekend, too. Hank's silver bracelet had haunted Ellen since the minute she read the inscription. Right off she had wanted to close it up tight in its box. But then she'd have to hide it somewhere safe. Robin nosed around. If she found it, she'd ask a dozen questions that Ellen didn't want to answer. Even worse, her mother might chance on it. Her mother liked Hank and would know the words meant a lot to him, and she *knew* where Ellen's heart really was.

Worse than the bracelet was Hank himself. One of the things she liked best was how sensitive he was. He'd see right off that she was changed. And he would be angry, cold angry the way he'd been about Luke. She shuddered to remember the way his eyes had turned to blue ice.

She really yearned for Cricket. She needed to tell Cricket about Michael. Whether Cricket understood or not, she'd care.

That last Friday morning, Maggie called. "I don't know where this holiday went," she told Ellen. "I've really missed you and I have tons of presents to exchange. Want to go to the mall?"

Ellen jumped at the chance. "How about right now?" she asked.

Maggie laughed. "More like in ten minutes. Mom

will drive." Maggie was radiant as always. She had also exaggerated shamelessly. Three gifts was hardly the same as a ton.

"Let's do them first," Maggie said. "Then have lunch. I don't have to be at the skating rink until three."

It was impossible to stay down in the dumps with Maggie. She was so happy that it was almost catching. It didn't matter that she mentioned Luke in every second breath. In fact, it was fun.

She traded a gold sweater for a blue one because "Luke never compliments me when I wear gold." A belt from an aunt went back for a smaller size. Her last stop was the sporting goods store.

While Maggie agonized between two skating skirts, Ellen shopped for jackets. She had one on when Maggie joined her, loaded with packages. "That looks great on you," Maggie said, cocking her head. "But it's awfully lightweight for this weather."

"It's for running," Ellen told her. "You get hot running. You only need something to cut the wind."

Maggie frowned. "I don't remember your running all fall."

"I really didn't do much," Ellen admitted, taking the jacket off. "And I didn't sign up for any races at all."

Maggie stared at her. "I don't know how you can get so good at a sport and then drop it. I'd explode if I didn't skate."

Ellen shrugged. Being crazy about Luke hadn't

dimmed Maggie's passion for skating, but that was different. Let Maggie try being in love with somebody who didn't love her back!

When they had settled and ordered lunch, Maggie grinned at Ellen, dimpling with excitement. "Want to hear my resolutions?"

"Not you, too!" Ellen groaned.

"Resolutions are fun!" Maggie said. "Luke and I even made some together. We're both going to make dean's list second semester. What about you?"

When Ellen only shrugged, Maggie stared at her. "Come on! You can't mean that. You've always made resolutions. I remember the year you joined that running club and decided to take two minutes off your running time. You did it, too, didn't you?"

Ellen smiled. "Actually, I took off three minutes, but I'll never do that well again."

"Not without trying, that's for sure," Maggie said. She dipped her cola straw in her glass, then licked it. "My other resolution's a secret because it's so conceited. I've only told Luke, but this year I'm going to qualify for Olympic tryouts, or bust! Come on, Ellen, think of something!"

When Ellen didn't answer right away, Maggie went on. "Okay, maybe you need to forget running and try something new."

"I do want to run," Ellen told her. "I love running. I just ran out of steam or something last fall."

"Don't give me that!" Maggie said, giggling. "Admit it! You got distracted. That hunk Hank Ober would distract anybody!"

Ellen half-listened to Maggie's chatter. Maggie was dead wrong. She had run out of steam or energy or whatever it took to get out there in the dark before dawn every day the way she used to. That awful tiredness that got worse every time she saw Michael had been a lot of it.

"If you're not going to eat your chips, can I have them?" Maggie asked. When Ellen pushed the plate over, Maggie chewed thoughtfully a minute, then giggled. "I've got it," she said.

She sparkled as she leaned across the table. "You need to do something you've never done before. How about you make yourself completely over and give the world a shock? You've worn your hair like that forever. And have been a blonde, too. And I bet you've never once tried fake eyelashes." She giggled. "Wouldn't it be fun if nobody recognized you? And you could take up some new hobby, too. Something exciting like acting instead of just hanging out with that drama group. You could even try ice hockey with Luke."

Ellen laughed. "No way!"

Maggie leaned over to look at Ellen's watch. "Whoops! Got to meet Mom. She's probably already at the north entrance." She made a face. "But if you're not running, get rid of that bulky black watch. Get something cute like a cat chasing a mouse all day."

As Ellen got out of the car, Maggie called back to her. "Think glamour. Purple eyelids. Fake fingernails!"

Ellen was still laughing when she got inside her house.

"What's so funny?" her mother asked.

"That Maggie. She was making up New Year's resolutions for me."

"That's not such a bad idea," her mother said.

"Purple eyelids and fake fingernails?" Ellen asked.

Her mother laughed. "Horrors! You'd better make up your own."

Up in her room, Ellen hummed as she put away her best jeans and changed into her pink warm-up suit. She'd forgotten how much fun it was to be with Maggie. And talking about running had reminded her of how much she had enjoyed it. She had always been happy when she was racing.

She fished the spring race schedule from her desk drawer. If she meant to race again, she had to get into training fast. The first race was on Saint Patrick's Day. She put the schedule back down. Could she possibly ever be that happy again with Michael gone? Connecticut seemed as far away from Chicago as the moon. But he had said he was coming back to finish up at Jefferson High. That probably meant he would be back for the summer.

Then it hit her. Maggie hadn't been giving her silly ideas. She could make a resolution worth keeping. She only had to think of a plan to make herself look older and more attractive to Michael by the time he got back, then work on it faithfully.

The idea was so exciting that she laughed out

loud. She had the whole second semester. She only had to decide what she wanted to do to herself. She locked her bedroom door, turned on all the lamps and stood in front of her mirror to study herself. She didn't need to be thinner.

Aside from being thin, she mostly saw hair, just that great mass of honey blonde curls with her face peeking out, pale and uninteresting, with regulation eyelashes and dark blue eyes.

Blonde! Maybe Michael didn't like blondes. His last girl friend at school had sleek black hair, cut very short. And the hair of the girl at the country club had been a rich wonderful red that shone in the light. And it was short! Maybe Michael didn't like blondes and or curls or long hair either.

Suddenly she could imagine the perfect scene.

She would have glossy black or red hair, very short and stylish. She wouldn't be wearing just the same old jeans and shirt but maybe leggings with a silver belt and earrings to match — anyway, something different for her. Her eyes would look bigger and more dramatic because she would get some kind of eye makeup even if she didn't do the false lashes.

She would walk slowly by where Michael was talking with friends. He wouldn't even recognize her. Instead he would turn and stare at her. "Who is that knockout girl?" he'd ask.

His friends would laugh. "Gosh, Tyler," they'd say. "You mean you don't know Ellen Marlowe?"

Shutting her eyes, she could imagine him run-

ning after her, calling her name, "Ellen," in that deep voice of his. Then he would catch both her hands and stand looking at her. She imagined him speechless because she couldn't decide what wonderful compliment he would pay her first.

Ellen caught her hair and pulled it back from her face. She looked absolutely repulsive with all that face showing and her naked neck sticking up out of the top of her shirt. Maybe it was the wrong color. She fastened a black scarf around her hair and turned her head this way and that. She looked like a vampire. A red scarf gave her skin a pale sickly look.

She left out the entrance form for the Saint Patrick's Day Race so she wouldn't forget to sign up. Later she would worry about how she could look by summer. Now she just needed to get through the rest of vacation and deal with Hank.

Cricket got home the next day. She must have run to the phone the minute she got there. She sounded so near to exploding with happiness that Ellen grinned with pleasure. Obviously, Cricket had gotten the horse she had dreamed of for so long.

"I've got to see you," Cricket said, all in a rush. "You'll never believe my wonderful news. Can you come over right away?"

"If Mom will drive me," Ellen told her. "Oh, Cricket, I've missed you!" she added.

"I've thought of you a lot," Cricket said with a crazy giggle. "Hurry fast. I'll fix us lunch." That was a switch. The most Cricket ever did in the kitchen was open a can of soda.

Cricket glowed as she opened the door and grabbed Ellen in a big hug. "Merry Christmas again and Happy New Year," she said. "Hurry up, come on in. I'm in the kitchen."

The air in the kitchen smelled rich and spicy and Mexican, and something was sizzling in a skillet. "Sit down," Cricket ordered, waving her to a chair. "This only takes a minute."

"I hope you brought pictures," Ellen said, watching as Cricket scooped steaming red stuff onto open buns.

"Pictures?" Cricket asked, turning with a confused look. Then, she laughed as she heaped potato chips on the plates beside the buns. "Oh," she said. "You mean the horse."

"What else?" Ellen asked.

Cricket grinned as she set down two glasses of milk and plopped down beside Ellen. "Think of the only thing in the whole world more wonderful than a horse," she said.

In spite of herself, Ellen laughed. If she said Michael Tyler, Cricket would probably choke on her milk. "I give up," Ellen said. "Come on, out with it!"

Cricket's eyes disappeared when she grinned. She leaned forward, smiling. "A baby," she said, her voice suddenly husky. "Dad and Lynn and I are going to have a baby. Isn't that glorious, Ellen? I'll have a little sister just like Robin. And I get to be there when she's born and help take care of her."

Ellen hadn't expected her own sudden tears. This had been Cricket's dream before she ever climbed on her first horse. Ellen grabbed Cricket's hand, unable to speak. "A baby, Cricket," she finally said. "Just what you've always wanted." Then she grinned. "Even more than a horse."

Cricket giggled. "Horses come and go," she said. "Babies are forever. I'm already working on being a big sister. How do you like my Wyoming Winner? That's what Lynn calls this sandwich."

Ellen licked the sauce from the corner of her mouth and nodded. "It's wonderful. I'm still in shock at seeing you cook."

Cricket shrugged. "Big sisters have to learn stuff like that," she said. "You did, didn't you?" Ellen grinned. Why remind Cricket that she'd only been four when Robin was born?

"I'm going to be the best big sister ever," Cricket went on. "Lynn is knitting. I tried but I'm all thumbs with those needles."

Ellen finished her sandwich, which was delicious and spicy. She remembered about training for Saint Patrick's Day and left the chips on her plate. It took Cricket a long time to run down enough to ask for news. By that time Ellen knew that she couldn't tell Cricket about Michael Tyler, not yet. She couldn't possibly talk about Michael without crying. If she cried she'd only throw a big shadow over Cricket's happiness.

"News!" Cricket insisted. Ellen told how Maggie and Luke still spent every possible minute together, and how dull it had been with the big storm and the bitter cold that followed. When Ellen paused a minute, Cricket leaned over and took her wrist.

"This bracelet is new," she said. "Boy, is it ever pretty! Who gave it to you?"

The minute before Ellen hadn't felt the least bit choked up. Suddenly she had trouble saying Hank's name. Cricket looked at her searchingly. "Trouble, Ellen?" she asked quietly.

"I don't know why you say that," Ellen said, turning away.

Cricket set a tissue box down by Ellen. "People don't bawl about a Christmas present unless there's trouble," she said.

Blowing her nose didn't help. When Cricket hugged her, Ellen really began to cry. "I don't know what to do," she wailed. "I like Hank so much, but I love Michael."

Cricket went to the sink to rinse their dishes and spoke quietly. "It was sure easier when we were just bratty little kids. Then I could just blurt things out. Now I know better."

"You can still tell me what you think," Ellen told her.

Cricket shook her head.

"Not even if I ask?"

"Not even if you ask," Cricket said. Then she turned and grinned that old way. "Even if you dragged me through cactus tied to a bucking steer, and put pepper in my boots, and a rattler in my bed-roll, I wouldn't tell you."

"Why not?"

"Because I don't ever want to be at odds with you again like we got over Luke and Maggie and the grades. Not ever again."

Ellen studied her. "That tells me what you're thinking."

Cricket shrugged. "Maybe you're right, maybe you're wrong. Not to change the subject, but come listen to the CDs Dad got me for Christmas."

Chapter 18

By the time Ellen got home from Cricket's house, Hank had already called twice. "He wouldn't leave a number," her mother said. "He just said not to bother, he'd call again."

"I talked to him the first time," Robin said. "I told him you were over at Cricket's about her horse. Did she have pictures? What did she name him?"

Ellen grinned and put her arm around Robin. "Cricket guessed wrong about her present," she said.

Robin listened to her explain about the baby with a puzzled expression, then shrugged. "Some people are awful easy to please." She glanced at her mother. "I'm not, you know."

Knowing that Hank could call at any minute sent Ellen into a panic. Even if Hank couldn't see the change she felt in herself, what should she do? All the kids at the Willoughby party had been from school. Someone was sure to tell Hank about her leaving with Michael Tyler. She didn't think Maggie or Luke would, but somebody would.

But telling him about the party wasn't the important thing. She couldn't live with herself if she let him go on thinking of her as his girlfriend. Before the party, it could have been just a crush. Now she knew for sure it was love. She *had* to talk to someone.

She thought of Brad and got a little angry. If he had been any kind of a decent brother, he would have given her a chance to talk with him over Christmas. Now it was too complex to explain. Even if she got Brad on the phone, could she make him understand?

Cricket was out, which left no one but Luke. She sat by the phone a long time before she got her courage up. His mother answered. From the way she was halfway laughing, Ellen guessed that Maggie was there. "He's right here," Mrs. Ingram said, "Cutting up with Maggie. I'll call him."

Luke cutting up? She heard his footsteps crossing the parquet floor and then his voice. "Ellen? What's up?"

"I have a problem," she said, keeping her voice low.

"Speak up!" Luke said. "We've got a rotten connection."

"Hank is home," she said swiftly. "I don't know what to do."

For a minute she thought the connection was broken. But when she spoke his name, he said he was there. "Was that a question, Ellen?" he asked.

"I don't know what to do, what to say to him," she said.

"If you expect me to tell you, you're way off base," he said. "For one thing, I like the guy."

"I just want to know what you think," she said.

"That's easy," he said quietly. "Unless you were struck with amnesia the night of the party, you must have known this was something you had to face."

"But I didn't think."

His tone softened. "Ellen, once you told me to stay out of it. I'm doing that."

She barely replaced the phone before Hank called.

"At last," he said. "Happy New Year and all that. How are you, anyway?"

"Fine," she fibbed, feeling a little shivery in her knees.

"Did you have a good Christmas?" he asked.

The hard, painful lump that she associated with Michael suddenly came in her throat. "You know I did, Hank. That's the most beautiful bracelet I've ever seen."

"Then you liked it?"

What could she say? She couldn't say she loved it when she had spent so many hours agonizing over it. "I haven't had it off since Christmas," she told him, instantly regretting it. She'd told the truth but her words were still a cop-out.

"Those were two *long* weeks," he said. "Can we get together this afternoon?"

"It's awfully cold," she said doubtfully.

"Jay said he'd drop us at the pizza place and pick us up before he goes to work, a little after five."

Even if she thought of an excuse, any excuse, she would only be buying time. She would see him for sure on Monday at school. At least, they had a reasonable shot at privacy in a booth at the pizza shop.

"That sounds great," she said, holding the phone with both hands. What if she cried? What if he guessed and turned that cold icy face to her and she was stranded there until Jay came?

"Is right away all right?" Hank asked. "Jay's got some stuff to do before work."

"Right away is fine," she said. "I'll watch and come out. It's so cold."

Hank barely waited for Jay to stop the car. He was out and halfway up the walk as she started down. She expected him to catch her around the shoulders in one of those bear hugs of his, but he only touched her arm and walked to the car beside her. Right then she began to feel the strangeness. Was Hank acting differently, or was she so nervous that she imagined it?

Jay grinned back at Ellen as Hank helped her in. "Good thing you gave in to the clown," he said. "Caged tigers bore me."

Hank said nothing, but sat staring straight ahead.

The clock in the pizza shop read ten minutes after four. If Jay picked them up a little after five, they had just about an hour. If she could only get over this weird feeling of dread, an hour would be nothing.

All of the booths were full but one, which the waitress wanted to save for a party of four. Hank charmed her out of that. "Hey," he said grinning at her. "I haven't seen my girlfriend since last year. And those tables by the door would freeze a reindeer."

She winked at Ellen and handed them menus. Instead of sliding in next to her, Hank sat on the bench facing her. He had never ever done that before. Then he reached over and lifted her wrist and looked at the bracelet. "Looks even better than I thought," he said without smiling.

She closed her hand around his. "It's the prettiest gift I've ever had."

"I meant it to be," he said, pulling his hand back as the waitress came back. "I hope you're hungry," he told Ellen. "I'm starved. My father's wife turns good groceries into cardboard."

"Cricket fed me," Ellen told him. "I'll just have a coke."

"Now I want to hear all about Christmas," he said, his eyes intent on her face. She had to force herself not to look away. Either he had become even better-looking in those two weeks or she had forgotten. Part of it was probably his warm high color from the cold. And his eyes were positively brilliant.

"You tell first. You were the one who went away."

"Ohio isn't away. It's off there. It's where my dad and his wife have their lives and I have a TV. That's where I watched your Christmas snow falling all over Chicago. It looked like a blizzard on the news."

Ellen stirred with restlessness. He looked at her as if he were waiting for something. What was he waiting for? Why wasn't he loose and funny and affectionate the way he had always been before? His tenseness made her edgy and a little fearful. Maybe the party wouldn't even come up. Then if someone else told him about it, she could say it hadn't been important enough to mention. But that would be a lie, with more guilt dragging along with it.

He asked about Cricket's horse, and grinned when she told him about the horse that turned out to be a baby on the way. "And are Luke and Maggie still an item?" he asked. At her nod, he smiled a little. "That should take care of Luke's problem with understanding Burns's love poems," he said. "I guess you all went to that famous Christmas dance?"

She nodded, her breath coming short. Their order came, her coke and his pizza. "That was the Saturday night of the snow, wasn't it?" he went on. "It's a wonder the storm didn't muck it up."

She caught her breath hard. "It did, for some people," she said. "Maggie and Luke had to leave early because of the snow."

He looked at her, his head cocked a little on the

side. "Finally we seem to be getting someplace," he said. "Now I'm waiting for you to tell me who took you home." His eyes were watchful.

She forced herself to meet his eyes but her voice tightened in her throat. "I went there with Maggie and Luke," she said. "But another friend took me home."

"A guy?" he asked.

She nodded. "Michael Tyler took me home about eleven."

"Straight home?" he asked, his pizza lying unheeded.

She couldn't have kept the resentment from her voice if she had wanted to. "What made you ask that?"

He shrugged and made a big deal of picking up a pizza slice. "Because I wanted to know. I go to that school, too, if you remember. I know who Michael Tyler is. I know he's not only BMOC but every other girl's dream guy. I've seen you up there on the balcony mooning over him at swim practice."

Her resentment was turning into anger. He had deliberately set a trap for her. This was the same as saying she wouldn't have told him anything unless she was forced to. But would she have?

"Hank!" she cried. "What's your problem? Michael and I are friends. He was a big fan of my brother's. To him I'm just a kid. He says so in that many words."

He didn't even seem to be hearing her. "So where

did Michael Tyler BMOC take you after the party?"

"Out to Salt Creek to look at the snow," she said angrily. Why couldn't she control herself when she needed to so badly? But she was completely startled to learn that he had been spying on her all that time.

"And I guess he kissed you," he said flatly, not looking at her anymore.

"Once. At the front door," she said, not caring that her voice sounded angry and defensive. She was furious with him. So maybe she was his girlfriend, that didn't mean he owned her! She was almost as mad at herself as she was at him. How old would she have to be before her face quit turning hot when she was embarrassed or upset? And wasn't the hand of the clock ever going to move past five?

He pushed his uneaten pizza away and drank a little of his cola. "I could gladly smash that face of his," he said in the coldest tone she'd ever heard him use.

She leaned toward him, trembling with fury. "And I could do exactly the same to yours!" she said, suddenly fighting tears.

He stared at her.

"I could," she said, staring right back at him. "I don't know why I let you put me through a third degree like that. Most of all I don't know why you bothered to do it. You'd already made up your mind. Couldn't you trust me to tell you on my own?"

"Hey," he said, shoving a paper napkin toward

her. "Who are you kidding? You weren't about to tell me and you know it."

"I certainly was," she said, glaring at him and wiping off her tears with the napkin. "I dreaded it and I knew it would be tough, but I was going to tell you anyway. Now you've just made it harder to explain."

He straightened in the seat, swinging his elbows back as if his shoulders hurt. He stared at the edge of the table and spoke carefully, as if he were fighting for control as hard as she was.

"Come on, Ellen, let's not just sit here spitting at each other. Let's go whole hog. You're not the only one who has it tough, you know. You see, I first noticed you with Cricket on book day. Then right away I saw you and Michael Tyler head-to-head on that bench out by the tennis court. When somebody told me he was giving you your orientation tour, I relaxed a little. Maybe too much. I probably wanted to fool myself, but I couldn't help watching. I'm supposed to be the actor, not you, but you fooled me. You had me thinking you liked me enough that I could win out over Tyler's famous killer charm."

He paused and caught a deep breath. "So I go off to count the days until I see you again, and what do I come back to? The hot news that Michael Tyler had added your scalp to his belt over Christmas. One of the guys who works with Jay saw you at that party and told me. Can you blame me for asking?"

Ellen shook her head helplessly. "I wasn't fooling you, Hank. I do like you a lot. I always have."

He leaned to look straight into her eyes as if she would lie unless he pinned her down. "But not the way you like Michael Tyler?"

Her chest hurt so much she wanted to bend over double. She was angry and hurt and too close to tears even to try to put her answer into words. She only shook her head and started to slip off the silver bracelet with trembling fingers. He reached over and gripped her hand hard, stopping her. His fingers dug into her flesh painfully.

"No," he said, too loudly. "Keep it. It's yours."

"Please, Hank," she said.

He shoved her hand away and fished out a tip. "Believe me, Ellen, I don't ever want to see that thing again."

It was ten minutes after five when they stepped out into the bitter wind. Hank shielded her in the doorway as Jay drove up, but he didn't touch her. He didn't even look at her as he opened the back door of Jay's car, watched her get in, and then got into the front seat beside Jay.

Back home she cried in a way she had never cried for anyone but Michael Tyler. Losing Hank hurt. Worse than that, never mind how much she had been hurt because of loving Michael, she couldn't bear causing Hank that much pain.

Chapter 19

The first day of school after the holidays, Robin came down the stairs singing. Ellen, trying to get cereal to squeeze past the lump in her throat, groaned. "What's she so happy about?" she asked her mother.

"New clothes," Ellen's mother reminded her. "Don't you remember when it was a big deal for you to go back to school after Christmas with new clothes?"

"I guess," Ellen said listlessly. She'd like to see the clothes that would make her happy to go back to Jefferson High. This second semester would be an eternity without Michael. She might not even get through it. She might just curl up and die and not even be here when he came back in the summer.

Connecticut was a world away from Chicago. What was it like? Would he be happy there as a new student after being so popular back at Jefferson? When he thought about Jefferson High, would he ever think about her? She couldn't let herself think about the girls in Connecticut. He'd be popular with them quickly enough!

If that wasn't bleak enough, she had to face Hank. The very thought was enough to make her give up on breakfast. It would be heaven to walk out the door and just keep walking, never to see Hank again with his cold, angry face closed against her.

All the time she had dreaded seeing Hank again, she was only thinking about him and herself. She hadn't thought of the other kids at all. Walking into English class was a total icy shock.

She knew she wasn't just being self-conscious. She actually saw the class, almost as a unit, stare first at her, then at Hank who was cutting up at the back of the room with a bunch of guys. She felt her face turn hot as she took an empty front-row seat. She felt a little sick when she heard a low rumble of laughter come from back there. Hank couldn't be making cracks about her, he couldn't! But she cringed inside, wishing she was dead.

Even Mr. Burns glanced at each of them in turn before bringing the class to order. "Happy New Year," he said, raising his voice for silence. "And happy countdown to the end of your first semester. Four weeks from today it will all be over, your themes will be turned in, your finals taken, and you will have lived or died. On your own heads, be it."

The class groaned as he passed out an assignment list for the coming weeks. Luke, in the row behind

Ellen, leaned forward and touched her shoulder. "Wait for me after class, okay?"

Knowing she didn't have to walk out of there alone helped her get through that period. But Luke's question out in the hall caught her off guard. "Are you staying with the drama group?" he asked, his eyes thoughtful behind those awful glasses.

"I hadn't thought about it," she realized aloud, a sudden thump in her chest. Hank would be there. He would always be there, either ignoring her or glaring at her that cold way. But she loved the group and wanted to stay.

Mr. Quigley had already talked to her about the costumes for the touring play, which was set in the sixteenth century. He had said, "A court like that of Henry VIII is really something to costume."

Luke broke into her thoughts. "Think hard about it," he said with a sudden grin. "That drama bunch will give you a great political base when you run for student council next month."

"When I what?" she asked, stopping too suddenly.

He nodded. "Maggie and I talked it over," he said. "You're the pick of the class, and we volunteer to manage your campaign."

"But I don't want to run for student council," she wailed.

"That's okay. Nothing helps a successful political campaign like a little convincing modesty," he said in a ridiculously pompous tone. "Start right now by smiling at everyone who looks at you, even if it hurts. I mean everybody!"

"Luke," she protested, lost for words. What was the matter with him? He knew her better than that. What kind of a girl smiled at everybody she looked at whether she liked them or not?

He took her arm and spoke quietly. "Think about it, Ellen. Nothing will keep you and Hank from being gossiped about for a couple of weeks anyway. You want to come off as a discard?"

"I'm no such thing," she wailed, staring at him. "Luke Ingram, that's a terrible, awful thing for you to say!"

He shrugged and grinned at her. "How about clever?" He tapped her on the shoulder as he turned into his classroom door. She started after him. She wasn't having any part of that kind of acting out. It was embarrassing even to think about. Almost like cheating. She hadn't realized she had slowed to a crawl until Barb Sanchez caught her arm. "Hey, you," Barb said, with that brilliant smile. "Who died?"

Ellen blinked. "Nobody," Ellen said. "I was just thinking."

"Don't give me that, Ellen," Barb said, smiling at her. "I tried to catch you coming out of English but Luke beat me to it. I saw you and Hank in class. Want to join my club?" Ellen puzzled that for only a minute. Barb was alone. Barb was never alone. Where was Tom Winter?

Barb read her mind and nodded. "I don't know

what happened with you and Hank but Christmas break lasted too long for Tom this year." Her voice was nothing like as bright as her smile. Then she shrugged. "I keep telling myself I was sick of his jealousy anyway. Someday I might even start to believe it."

Barb hugged her arm as they went through the door. "Quit thinking in public," she whispered. "It gives a bad impression."

Ellen smiled back at her. She had never seen Barb Sanchez's huge brown eyes so dark with sadness.

Going to drama group the first time was the worst. Mr. Quigley had been right about their getting to know each other almost too well. Where Ellen only got stares and whispers from the rest of the school, these kids were into comments.

They ranged all the way from regret, "I can't believe you dummies messed up a good thing!" to a veiled hit from Ollie Samson, who had played the male lead in the November play and would play Henry VIII in the new one.

Ollie was a junior. In Ellen's very private opinion, he was the only guy who was even close to Hank in talent. He couldn't have looked any less like Hank if it had been planned. He was tall in a solid muscular way, dark-skinned with heavy eyebrows and deeply set black eyes. Although he only had to knit his brows to look the perfect villain, when he turned on the charm, he was ruggedly appealing. And sure of that charm, too.

Ellen looked up at Ollie with surprise when she felt his arm slide around her. He shrugged and grinned. "It won't be the same without you and Ober thick as thieves. Whatever happened is a rotten shame," he went on. "You two had it hands down for the best-looking freshman couple. But it does open up the field for the rest of us, doesn't it?"

As she smiled and wriggled free of his grasp she saw Hank glaring at her from the back of the room.

As Luke predicted, she and Hank were gossiped about for only a couple of weeks. The third week the curious stares were aimed at a junior couple who hadn't read the fine print in the student handbook. They got hauled into the dean's office for offensive public displays of affection. He only gave them a warning. The rest of the kids gave them a ribbing that would have sent Ellen right down through the floor.

Luke had been right in telling her to smile, too. Every time someone gave her a curious stare, she smiled back. Right away a lot of kids she hadn't known before were smiling first. Some of them even caught up in the halls to walk along and talk with her.

Their company helped dispel the loneliness of Michael and Hank's absence. Knowing Michael wasn't there was even more painful than seeing him had been. She looked for Michael without meaning to. Sometimes she saw some tall boy with that dark hair down the hall and shivered until she remembered. Missing Michael even hurt worse than Hank's glares every day at drama group.

With the worst of the cold weather over, she forced herself back to running. She had only two choices in time, very early in the morning, or late after school. Since it was dark both times, she chose the morning. There wasn't much traffic on the village streets before dawn and the air was crisp and sweet.

The first few days she hated it. Muscles she didn't know she had ached all night. She was so discouraged at first that she refused even to time herself. But by the last week of January the old excitement began to come back, the thrill of feeling her muscles harden, the giddy sense of achievement that followed a good run.

She played a game with herself. Each morning that she took even a few seconds off her time, she got to run past Michael Tyler's house. Usually she passed just as the automatic timer switched the house lights on. She pretended that he was there, waking up, getting ready to come to school. It made him feel closer, easing the ache of his absence just a little.

The semester exams made the midterms look like child's play. But Maggie and Luke both made honor roll, and Ellen stayed on the dean's list. It wasn't any of her business but she felt bad that Hank wasn't on either list this time.

A lot of important changes came with the start of the new semester. The one that affected Ellen's daily life the most was her mother starting her college courses. "I worry about your schedule," she told Ellen. "I'll have to spend lots of library time. And your father often has night meetings. I hate to have you hung up with Robin so many evenings."

Ellen laughed. "As early as I get up to run, Robin will be lucky if I don't beat her to bed."

"I wasn't really thinking about that," her mother admitted. "You don't have any social life at all except on weekends."

Ellen hugged her. "You can't be talking about my running out of boyfriends, can you, Mom?" she teased.

Strangely, her mother stiffened. "That's exactly what I meant. You've only gone out with girlfriends — Cricket and Barb Sanchez — since you and Hank quit seeing each other. It's nice to have boys as friends, too."

"Oh, I see Hank plenty," Ellen said, not caring that it sounded sarcastic. "He glares at me across the auditorium every day for an hour and a half. Not counting English class."

Her mother turned away as if to regain her self-control. "You know what I mean, Ellen," she said with just the tiniest hint of irritation in her tone.

Her mother might as well have written FORGET MICHAEL TYLER in giant block letters in the air between them. Her mother couldn't seem to forget that Michael wasn't Ellen's age. But Michael had the same problem, Ellen reminded herself bitterly.

* * *

Luke and Maggie were serious about getting Ellen into student council. Over Ellen's anguished protests, they nominated her and plastered the school with impressive posters. When it came down to Ellen making her candidate's speech, she didn't have the heart to back out on them. That was all right. She was running against two popular boys and one of the cheerleaders. She wasn't going to win anyway.

Or so she thought. She did win, and by a good margin. She saw the election returns with a sinking heart. Her life was already on overload. She was just getting on top of her second-semester classes. She couldn't give up her running. It helped her fight the emptiness caused by Michael's absence. And Mr. Quigley had made a monster understatement when he described dressing a cast of twenty-seven actors and actresses for the play as being "difficult." All of that was too much with her added duties the nights her mother studied and her father was at his office.

She was ready to throw up her hands and resign from the world the day the letter came. Robin tossed it on the hall table along with a sports catalog and the entrance form for an April race. Then she went back and looked again.

"Can I have the stamp off this letter of yours?" she asked, following Ellen into the kitchen.

"What letter?" Ellen asked, setting things out

and making lists in her head because she was late in starting dinner.

"This one with the killer whale stamp on it. The postmark is Connecticut," Robin said.

Ellen felt the word register in her mind with a thump. She tried to keep her tone level. "Let me see it first," she said as Robin skipped after her, the letter in her hand.

She took the letter with trembling hands. She had never seen that handwriting before.

"Want me to do place mats?" Robin called.

"Help yourself," Ellen mumbled. There was no return address, but the postmark was Darien, CT. Connecticut. Robin was right. But it couldn't be.

She opened the envelope carefully, dreading the inevitable disappointment. Notebook paper, regular lined notebook paper, neat lines of printing with a felt tip pen in very black ink.

He hadn't written, "Dear Ellen" or anything at the top. It just read, *Dean's list again and student council! Wouldn't you know? Congratulations! Onward and upward, Ellen Marlowe. You're making my old school paper worth reading.* Then the single word. *Michael.*

She wanted to do a thousand crazy things at once, dance, shout, hug the letter to her chest, and cry. She only stood, reading the words over and over. He remembered. He was proud of her. He was homesick.

And he still read the school paper.

Robin came to the doorway. "I finished the table," she said, then paused. "Are you okay?"

Ellen folded the letter into the pocket of her jeans and grabbed Robin by both shoulders. "I have never been quite so okay in my whole entire life." She told her. She began to spin around. "Come on, Robin. Let's dance."

Robin shook her head and pulled away. "I think you're sick," she said. She reached for two apples from the wooden bowl on the table and stamped off upstairs with them.

Ellen went up right after her, taking the steps two at a time, startling Tawny from her nap at the top of the stairs. She carefully put the letter in between the pages of the book of love poems Mr. Burns had them buy for first semester.

When she saw Luke and Maggie, she was going to kiss them both hard, but not explain why. Then, for the very first time, she talked to Michael in her head as if he were actually there.

"Thank you," she said very quietly, then laughed out loud. Linda Garner was always asking for news for the freshman column. From now on she was going to get Ellen's news without any coaxing at all.

Chapter 20

The new semester brought one really super change, a transfer student from Pebble Beach, California. Valerie Frederick was a junior, as tall as Ellen and blonde in the same golden tan way. Everything about her — posture, clothes, even her slow smile when someone spoke to her — was streamlined. Ellen liked her the first time she saw her, and respected her, too, for the cool, yet friendly way she handled the guys in the drama group who made instant fools of themselves trying to get her attention.

The minute Val walked across the stage to read for a part, Ellen became her fan. She could act! And this was a girl to design an Elizabethan dress for, broad-shouldered, narrow in the waist and hips, with a graceful angle to her head.

In fact, Ellen was so busy sketching that head in an Elizabethan headdress that she didn't notice that Valerie had slipped into the seat beside her. She glanced over to see Valerie studying the sketch with absorbed interest. "That's wonderful, you know," she whispered to Ellen.

Ellen nodded her thanks and whispered, "Welcome," and told Valerie her name.

"Can we talk after?" Valerie asked as someone looked back, frowning disapproval. Once they were outside, Valerie suggested going somewhere to get acquainted.

"How about you come to my house?" Ellen asked. "I have to beat my younger sister home from the sitter."

Ellen couldn't remember ever liking a girl so much right off. Val settled on the kitchen bench with Tawny on her lap while Ellen started dinner. "I can't believe how good you are," Valerie said when Robin wandered off to do her homework. "Tell me about your drawing."

Ellen handed her the sketchbook for the play. While Valerie studied the pictures, they talked about Ellen's love of designing and just about everything else. Val was as crazy about golf as Ellen was about running. She was honors in English and social science but "rotten" with numbers. "Mostly I love acting," she told Ellen. "I didn't see you try out."

"I like the costumes and settings," Ellen explained. "But Mr. Quigley has been on me all year to audition for something."

Val's eyes were a pale clear blue, rimmed by dark lashes almost too thick to look real. She stared at Ellen thoughtfully. "Why don't you? You must have a good reason not to."

Ellen laughed. "I'm too self-conscious, I guess."

Val laughed softly. "That's all the more reason

to try. You get to be somebody else up there on stage. It's wonderful to live another life even for just a couple of hours."

"I never thought of it that way," Ellen admitted, gathering up the sketches.

"Wait!" Val said, pulling one toward her. "How do you know all this stuff? The clothes Anne Boleyn wore and all that."

"I research," Ellen said. "I like doing things right."

"Isn't that a big cast? Will you design for all of them?"

"Twenty-seven," Ellen told her. "But some dress alike, the choristers and the servant women, for instance."

Val glanced at the dark beyond the window. "I've got to run. Thanks for taking in a stranger, Ellen. This was super."

A stranger. Val was like Michael, coming in mid-year to a strange school, different kids. "This has to be tough," Ellen told her. "Moving and all."

Val narrowed her eyes thoughtfully. "Good stuff and bad," she said with a shrug. "The bad is that I miss California and my friends. The good part is that I'm forced to be away from a guy I am out of my mind about." She smiled that slow smile.

"What could be good about that?" Ellen asked, horrified.

"Hey," Val said, shrugging. "I'm only sixteen, a lot of years away from settling down." She fished in her purse and handed Ellen a small picture of a smiling dark boy, his arm around a radiant Valerie. "This is Eric," she said quietly.

"It's a great picture," Ellen said, letting herself down on the bench. "Does he love you, too?"

Val nodded. "We decided that if the way we feel lasts, we'll be back together again. If it doesn't survive this separation, then Dad's transfer saved us from doing something stupid." Val rose, smiling. "You wouldn't be a little bit in love, would you, Ellen?"

Ellen shook her head. "No," she said. Then she laughed. "More like a whole lot? How did you guess?"

Val laughed and touched her arm. "It takes one to know one," she said. "Thanks again for everything."

Ellen went to bed that night thinking about Val and her boyfriend. Most of all she envied her that picture. What wouldn't she give for even a silly little class picture of Michael! Tawny glared as Ellen sprang from the bed, dumping the cat from her coverlet.

Brad's room was neater than it ever was before he went off to college. His high school yearbooks were on the bottom shelf of the bookcase, four of them. She found Michael's picture at once. In fact she found a half dozen of them in the last yearbook. She didn't dare cut one of them out. Brad would kill her. She sat staring at it a long time before taking the book back to her room and sticking it in her book bag.

The next day she copied the whole page of sophomore class officers and then cut the other faces away. The shot came out grainy but the smile was right, humorous and a little mischievous, with those dark eyes looking right into hers.

She didn't dare carry it with her the way Val did. Instead she put it into the poetry book inside his letter. Knowing that picture was there was like being with Michael himself, joyful but miserable at the same time.

Ellen's first race was run along Lake Shore Drive in Chicago. It rained that Saint Patrick's Day, a cold, slow rain that kept many of the runners home. Ellen had been the youngest member in her running club the year she joined. Her old friends crowded around her, welcoming her back like a long-lost daughter.

"I hope you're in trim," one of the older runners said with a concerned frown. "You can't just jump back in."

"Listen to him," his wife scoffed. "He's just afraid you'll beat his time."

A gray cold drizzle fell on them the full length of the course. White gulls swayed in from Lake Michigan as Ellen paced herself among the runners. The drive was so quiet that she only heard the lapping of the lake on the shore and the whisper of the other runners' feet. She forgot time, not even listening to the chant of the mile markers who droned the minutes and seconds as they passed. She tried to ignore the slow burning that began in her legs as she neared the end of the course. She heard shouts ahead as the first runner hit the final ribbon. Then she was at the end, too, turning right into the woman's chute and handing over her identification and number. As a volunteer handed her a cup of steaming cider, she glanced up at the clock. She hadn't really absorbed her final time before the congratulations began.

She'd never had so many people grinning right up in her face like that. She stared at the smiling judge in amazement. "Third in your age group," he said, handing her a ribbon along with her bright green T-shirt.

Someone slapped her back, sloshing hot cider out of her cup. "Twenty-two minutes, forty-seven seconds," he said. "That's your best personal time ever, according to club records."

Ellen couldn't tell whether it was rain or tears of joy streaming down her cheeks as she danced to cool down and changed out of her wet clothes. She clung to her ribbon and shirt all the way home, wondering if Michael would read the race results.

But that was her spring for winning. The dress rehearsal of the play went off without a hitch before the play started its tour. When Mr. Quigley asked to borrow her costume sketches, she didn't think much about it. "I do want them back," she told him.

"When I'm through," he promised her.

Not until the final performance, back at Jefferson High, did she see the exhibit that had traveled with the play. Her sketches, matted in white with black frames, were displayed in neat rows on the long walls outside the auditorium.

Val was there grinning with delight. "I plotted against you," she told Ellen. "They're too good to go unseen. And Mr. Quigley agreed with me. Neat, huh?"

Maybe once Ellen would have been embarrassed by the praise, and shy about having her picture taken against that background of Elizabethan costumes. Now she only grinned with joy that the picture, would run on the cover of *The Monticello* in full color, where Michael Tyler would see it.

When Ollie Samson asked her to go with him to the cast party, she said she really couldn't. The second and third time he asked, she was equally firm. Then Val talked to her.

"You're not thinking, Ellen," Val said seriously. "If I can go to that party with Thomas Cromwell, you can sure go with Henry the Eighth. In fact, the guys want us to double-date."

Ellen laughed. Val had played Anne Boleyn with Ollie playing the king. Val didn't laugh. "I know more than I knew when we first met," she said. "If you're trying to avoid Cardinal Wolsey because of your real mystery love, forget it. That's Hank Ober's problem, not yours."

Ellen studied her. Hank had played the Cardinal Wolsey role with unbelievable depth. She had been at the point of congratulating him when he had given her one of those cold, hateful stares. But Val was right. The fact that they couldn't even be friends was Hank's problem, not hers.

In fact, it was a wonderful evening. She had laughed until her stomach hurt before Ollie walked her to the door. "Hey, Marlowe," he said. "Tonight was worth that sales job. Thanks."

"Thank you," she said sincerely.

He took her gently by the shoulders and looked at her in the dim glow of the porch light. "You wouldn't want to lose your head for saying no to a king, would you?"

"Not on my life," she said, laughing. She stood on tiptoe as he touched her lips with his.

He held her close a minute, then sighed. "I guess that'll do for starters," he said, releasing her. "But just as starters."

Ever since she got his letter, Ellen had talked to Michael silently in her head. Sometimes she talked to his picture. That night, she took the picture out before she even undressed.

"All right, Michael Tyler," she told the smiling face. "There are some sixteen-year-old guys in this world who think I am an actual grown-up girl."

Chapter 21

With April the dawns had begun to come earlier. That Sunday morning after the cast party, the first pale light shone on a curtain of trailing mist. Ellen let herself out the back door and set off, running slowly. If she hadn't placed so well in her first few races, she couldn't possibly have forced herself out of bed. But she was still glad she'd gone to the party. It had been fun. But getting only four hours of sleep made running a chore.

She was only a block from home when she heard running footsteps coming up behind her. Her heart leapt to her throat. Should she turn, pick up speed and try to lose whoever it was? Before she could even decide, she heard that familiar voice call her name. She whirled, her heart thundering.

"Hank!" she said angrily. "You scared me to death!"

Then he was there, facing her. "I'm sorry, Ellen," he said. "I really am. I just needed to talk to you alone."

She was still fluttery from that moment of fear, and resented it. "How did you know where to find me?"

He shrugged. "I just did." Then he grinned, running his palms down the dew-covered front of his leather bomber jacket. "As you can see, I waited a while. I'd almost decided you weren't going to run today."

"Late night," she said.

"I was there, too," he reminded her. "Can we talk?"

"After I run," she said. "I'm in training."

He nodded and grinned. "I know that, too. How about we do a mile together and have breakfast?"

"A mile!" she scoffed. "I'd only be warming up!"

"Just this once."

Looking at him made her weaken. What a nice guy he was when he wasn't imitating an iceberg. A mile, he'd said. Could he keep up with her for a mile? And wouldn't it be great if he couldn't!

"You choose the mile," she told him. "None of my runs end up at restaurants."

He grinned and let out a huge breath. Relief? The minute he named the streets, she knew what all-night restaurant he meant. "Do we need a starting gun?" he asked.

She giggled. "Not unless you want to get a couple of cops on us in about ten seconds flat. On your mark. Get set. Go!"

She was off like a shot. With only a mile to run

she didn't have to pace herself. She lost him within a block only to have him gain on her farther on. He had almost caught up when she reached the door of the restaurant and stopped to wait for him.

"I bet you think you're pretty smart," he said, gasping for breath as he braced himself against the door.

"Just fast," she told him, trying not to let him know that she was pretty winded herself.

"We've never had breakfast together before," he told her over the menu. "It's my first favorite meal of the day."

She laughed. "Like lunch is your second favorite meal and dinner your third?" she asked, handing her menu back to the waitress. "I'll have one egg scrambled, hash browns, and whole wheat toast."

"You got it," Hank said, giving his own order.

He fell silent as the woman walked away. Ellen watched him. She knew that look. It was always hard for him to say anything that really mattered to him. She didn't mind helping him out. "You were great as Cardinal Wolsey," she told him.

He looked up and grinned. "It was my costume that was great," he said, "But thanks anyway." Then he reached over and took her hand. "Something to hang onto," he explained. "I want to talk to you about tough stuff."

Ellen stifled a sigh. She didn't want to talk about tough stuff. It was nice just being there with him as friends, the way they had in the old days. The feeling of her hand in his brought back all that tenderness she had felt for him before the Christmas fight they'd had.

"I've missed you," he said quietly. He leaned toward her. "Then I noticed that your friend Tyler was missing, too. One of the guys said he'd gone back east. Did you know he was going?"

She took her hand away and stared at him. "Did we come here to talk about Michael Tyler?" she asked.

He reddened at the question. "We came to talk about us, but he's part of the package. Don't you agree?"

"Maybe," she murmured. "And yes, I knew he was leaving."

"Is he gone for good?"

She sighed. What could be good about Michael being gone at all, for any reason? "Only for this semester," she said. "He's staying with his aunt while his father does a project in Egypt."

"Why didn't you tell me that?"

She stared at him. "You didn't ask me," she said. "As a matter of fact, you didn't give me a chance if I had wanted to."

"Okay," he said, pulling back a little. "I'm making a mess of this. Let's start all over. I miss you. I wanted to kill Ollie Samson last night. I hope you noticed that I didn't."

"I did notice," she said, grinning at him.

"This is not funny," he said crossly. "I'm working

on self-control. You're supposed to like that. It's the pits for me when you're with some guy. You know I never liked a girl this much before. I couldn't deal with your not feeling the same way."

He was explaining instead of apologizing but she nodded anyway. "I've done some heavy thinking," he went on. "We've got so much going for us, Ellen. We've had great times together, and we've got lots in common. That's the tough part. It took me forever to figure out how much we really do have in common."

When she looked at him, puzzled as to where this was going, he nodded. "Look at it, Ellen." He leaned toward her. "You have this thing about Tyler, and I have the same kind of thing about you. We're flip sides of the same dumb record. I can't do anything to change that, and neither can you. But we could maybe just face up to it and be friends again. It's not the way either of us wants it, but that's how it is. I messed up a real good thing by losing my cool. I know better now. I'd give anything to go back like we were, hanging out together, sometimes dating, but both of us knowing the other one understands."

She felt her breath come short. She was too stunned by what he had said to think clearly. It really hurt to think that Hank was as miserable over her as she was over Michael. But there was something more, something that he hadn't said.

"What are you thinking?" he asked.

She shook her head. "I don't know, Hank," she

admitted. "Maybe that people can't just go back places. They change."

His smile was brilliant. "That's it. That's what's so great. People do change. Who knows? Maybe you'll get over Tyler or I'll get over you. In the meantime, we could be together again."

She needed to say one more thing but couldn't find the words. When she tried, they stumbled out sounding funny. "Just so you don't bank on *my* changing."

He frowned. "So I'm not supposed to be hopeful?" he challenged her. "You are, aren't you?"

She nodded without meeting his eyes.

He surprised her by laughing softly. "Okay, we make a deal. We'll go together just like before, but both keep shopping."

"Shopping?" she asked, confused.

He shrugged. "If you see somebody else you like — not Ollie Samson please, just tell me. I'll do the same. Shopping! Are you game to try?"

"You're crazy, Hank," she told him. "It's a ridiculous idea, but I'm game. I've missed you, too, you know. A lot."

Outside, he held her face lightly and kissed her a long time. He walked her home with one arm loosely around her shoulders. "Did you know I had a middle initial?" he asked her.

When she shook her head, he said. "It's *S* like in stubborn." When she laughed, he shook his head. "That's on the level, it really is. For once my stubbornness worked."

Ellen's family was all at the back of the house eating breakfast. As Ellen stood at the front door Hank leaned both hands against it on either side of her. She had forgotten how warm she used to feel when he sheltered her like that, against the wind.

"Ellen," he said gently, "don't let's blow it again. It's too great." His expression was shy, the way it had been on their first date.

They took a lot of kidding those next few weeks. Ollie Samson was the worst, but Hank only grinned. "Winners can be generous," he told Ellen when she congratulated him on his cool. She enjoyed Hank; and loved him that tender way she always had, but she was marking time for Michael.

In May, Ellen took her advanced placement tests, ran in the warming dawns, and raced almost every weekend. As the end of May neared she had to pack away a bunch of books to make room for the running trophies on her bookshelf. After May would come June — the end of school and summer. Michael back home again.

That last week of May Ellen's mother was offered a job with a local accounting firm. Ellen had never seen her so happy.

"This is exactly the job I wanted," her mother said, glowing with excitement. "I only wish I had more time to get things arranged here at home, but they want me to start next Monday."

That Friday night they celebrated with dinner

at the country club. Even Hank came. Ellen's mother laughed and hugged Hank when she saw the card he had brought with her flowers. It was signed, "That nice Hank who bikes Ellen home." Brad, who loved to tease, sent a telegram asking her to lend him money.

Ellen's happiness for her mother only lasted until the next morning. She was running longer distances now, training for a ten-kilometer race. She got back home too late for breakfast with the family, but they were still around the table. "Shower fast and come back down," her mother said. "We have wonderful news."

Ellen didn't notice the pile of brightly colored brochures by her father's plate until she slid into her chair.

"Let me tell!" Robin pleaded. "Please let me tell Ellen."

When her mother nodded, Robin thrust a pamphlet in Ellen's face. "I get to go here," she said. "It's a horse camp and I get to ride every day all summer. Look at that great horse."

Ellen glanced at the horse and its child rider and looked over at her mother. "What's all this?" she asked.

Her mother beamed. "Your father and I have spent weeks figuring out what to do if I get a job. That western riding camp is highly recommended. It's perfect for Robin."

Ellen's eyes strayed to the other brochures with suspicion. "I'm not going to camp," she said quietly.

They all stared at her. "You haven't even looked at what we've chosen," her father said.

Ellen got up swiftly, shaking her head. "That's not the point. I don't want to go to camp," she said, "I want to stay here. Robin can go if she wants. Brad will be here. I'll stay with him."

"That's impossible," her mother said. "Brad will be working in the loop, long hours, weekends even. You'll be better off doing things you like, meeting new friends. We checked camps everywhere. This Jayhawk Running Camp sounds perfect. Sit down. Let's talk."

Ellen sat down, fighting tears. "There's nothing to talk about. I don't want to leave home. Jim Spivey gives running clinics right here in DuPage County," she said. "He was an Olympic runner. I can work with him and not have to leave home."

"Ellen," her father said, his voice almost threatening. "Quit carrying on and listen to our plans. Brad isn't even going to be around. Your mother and I will still be adjusting to work she's been away from for a long time. You know how much I travel in the summer. Camp is where you girls both belong."

Ellen glared at him with streaming eyes. "You're not even thinking about us at all. You've made all these plans for your own convenience and Mom's. That's just plain selfish. I don't care what Robin does but I don't want to leave home."

Robin got up, cried, "Giddy up," and galloped

out of the kitchen, slapping her thighs with both hands.

Ellen sat staring at her lap, not looking at her parents or the two brochures her father put in front of her. When her mother tried to take her hand, she pulled it away and put it in her lap.

"There's something going on here that I don't understand," her father said quietly.

Ellen flamed with anger. "It's not complicated," she said hotly. "I simply don't want to leave home."

Her mother was suddenly on her feet. She crossed to the stove in quick, angry steps. "If I had any question about your being mature enough to stay here alone, it's gone now. You're acting like a seven-year-old. You're not being banished for life, Ellen. You're getting a chance to do two of the things you like best and meet other young people with the same interests. Like Maggie and her skating camps."

"I'm not Maggie," Ellen reminded her. "I won't go to camp."

"Ellen," her mother said quietly. "Is there some special reason you don't want to leave this summer?"

"Hank's going to be off in Ohio," Ellen's father said. "He told me that last night at dinner. You two can write."

Ellen stared at him. Hank! Did her father really think she was worried about missing time with Hank? She looked at her mother without wanting to and knew what she was thinking.

Her mother knew. How had her mother figured out that Ellen was counting the weeks until Michael Tyler came home? "We do know what's best for you, Ellen. You are going to spend your summer at camp."

Ellen fled the room, helplessly crying.

Chapter 22

That began the worst weekend of Ellen's life. She cried until her face was puffy, her eyes red, and her nose running. When Robin called her for lunch, she said she wasn't hungry.

It was the unfairness. She had waited, counting the days until Michael would be back. She had thought of him every single day. Although she decided changing her looks was silly, she had really tried to get more grown-up and mature. Hadn't she done student council when she didn't want to? Hadn't she made herself go back to running to shake that awful depressed feeling? She had earned the right to be here when Michael came home.

She heard the family leave in the car a little after two. She had run and missed two whole meals. Down in the kitchen nothing looked good except apples and graham crackers. She ate them out on the back steps, feeling like Cinderella. The phone rang inside but she didn't answer it, then or later. She didn't even care who was calling. She didn't care about anything.

When she told Robin she wasn't hungry for dinner, her father came upstairs. He closed her door and stood with his back to it. "I can't speak for your mother, Ellen, but I've had my fill of this. You are coming to dinner and you will be polite about it. Don't worry about looking awful, your mother cried all day, too. And about being selfish — who is worse, a child who refuses to accept the best her parents can do for her, or the parents whose main concern is her well-being? I'm sorry you don't want to go, but the plans are made. The best you can do now is accept our decision gracefully."

Fortunately Robin was full of chatter about her afternoon. No one else seemed to have anything to say at dinner anyway.

The next morning when she set out to run, she couldn't make her body obey. She jogged to Jefferson and sat on the bench where she had first sat with Michael. When the tears started again, she gave up and went back home, completely sick at heart.

She should have known better than to expect any understanding from her friends at school that Monday.

"Why so down in the dumps?" Hank asked. "Let me guess! It's because you'll miss me so much when I'm off in Ohio."

She glared at him. Talk about conceit! "I just had my whole summer ruined," she said, telling him about her parents' plans.

When she tried to tell Val how unfair her parents

were, Val missed the point. "What's so big about staying here?" Before Ellen could reply, Val narrowed her eyes. "The guy?" she asked.

Ellen nodded, afraid to speak for fear of tears.

"I don't even know this mystery man's name," Val said. "Does this mean that he's been gone and is coming back this summer?"

Ellen nodded again. "I've waited forever to see him."

"Will he be going away again in the fall?"

Ellen shook her head. "Then there's no problem," Val said, smiling at her. "Let him look for you for a while. Do him good!"

Cricket listened without really hearing Ellen. "Leave me your address," she said. "So I can tell you when our baby comes."

Luke was the worst. "Don't complain to me," he said. "I'm doing the grandson act in Florida! But Maggie loves her camp."

Ellen honestly believed her parents would back down. She tried everything, tears, arguments, even silence. They never gave an inch. She even talked about the money. It would be cheaper to keep her at home.

Wasted breath!

She had no more than said good-bye to Hank than she started packing her running gear. The one extra thing she took was her yearbook. Michael had seven pictures in it and all of them great!

Ellen lost track of the new experiences she had

that summer. She had never flown alone before that flight to Kansas City where the camp bus met her. She had never lived in a dormitory before or shared a room with anyone. She'd certainly never seen that many young distance runners together at one time before. The campers ranged from twelve through juniors in high school and split equally between guys and girls. And they were from everywhere — as far away as Alaska and Spain.

She couldn't have moped if she wanted to — there wasn't time. Days began at six-thirty in the morning with lights out at eleven-thirty. They ran and ate and ran and ate again. Even the lectures were great, with famous runners and experts on everything from equipment to agility. By the second day she and Christy, her roommate, were fast friends. Before camp was over Ellen was astonished to be planning with Christy to come back together the next year.

She even got some sketching done when her age-group wasn't competing. A lot of her drawings were of a boy they called Scott from Scottsdale. Everybody kidded him about being named for his hometown, but nobody kidded him about his racing form or speed. She watched him as they ran in a group and again when his age-group ran. When he saw her and Christy cheering his win, he came over, tugging on his warm-ups. Even streaming with sweat and flushed from the heat, he was handsome. He stuck his hand out to Ellen. "Thanks for the cheering section," he said, still holding her hand.

"Do me a favor and wear that shirt again tomorrow."

When Ellen looked puzzled, he laughed. "I ran a Bastille Day race, too, but not in Chicago." When one of the coaches whistled them over, Scott danced in place. "See you in the lounge later?"

Christy sighed as he ran off. "Remind me to dye my hair blonde and grow three inches," she said. "He's a winner."

Scott was a winner, both on track and off. He was funny and bright and wonderful fun to be with. He and Ellen talked running and music groups and movies and school. He hugged her after races but didn't make any moves on her. They did hold hands walking on campus at night while fireflies winked around them. "I hope your boyfriend doesn't mind if we write to each other," Scott told her the last night. "I like you too much to lose track of you."

Ellen looked at him, startled. "Hey," he said. "A girl like you has to have a special guy. Tell me about him."

Ellen walked on silently. Scott was a junior, Michael's age, and just as great in his own way. Maybe greater. Her age had never even come up between them. He had only liked her and chosen to be with her every minute they weren't on camp schedule.

She looked up to see him almost laughing at her. "Tongue-tied?" he asked. "Surely you've talked about him before."

She shook her head. "Nobody ever asked me. They know him."

He frowned. "Big Man on Campus?"

She nodded even though she hated that phrase.

"A runner?" he asked.

She shook her head. "A swimmer." Only at that moment did she realize that Hank hadn't crossed her mind. She had thought of Michael Tyler and nobody else. She looked up at Scott. How could she trust a brand-new friend this much? But she did. "He's not really my boyfriend, Scott," she told him. "I just wish he was."

He turned, frowned, then put his arms around her. "That poor boy is sick," he said soberly. "Listen, Ellen, stay away from sick people. You could catch stuff from them, germs, viruses, bacteria. You'd have to drop training, start from scratch."

She laughed without pulling away. "I'm the sick one, Scott. Smart girls don't carry torches."

He laughed. "Except in the Olympics." Then he sobered and studied her face. "No kidding, Ellen, will you give me your address? Will you write me? Sometimes I could maybe even call."

"I'd love it," she admitted. His body was hard from running but his arms gentle around her as he kissed her. A night bird called from a nearby tree as they started walking again, arm in arm. She felt peaceful and beautiful.

On the way back to the dorm she told him about the rest of her summer, an art workshop in Pennsylvania that she was going to and how much she'd rather be back home. "Give me that address, too," he said. "I earn camp and my race fees by working the rest of the summer for my dad."

Ellen was only home long enough to repack before leaving for Pennsylvania. She thought only of Michael while she was home. Where was he? What was he doing? She yearned to dial his number just to hear his voice. Instead she put her annual in with the things listed for the drawing and painting workshop.

Three pieces of mail beat her to Pennsylvania, a card with a cactus on it from Robin, a letter from Scott, and an announcement from Cricket.

Robin missed her and rode a "hard" horse named Buster.

Scott missed her and said he pretended she was there beside him on his training runs.

Cricket gave the baby's weight and length and what minute he had been born. "For a kid that was supposed to be either a horse or a girl, he's something else. We named him Zach, and he likes his aunt Cricket the best already."

The buildings of the workshop were among ancient trees in the rolling Pennsylvania hills. Going so swiftly from strenuous exercise to quiet lectures and hours of sketching sent Ellen into a kind of culture shock. But the shorter hours and leisurely pace enabled her to run daily and keep up with her classes, too.

She had been placed in an advanced class on the

basis of work her parents had sent. The work was a challenge — anatomy lessons for figure drawing, precision drafting for perspective, and endless experimentation with light and shade. The other students were a challenge, too. They took themselves more seriously than any kids she knew — arguing endlessly about politics, art theories, and bad movies. And they didn't understand her running.

By the second week she had made a couple of fairly close friends, a girl named Aida, who hummed off-key as she painted and dared impossible colors that always worked, and a quiet scholarly boy named Brian, whose style was as flamboyant as he was shy. By the end of the month, she completely fitted in, going to movies with a boy named Matthew from Baltimore, who was masterful in oils, arguing theories with the loudest of them.

Through the days she lost herself in the drawing and painting only to find herself again when she ran at dawn through the green countryside. She loved the mail, letters from her mother with a scratched insult from Brad at the bottom, a card from Maggie at skating camp, and Scott's occasional letters, which were cheerful, full of his running, and somehow terribly lonely.

By the second week of August she had quit digging the annual out of her bag to look at Michael's pictures. She thought about Hank a lot. What he had said was wise. Had he seen anybody he could care for when he was out shopping for girls?

She celebrated her fifteenth birthday the week

before she was to leave camp for home. She got fifteen red roses from Hank, who had called her mother for her address, a new cold-weather running jacket and her first set of really good oil paints from her parents, and a picture of Zach from Cricket.

Instead of that strange wistful longing that had haunted her fourteenth birthday, she felt an almost giddy freedom from her obsession with Michael Tyler. She hadn't seen him since that night at the Willoughby party. She hadn't talked to him except in her head, and that not for a long time. She had been able to establish an honest, almost loving relationship with Scott, whom she really respected, and had learned to enjoy other boys like Brian and Matt. Then there was Hank whom she really looked forward to seeing again. It was good to be going back home again believing in herself and the time to come.

Some day she'd meet the boy who could stir her heart the way Michael had. She was willing to wait for that, but she wasn't in any big hurry to go through *that* again!

Chapter 23

Summer ended as swiftly as it had begun. Ellen and Robin both came home the Sunday before book buying day. Cricket had come in from Wyoming the day before.

Cricket came by for Ellen wearing a T-shirt that said in block letters: HANDS OFF, PODNER! THIS COWGIRL BELONGS TO ZACH. After Cricket showed Ellen the baby's pictures, she told Ellen she had to get through at school as fast as possible. "I have to be home when Lynn calls," she explained. "She promised to let me know about Zach's checkup."

Ellen laughed even though she was disappointed. She had hoped they could bike home together like in the old days. Because the good old days were back to stay. She knew that as a fact!

Cricket got through before Ellen and was gone when Ellen saw Michael. He was down at the far end of the hall, laughing with a bunch of guys. He was more deeply tanned than she'd ever seen him and even more handsome than she remembered, wearing shorts, a white shirt, and sneakers.

The shock was physical. She clutched her books tight and started for the door. This couldn't be happening. All the grief and pain and problems that had come from loving Michael Tyler couldn't be closing back in on her again at the first sight of him. She had been so completely sure she was past all that.

She hurried for the door, feeling as if she were running for her life. She thought she had made it when she heard him call her name. Then he was there, smiling at her. "Ellen," he said again and caught her arm. His touch was enough to make her shiver with delight. "Are you ever something to see! Or are you too famous now for your old friends?" Then he laughed. "Talk about history repeating itself. I met you before, loaded down with junk like that. I hope you're through?"

At her nod, he grinned. "I am, too. Let's go get our bench. We need to catch up."

She could have made up some excuse. She could have really run for her life. Instead she followed him out.

"Where were you all summer anyway?" he asked.

"At a running camp out in Kansas," she told him. "Then an art workshop in Pennsylvania."

He whistled softly. "You are something else. And all that time I was only shouting at monster kids in the golf club pool." He checked his watch, then asked what Brad was doing. "I saw him from a distance at a movie but never got to talk to him oncc."

She couldn't look away from him. He seemed older, his voice a little deeper, but his smile still made her weak. He had liked Connecticut okay but was glad to be back home. "Dad's project went well, thank goodness. Otherwise I couldn't have come back here to finish up at Jefferson like I always wanted to."

She wanted to stay there with him forever, just talking and watching him smile. But he kept checking his watch and looking at the side door they had come out of. He finally explained that he'd asked someone to join them. "A surprise," he says. "Someone we have in common."

Suddenly, halfway through a sentence, he got up and looked toward the door. Ellen turned to see Valerie Frederick coming toward them with that sweet, slow smile. He met her halfway and put his arm around her, kissing her lightly on the cheek. "I nearly flipped when I found out the club's newest good golfer was a friend of yours, too," he told Ellen.

Val grabbed Ellen and hugged her tight. "Welcome back! Have I ever missed you! And your ears should have burned all summer when Michael and I compared notes on our astonishing Ellen."

"Hey," Michael said, his arm still around Val. "Since we're all through here, how about going someplace and catching up?"

All Ellen could think about was getting away. Being with Val and Michael together was more than she could handle. Now Michael was threatening to turn a ten-mile race into a marathon.

She picked up her books. Her voice even sounded strange in her own ears. "Sounds great," she said, "But I'm due home with Robin. It's great — really great to see you both."

She made it to the deserted bike rack before she felt her insides crumble with grief. She biked home with her wheels playing the rhythm over and over. Val and Michael. Michael and Val. This was like a tragic play whose ending she should have guessed. The girl she idolized and would most want to be like had connected with the guy she idolized and loved hopelessly.

She dumped her books on her desk and threw herself across the bed. Her life might as well be over. Nothing was ever going to work again. They were seniors. They would do all those great senior year things together and then he would be gone — forever. Why hadn't she thought about this happening? Val was a golfer. He was lifeguard at the golf club pool. She wanted to die.

Then she sat up and wiped her cheeks with the back of her hand. It had been pure luck that she had never mentioned Michael's name to Val. Somehow she had to keep Val from ever knowing who her "mystery man" was. It wouldn't be easy.

She had been so sure of herself, so positive she had gotten over this awful obsession with Michael. She had spent this entire summer being a person all on her own and thinking she was getting along okay, thank you. She had been wrong, wrong, wrong. She had only been safe because she was so far away. And Michael wouldn't graduate and leave for nine whole months. She didn't know how she was going to deal with it.

Hank came in from Ohio that weekend. She hated herself for fitting into his arms so willingly. But how could she explain that nothing had changed except that hearts can be broken more than once and still beat regularly.

"Well," he said, holding her close. "I'm in luck. Does this mean that the shopping wasn't that great?" She smiled and clung to him. Any warmth she felt had to come from outside herself.

School started even though her world had come to an end. For the life of her, she couldn't get interested in any of her sophomore classes. For the life of her she could hardly stand even her best friends. They were all too happy. Maggie with Luke, Barb Sanchez with a quiet, dark boy who had transferred in. Cricket with her endless chatter about baby Zach.

That fall she felt herself taking a long, slow slide into nothingness. Seeing Michael and Val together at school was an ache that only got worse with time. It only made it worse that neither of them seemed to have any idea of her feelings. They were always glad to see her. She and Val still worked together closely in drama group. Michael was forever stopping to say something funny (and big brotherish) to her.

Her one good grip on reality was running. She

was out for a ten-mile run every morning regardless of the weather. She ran compulsively, the way she loved Michael. She went to bed tired and woke up feeling even worse. Hank, confused but devoted, suggested that if she didn't run so much, she'd be her old self again. She couldn't explain that when she was running she wasn't thinking. Thinking was one thing she couldn't afford to do.

They dated but finally quit going to movies. He thought she was sleeping on his shoulder when she really was just making herself not watch. The dumbest love scene in the stupidest movie was enough to plunge her into helpless tears.

The same old things came around, class pictures, the sophomore play, the midterm tests. Then the letter came with warning notices on Ellen's progress in three courses.

Her mother tapped the envelope on her hand thoughtfully, then went to the phone. "You and I are going out to dinner tonight. Your Dad is working late," she told Ellen when she came back.

"But I have dinner almost finished," Ellen told her.

"Ellen's night out," her mother said with an unconvincing smile. "I called Cricket to come sit and have supper with Robin. You decide where you want us to go."

Her mother was too easy to read. They were going to have a talk where they couldn't be interrupted. On the surface they would talk about the first bad grades Ellen had ever gotten in her life, but the unspoken subject would be Michael Tyler. Ellen was sick with dread by the time her mother parked outside the restaurant. "We're in luck," her mother said. "It doesn't look crowded."

By the time they ordered their meals, Ellen knew her mother wasn't going to make it easy for her. She toyed with her fork without meeting Ellen's eyes. "German, geometry, and chemistry," she finally said. "Would you like to talk about those classes?"

Ellen sighed. "I'm having a lousy year."

Her mother leaned back a little as the waitress set down her salad, and then Ellen's. "Problems with teachers? Anything like that?" her mother asked. Ellen shook her head.

Her mother sighed. "One more time. Ellen, will you talk to me about what's ruining your high school years or do I have to?"

Ellen looked at her. A lot of the kids had real trouble with their parents. Kids like Cricket who had a mother who didn't like her and a stepfather she hated. Kids like Hank who couldn't even bear to mention his mother's name. She'd been lucky. She and her mother had always been close except for small passing differences that Ellen couldn't even remember anymore.

Ellen sighed. "Michael Tyler," she said in a defeated tone.

Her mother bent her head. She looked very graceful with her dark hair catching the light and her hands still beside her plate. "Michael Tyler," she repeated in a whisper. "Now that we've named the problem, Ellen, how can we solve it?"

Ellen shook her head, feeling tears hot behind her eyes. "I've tried," she whispered. "I've really tried. But what can I do when I can't think of anything else? When I can't feel the same way about anyone else? I've tried."

"And this summer away didn't help at all?"

"It helped while it lasted. Then I came home and saw him."

Her mother sighed. "Honey, I know you expect me to give you a lecture on how important your high school grades are to your college chances, to your future success. You know those things as well as I do. I was slow to see what was happening. It only dawned on me a little bit at a time. I know how strong you are in other ways, at disciplining yourself for running and study and just being responsible. I kept telling myself that all those good gears would kick in and help you get over this."

Her lips smiled but her eyes didn't as she looked at Ellen. "Now I'm scared. More than those grades, I'm worried about you. A lot of forbidden things come along in life, forbidden, tempting things, that only you can resist. Nobody can do it for you. This is a tough test. Apparently this Michael is a wonderful kid for everybody else. But to you, he's poison."

Ellen remembered walking with Scott from Scottsdale under the campus trees. She almost heard his words echo in her mind.

Her mother watched her. "What are you thinking about?"

"A boy I met at running camp," Ellen said quietly. "The one in the portrait I painted at art school and framed for my room."

"The runner," her mother nodded. "That's a great picture."

"He's a great guy," Ellen told her. "He's the one who writes me now and then. We were a couple all the time we were there. I told him I'd been carrying a torch for a guy for a whole year. He said that the boy was sick. He was wrong. I'm the sick one. But, Mom, I don't know what I can do to help myself."

"There are drastic things we can't afford to do," her mother said. "Like send you off to boarding school until Michael is gone or you get over it. But that's only running away. It doesn't solve the basic problem. Sooner or later Ellen has to take charge of Ellen. You have to decide how big a price you can afford to pay for something that is destroying you."

"I can't afford any of it, Mom, not the hurting, not making bad grades, not even that awful tiredness I get from fighting something I can't win against." Her mother looked so sad that Ellen wanted to hold her tight. "Surely *somebody* gives lessons in falling out of love?" Ellen said, hoping to make her smile.

It wasn't a smile, just a good try. Then her mother shook her head. "If you could just manage to live like you run, a step at a time, a minute at a time, ignoring the wind and the stinging muscles, but just keep pushing on because of where you're going."

"A step at a time, a minute at a time," Ellen repeated. Except for this summer when she'd been away, she had fanned the fire herself, by watching for Michael constantly in the halls, by letting herself think about him all the time, by running past his house and imagining him there, by copying that picture and talking to him in her head. "Will you pay to have that tattooed on my forehead?'" she asked.

Her mother tapped her hand gently. "You're as bad a tease as your brother," she said, smiling.

"But you have to catch me if you see me slipping," Ellen told her. "I know it will help that we can talk about it."

"I hope so," her mother said. "I've bitten my tongue too long trying not to mention his name."

"A step at a time, a minute at a time," Ellen whispered.

Luckily she had finished her work on the sets and the costumes for the November play. Mr. Quigley was completely understanding about her going to the library to study instead of drama group the rest of that semester.

Hank said he understood, but admitted that her being gone gave him a different problem to deal with. Although he only had the second male lead in the November play, it was the most demanding part he'd ever tried. "When you're not there at practice, I just can't get myself into it," he told Ellen.

When Ellen tried to convince him without success, he came up with a suggestion that made her want to cry.

"Maybe if you would start wearing that bracelet again," he suggested. "Just knowing it was on your arm might bring me luck."

Catching up in German class was the hardest until her father bought her a set of tapes that she listened to when she ran. When she went back over the geometry, she was able to catch up with it by herself. Chemistry was one miserable smelly lab day at a time. She was so busy bringing those grades up painfully, one day at a time, that she hardly noticed it when Michael and Val quit always being together.

"None of my business," she told herself over and over. "None of my business at all."

Then it had to snow.

Chapter 24

Instead of a typical early snow that fell and melted, this was a real snow. The snowplows shoved it up into gleaming crumpled drifts and when the sun came out, the glare was blinding. The roads were so bad that Ellen had to quit her training runs, which had helped after her talk with her mother.

She didn't need this. She didn't need the village looking like Christmas until the day actually came. Everything she saw buried in white reminded her of standing with Michael, warm and smiling beside her, at Salt Creek Bridge. In spite of all her mother had said and her own painful effort, you could be watching every step and still stumble. For the first time ever, she dreaded Christmas.

As always, the drama group had their traditional pizza party following the last performance of the November play. Ellen went to the party with Hank. After they'd put in their huge order, but before the food came, Mr. Quigley rose to command the noisy group's attention.

"Okay, clowns," he shouted. When they settled

down enough to listen, he dropped his voice, grinned, and waved a large manila envelope in the air. "I have a surprise for you," he said. "I hold in my hand a compliment in the form of an invitation. We've been asked, as a group, to give one more performance of this play on the afternoon of Saturday, December twenty-first."

Somebody groaned. "But school will be out," somebody called.

"Yeah," another boy chimed in. "I'm on my way out of town that morning."

Mr. Quigley acted as if he hadn't heard them. "This isn't just another performance," he went on. "We've been asked to do a performance to be taped for television. The sponsor is an educational network whose scouts have been auditing our work for the past couple of years. If any of you are crazy enough to think you're going to make a living in the theater later, this will be a valuable professional credit. For you who intend to be commodity traders or market analysts like your parents, you will have evidence that once, when young, you had the wit to put art over numbers. Before I go on, did I hear something about school being out and leaving town?"

During the chorus of people backing off, Hank tightened his arm around Ellen's shoulder. "Boy is that man lucky! Last year and next year I'd have to be off there in Ohio. But since I'll be around, I suppose I can spare him that day."

She laughed softly. "Don't give me that!" she

said. "If you were any happier you'd be dancing on the table."

"I may anyway," he said as Quigley gestured for silence.

After Quigley had explained the details of the planned taping, he added, "When it's over, hopefully without mishap, my wife and I want you to join us for a probably inedible buffet supper at our place. Just to thank you for the honor you've showered on me as well as yourselves."

Ellen covered her ears against the chorus of shouts that followed. "This is being struck by lightning, isn't it?" Hank whispered, his eyes shining.

She nodded. Hank would never realize how true his words were. Not only was she thrilled and proud and excited about the TV taping, but the date would make Christmas easier. The white engraved invitation to the Willoughby Christmas dance had already arrived. When she reminded her mother that Michael would be there, her mother had promised to help her think up an excuse.

Now she didn't have to worry. Her aunt Silvie and uncle Alex would be as thrilled as she was. This was one excuse they would be happy to accept!

In spite of her constant battle with her own mind, a lot of things were more fun that Christmas. Especially the shopping. Maggie wanted to buy everything she saw for Luke. Cricket did buy practically everything she saw for her little brother, Zach.

The year before, Ellen had only seen things she thought Michael would like. She concentrated on not thinking about him. It worked until they were in the kid's department to buy a hideous lamp with a rearing horse on it that Robin had fallen in love with. While the clerk was getting the boxed lamp out of the storeroom, Ellen waited by the cash register, looking at a display of trinkets for a little girl's room — musical jewelry boxes, light catchers, and fancy picture frames.

One thing in the display didn't make sense to her. It was a long wide red ribbon boxed with a package of white hat pins. Across the top of the ribbon were two huge red padded hearts followed by the words, I HAVE BROKEN.

"Isn't that cute?" the clerk asked. "Hearts I have broken. The little girl pins her boyfriend's school pictures on it and hangs it on her bedroom wall."

Ellen caught her breath and blinked. Now that was the perfect gift for Michael if there ever was one. The bitterness of her thought startled her. Had carrying the torch for Michael so long burned out some of her gentleness, leaving something ashy in its place?

When the three of them left the mall loaded with packages, Cricket frowned at Ellen. "I know that lamp is a big enough thing to carry, but you only bought that one present. What about Hank?"

"I got smart and ordered his this year."

Maggie glanced over at her. "So what did you get him?"

Ellen hesitated. They had to know Hank as well

as she did to know how perfect the gift was. "Some cassettes," she said.

Maggie narrowed her eyes. "What group?"

Ellen laughed. She couldn't pass up that straight line. "The Royal Shakespeare Company," she said. "Gielgud and Burton."

Maggie frowned. "I guess that's no sillier a name than the Rolling Stones," she said. "It sounds British."

Ellen giggled. Even if she explained, Maggie would think it was a stupid present. Cricket frowned a minute before she got it. "From the Smithsonian?" she finally decided out loud. "Lynn likes that highbrow drama, too. But it's all words and no music."

That was all right. Ellen knew that the words in the four Shakespearian tragedies she'd chosen for Hank would sound better than music to anyone who loved drama the way Hank did.

The taping of the play went off beautifully. It seemed to take forever with the constant adjustment of the light and sound checks. The Quigleys' dinner was delicious, long tables of both hot and cold food that tasted fabulous after the long, grueling afternoon in the chilly auditorium. Hank and Ellen crunched toward home together on yet another fresh snowfall.

Hank seemed as buried in thought as Ellen was. That day had been some kind of a record for her. Only once had she been struck with that intense longing for Michael that still came without warning. In the final scene the male lead realized, almost too late, that he was losing the only woman who had ever truly loved him. Ellen had shivered in recognition of the girl's anguish. But Michael Tyler was going to do that exact same thing. He was going to graduate in only a few months. He would go away to college and forget her without ever knowing how deeply she loved him. Real life wasn't as tidy as a play. And there was nothing fair about it.

They were almost to Ellen's corner when Hank spoke suddenly. "You're missing that big Christmas party you went to last year."

She nodded and smiled at him, tightening her arm in his. "I went to a different one tonight and loved it."

"Bud Leonard was going again tonight. Rented a tux and everything. Probably Michael Tyler's there, too, like last year."

Bud Leonard's name caught her off guard. Bud had been at the Willoughby party. She had danced with him before Michael came in and sort of took over her evening. Was it possible that Bud had been the one to tell Hank about that evening?

"How come you know Bud?" she asked him.

"He works with Jay," Hank said.

As he spoke, he stopped suddenly in the shade of a huge oak tree. He caught her by the shoulders and pressed her back against the rough bark of the tree. Before she could catch her breath, his lips were on hers. This was no gentle, loving kiss with his mouth tender on hers, but an angry kiss, with his teeth hard and cutting against her lips, and his breath hot on her face.

She tried to twist her face away but his mouth clung to hers, following her movements, rough and demanding. He was holding her so tight that she was actually scared. She felt panicky and helpless and could only think of getting away, pulling herself free of that awful, painful kiss.

Her mouth felt bruised and swollen when she finally wrestled herself loose. He had cut off her breath so long that she was gasping as she ran awkwardly along the icy, snow-covered walk.

"Ellen," he called after her. "Please, Ellen."

She knew it was hopeless but she only shook her head and tried to keep ahead of him. He caught up with her almost at once, grabbing her arm so she couldn't pull it loose.

"Let go," she whispered. "Let go of me."

His hands fell away at once. He stood perfectly still, his arms loose at his sides, his face unreadable. She stopped a few feet away, fighting to catch her breath. She pressed the palms of her mittens to her face to soak up the tears she hadn't realized were falling. She felt dizzy and unsure of her balance.

"Ellen," he said quietly. "I'm sorry."

She couldn't speak. She kept having to catch her breath around an awful thumping in her chest that wouldn't stop.

"I really am sorry," he said again, still not making a move toward her. "Maybe it's just that a year ago, *he* was kissing you."

"And you *wanted* to hurt me!" she sobbed.

"I guess I did there for a minute," he said. "It wasn't really you. It was just," he paused. "I don't know what it was. Please, can I come walk with you now?"

His face was in shadow but the lamp at the corner lit the smooth strong line of his jaw and the sadness of his mouth. "I don't understand," she stammered. "I just don't understand." He didn't move until she finally held her hand out to him. He took it and drew her close to him, putting her head against his chest just under his chin.

He sort of rocked her back and forth against him, whispering into her hair. "I'm sorry. I'm so awfully sorry. It's not really you I want to hurt. But it's not fair. It's just not fair."

She slid her arms loose from his grip and put them around him. She knew what he meant and he was dead right. It wasn't fair that he had so much more love for her than she could ever feel for him. But neither was it fair that she felt the same way about Michael in spite of every effort she had made. She wasn't letting it get in the way of her studies anymore. She was forcing her mind away every time she started to daydream, but how many times had she been furiously angry at Michael for her own obsession with him? Was she somehow better than Hank that he wasn't allowed to feel the same way?

"How about we go on home?" she asked after a minute.

He nodded and held her away from him, just looking at her face. Then he shook his head and put one arm across her shoulder to walk her home. "I don't think I'll come in," he said at the door. "Do you still want me to come to Luke's party with you on Monday night?"

She sighed. "Of course I do, Hank. And so does Luke. He didn't ask you just because of me. He really likes you."

"Well, then he's one up on me," he said with that funny cockeyed grin she loved. "I can hardly stand myself sometimes."

She laughed softly and rose to touch his lips with hers. Maybe she ought to be angry and furious and unforgiving. But how could she feel like that when she and Hank were both caught in the same hopeless situation?

Chapter 25

The week before Christmas, Hank auditioned for a part in the cast of the drama touring show. Luke caught up with him as he was dropping Ellen off at her classroom. "Hey, Hank," Luke said. "Don't forget about my bonfire and skating party next Monday. Maggie and I really want you both there."

Hank looked doubtful. "I've been thinking about that since you first asked," he said. "You were great to include me but I'd better not come. I've never been on one ice skate in my life, much less two."

Luke shrugged. "No problem. Lots of kids don't skate. They just play games or sit around and eat." He grinned at Ellen. "I even remember when Ellen mostly skated sitting down."

"Not fair!" Ellen cried. "Nobody's born ice skating!"

"Except maybe Maggie," Luke corrected her. Then he got that glazed look that he got when he thought about Maggie. "I mean she's so good it scares me. But wait and see for yourself, Hank.

Nobody around here is within an Olympic mile of her."

Ellen had to break in. He was good for a half hour of bragging about Maggie without catching a breath. "I'm sorry, Luke, but it's almost class time. See you later, okay?"

Luke glanced at his watch and winced. "Wow. You're right. Oh, and Hank," he called after them. "Don't worry about skates. We have tons of extras." He grinned. "Some of them even match."

Hank frowned and shook his head. "I have no idea of what I'm getting into with this party. Is there some way I can bone up on skating in about two weeks?"

"You could try squinching your feet down real narrow and scooting them along ahead of you instead of walking," she said brightly.

"And you might try not being such a smart-aleck," he said, laughing. He caught her wrist at the classroom door, his hand covering the silver bracelet she'd worn every day since he asked her to put it back on. "My lucky charm. Just so it works again."

"As good as you are, who needs luck?" she asked.

Hank was still auditioning when Ellen came out of class and saw Michael Tyler for the first time in weeks. He was coming toward her down the hall beside a small girl with short, dark hair. Ellen stiffened, bracing herself against her own feelings.

Michael spotted Ellen and waved. At first she didn't realize that the girl at his side was with him.

She waved back and would have gone by if he hadn't practically blocked her way. "Hey, Ellen," he said. "Too bad you couldn't make the Willoughby bash. But taping that play for TV was great! The stars of Jefferson High!"

She couldn't read his grin. Was he making fun of her or did he really think the taping was great? It didn't matter. She only needed to be polite and get away as soon as she could. If only she didn't feel like she was teetering on the edge of a cliff.

She did manage to smile. "They're stars, all right, but I'm not," she told him. Hank had said that Michael had "killer charm." As he smiled at her, Ellen couldn't argue with the term. Michael's oxford cloth shirt was open at the neck above a chestnut brown crew sweater about the shade of his hair. Those dark brows that might have looked like overkill on anyone else only made his eyes look deeper set and somehow mysterious. And as always, his eyes seemed to smile all by themselves.

Although the girl was about Cricket's height, there any resemblance ended. How could anybody stay that perfect-looking all in winter white? Her only touches of color were an apricot-colored silk scarf tossed over her shoulder and matching lipstick. As Michael talked to Ellen, she caught her lower lip between her teeth and stared at Ellen.

Michael must have sensed her annoyance. He turned and put his hand under her elbow. "Ellen, have you met Allison Grant? Ellen is Brad Marlowe's little sister. You remember Brad."

The girl wasn't anything like as pretty as Val and she didn't look as pleasant either. She not only had a cross expression, she acted hateful. She kept staring at Ellen without smiling and barely nodded. "Ellen Marlowe," she repeated, as if memorizing the name to hang on a dart board. "Aren't you the one who goes with Jay Ober's little brother?"

Michael saved her from having to answer. "Hey," he said. "Hank Ober's made a name for himself on his own. That kid has real acting talent. Don't you think so, Ellen?"

"I do!" she said, prickling with annoyance. If Hank was a "kid" who could be known apart from his brother, why didn't she get the same privilege? Cool it, she warned herself. It didn't matter. Nothing Michael said was allowed to matter.

But the fact that this Allison obviously knew Jay Ober hit Ellen hard. What were Ellen's chances that Allison wouldn't mention this meeting to Jay? She needed to get away, and fast!

"Nice to meet you, Allison," she said even though it was a flat-out lie. "Got to rush."

Michael looked startled and caught her arm, holding her back. "And it's great to see you, Ellen," he said. "We'll miss you at Willoughby's, but have a Merry Christmas!"

She fled, trembling with anger at how her own skin betrayed her by tingling at his touch even through her shirt and sweater. Concentrating through the next period was impossible. She knew what Hank was going to say. And for sure, that girl would run and talk to Jay. Her stomach began to do that thing with knots. The very thought of Hank throwing another jealous fit made her both scared and angry. She couldn't deal with it. And she didn't have to. It was silly and stupid for him to carry on the way he did.

By the time Hank caught up with her later in the day her resentment must have shown on her face. He looked at her and laughed. "Wow. Do you ever look ready for a fight!"

She grinned sheepishly. "I'm sorry. A fight's the last thing I do want. So don't you dare start one when I tell you that I ran into Michael a while ago."

His smile died in an instant. "There must be a hundred Michaels in this school," he said coldly. "But for you, there's only one. You don't even need a last name, do you?"

"Stop that!" she whispered fiercely. "Do you want to hear what I have to tell you or not?"

"I won't know until I hear it," he said sullenly.

"Two things," she said, wishing she'd taken her chances with Allison's big pouty mouth and never started this. "Michael Tyler was talking about your making a name for yourself acting."

"So how did my name happen to come up?"

She glared at him. He hadn't even heard the compliment, but had gone straight into his jealousy mode. "When his girlfriend asked if I was going with Jay Ober's little brother, Michael said you were so talented you should be known on your own."

Hank studied her, frowning. "Doesn't he go with Val?"

"Not anymore," Ellen said. "This is a new girl."

"Who is it this time?"

Ellen chose her words carefully. She couldn't show her instant dislike for the girl or Hank would accuse her of being jealous. "Her name is Allison something, maybe Grant."

He groaned and slapped his head. "It's Grant all right. What a witch that girl is. Jay works for her dad. Maybe I'll be lucky and she'll wreck her sports car racing over to tell Jay about that." Then he looked sideways at Ellen. "But don't worry about Allison giving you any long-term competition. Her track record with guys is two weeks max."

"Brad's little sister can hardly be considered competition," she told him icily, turning to walk away.

He caught up and took her arm. "Level with me, Ellen. He really called you that?"

"It's not the first time," she snapped.

"I'm sorry, Ellen. I don't mean to blow up like that." He sounded genuinely sorry. "That's pretty stupid of him. I'll just cross my fingers that he doesn't ever get his head checked."

Ellen wasn't sure just why she dreaded Luke's party, but seeing Michael always left her down in the dumps. It was as if he had cast a spell on her. In two minutes he could sweep away all her good resolutions not to let him affect her. She tried to keep from plunging back into that old yearning.

But Hank bothered her, too. Twice now in a week, his jealousy had left her miserable. She didn't even like him when he flew off like that. She hated worrying about every word she said for fear he'd take it wrong. She'd really believed they would have the same warm relationship after they made up in the spring. They might have, too, except for his jealousy.

Adrienne already had Luke and Maggie in the front seat with her when she picked Hank and Ellen up at the Marlowe house.

"We've got a perfect night," she told Ellen. "Ten million stars and good smooth ice. How can we lose?"

"Not possible," Luke agreed, looking over at Maggie.

Once there, Ellen had to agree that the party promised to be a winner. The music sounded great in the crisp air. The flames of the bonfire lit the face of the frozen lake with muted rosy lights. While the crowd was still gathering around the fire in their brilliantly colored parkas and hats, Maggie and Luke clomped over on their skates. "Isn't this wonderful?" Maggie asked Ellen and Hank, her face dimpling with pleasure.

"We'll see," Hank told her. "I'm a first-timer on ice."

"No problem," she said. "It's almost as easy as it looks."

"Show me," he challenged her.

She looked startled and glanced at Luke. "I hate to be the first one out there." At Luke's smile, she shrugged. "So what? Somebody's got to break the ice, as they say."

In a few swift leaping steps, she reached the edge of the lake and took off. Ellen watched her in amazement. She had seen Maggie skate all her life, but never like this. Whatever the Martins had spent on Maggie's lessons had been worth it. Maggie belonged to the ice. She looked more like a ballerina than a skater, spinning and whirling in the air as if she were weightless. She moved in flawless timing with the music as the record came to an end and stopped.

Ellen hadn't realized that the whole crowd, Adrienne's senior-class friends as well as her own class, had gathered at the side of the lake. When Maggie dipped low to skate back to shore, they shouted and whistled their approval.

Ellen didn't recognize the tall, slender boy in bright green skating clothes who had come to watch near them. "Now that is what I call a ringer," he said quietly, as if to himself, before turning away to disappear into the crowd.

"I don't know what a ringer is," Ellen told Hank.

"It's somebody who comes into a competition without anyone realizing what an expert he is. He mustn't know Maggie."

"He must be one of Adrienne's friends," Ellen said. "Anyway, this isn't a competition."

"Want to bet?" Hank asked, nodding toward the

lake where a half dozen skaters were warming up. The boy in green was out there, too. After skating smoothly in a giant circle with both hands behind his back, he began to perform with a flair equal to Maggie's, only bolder because of his height and strength.

When the other skaters pulled back to watch the performance, only Luke and Maggie stayed on the ice. "Come on, you guys," Luke called to them. "Let's get a game going."

When Ellen didn't move, Hank turned to her. "Don't hang back for me," he told her. "I'm going to watch awhile."

"This is Luke's favorite game," she told him. "It's like a square dance on skates with the boys skating with one girl after another." She glanced back toward the stereo. "I guess Luke's dad is going to call the changes."

Self-conscious with Hank watching, Ellen skated onto the ice to join the ring of girls. As she glided across the ice, the cold wind swept away her doubts. It felt like the wonderful old times when she and Luke and Cricket had skated as kids together.

Maybe they were all watching for the expert skater in green to connect with Maggie, Ellen certainly was. As Luke slid his arm around Ellen, she smiled over at him. "You didn't exaggerate about Maggie, Luke. She's fantastic."

"And so is that Tony Harrel," he said with something like envy in his voice. "He's some guy from

Oakbrook that Adrienne is dating. She said he was a good skater, but I didn't realize how good. Look at them. There they go."

There were lots of good skaters on the ice, Adrienne and Luke among them. But they were just skaters. Maggie and Tony Harrel could have moved smack onto a TV screen as skating stars. Later Ellen wondered if Mr. Ingram forgot he was supposed to make the calls for the changes, or if he, like everyone else, was hypnotized by the beauty of Maggie and Tony Harrel's performance.

Ellen was glad that she was with Luke as the crowd pulled back again to the edge of the ice. She gripped his mittened hand in hers as they watched that incredible stranger whirl Maggie like a snowflake, then lift her above his head before circling again to go into a new routine.

Adrienne finally broke the crowd loose. "Waltz time!" she shouted. "The last one on the ice is a rotten egg."

Ellen barely glanced at Luke's face as he pulled her onto the ice. Even that swift look was enough to make her want to cry.

On the ice she saw Maggie glide by in Tony Harrel's arms. He was smiling down at her possessively. The adoring look on Maggie's face as she looked up at her companion made Ellen feel sick. Ellen caught her breath, snagging her skate so that Luke had to catch her arm to steady her.

"It's the way of the world," he said dismally. "The

king is dead. Long live the king. And all those other stupid clichés."

"They're only skating. Don't be silly," Ellen told him, nudging him in the ribs.

He smiled wanly. "Let's not kid ourselves, Ellen."

Chapter 26

Luke made some lame excuse about helping his folks and left Ellen with Hank.

"Maybe it's just tonight," Ellen told him. "I don't think Maggie's ever skated with anyone as good as she is before." She tried to smile at him. "Maybe she'll wake up in the morning."

"Who do you think you're kidding?" he asked, putting his arm around her and pulling her close. "Did I tell you how much I like the way you skate? Maggie's flashy but you're classy."

Ellen smelled the food before she saw Luke and his mother loading the long tables with huge vats of chili and trays of sandwiches and chips. "How can I be this hungry without even putting skates on?" Hank asked as they filled their plates. Then he paused. "I hope you don't mind it that I don't want to try skating. I hate making a public fool of myself."

"Just so you have a good time," Ellen told him.

"Hey," he said, pressing his shoulder against hers. "You're my good time."

The chili was so good that they both went back for seconds.

"You haven't really told me about the tryouts for the play," she reminded him as they sat by the fire with their food. "I only know that you got a good part. Does the play read well?"

"The greatest," he said, grinning like a kid. "Val Frederick read the female lead like a pro. Naturally she got it." Warm from the fire and full of hot food, Ellen leaned lazily back against Hank's shoulder. She loved watching his face when he was caught up in what he was talking about. Even if his features hadn't been even and strong, the vitality in his voice and face would have made him knockout good-looking.

Watching him like this, she felt wonderfully close to him. She hadn't felt this close since that awful night of the pizza party. She slid her hand out of her mitten and into his, lacing their fingers together. He tightened his hand on hers and leaned to brush her cheek with his lips. The music had started again, slower music, the kind of dance music on ice that Ellen liked best. She even imagined being out there, swaying on the ice with that music. It didn't matter. She felt happy there in the darkness against Hank.

When he suddenly stiffened, she should have been warned. Instead she only came out of her daze to look up at him. Her heart dropped. All that warm genial vitality had been replaced by a dark, angry scowl. Before she could ask him what was wrong, he took her hand out of his mitten and laid it back on her lap.

"I guessed right about Allison Grant on two counts," he said roughly. "She nearly killed herself getting back to the store to report on how you flirted with *her* boyfriend."

Ellen sat up straight and stared at him. "What brought that on?" she asked.

He glared at her. "The second thing I predicted, what else? She didn't even last two weeks with your BMOC. If you look over there, you'll see that he just walked in by himself."

"I don't want to talk about it," she said firmly, looking straight ahead, hoping Michael wouldn't see her or even be in her line of vision. But all the physical stuff started anyway, her stomach making knots around her chili, her heart thundering, and her hands moist with sudden sweat. Hank said nothing more, but leaned forward to stare at the fire as if she weren't there.

Ellen saw Luke picking his way toward them with a sense of relief. "Hey, Ellen," he said. "Want to skate?" It's pretty awkward skating out there alone.

"From that scowl on Hank's face, you're having about as good a time as I am," Luke told Ellen as they moved onto the ice.

"I hate the way he acts when he's jealous," she said.

"Turns the world to thin ice, doesn't it?" Luke asked, making a stab at being his old self.

"I hate it," she said hotly. "I mean, I can't stand it."

"I got news for you. Feeling jealous is as ugly as it looks," Luke said quietly. "Do me the favor of knocking me flat if I make a fool of myself that way."

She tightened her arm in his. "You'd never do that."

He shrugged. "I wish I could be that sure of it."

Luke spun her in a graceful circle as the music stopped. "Thanks, Ellen. Now I guess you'd better go back to unhappy Hank."

Michael Tyler caught up with them as they neared where Hank was sitting. "Great party, Luke," he said. Then he grinned at Ellen. "Want to give the Martin and Harrel act a run for their money, Ellen?"

She laughed at the very idea. "No way," she told him.

"Come on, kid. Don't turn chicken on me," he said, reaching for her hand. She had forgotten how persistent he could be about getting his way. But she hadn't forgotten that Hank was watching only a few feet away. Oh, if just once she could stay cool when Michael looked at her like that. She was sure that Hank knew how her heart was thundering at Michael's touch.

Hank had risen and come over. Michael turned and stuck his hand out. "Ober!" he said. "What a good job you guys did with that play. That taping will put Jefferson on the map."

As Hank ducked his head and mumbled his

thanks, Michael went on. "I'm having no luck talking this Marlowe out onto the ice."

"What's your problem, Ellen?" Hank asked, turning to her with cold eyes. His expression wasn't so much a smile as a challenge. "Go for it."

Ellen's chest was a solid hard knot. Surely Luke and Michael could see the same cold fury in Hank's face that she did. Maybe not. Maybe she just knew Hank too well. Entirely too well!

Hank had said he wasn't into making a public fool of himself by skating. What about doing it with this iceberg act? Jealousy was ugly and mean and she didn't have to put up with it.

She shrugged and smiled at Michael. "Okay, that's it. You talked me into it. Let's go."

Maybe Michael wasn't as good on the ice as he was in the water, but he was close. For the first few moments she was nervous and a little stiff. What if she fell? Sometimes even Maggie fell when she tried too hard. The fear vanished as she let herself relax into Michael's lead. She heard her skates whisper with the rhythm of the music. The faint stars that had shone early in the evening were gone. In their place came snowflakes, the big flat kind, drifting out of the black sky to twirl around them as they spun across the ice.

When one landed smack on Ellen's nose, she blinked. Michael grinned and leaned close to blow it off. "Nice," he said, grinning at her. "Where did you learn to skate like this?"

"Right here," she said, still breathless from the

nearness of his lips to her face. "Luke and I have been friends forever."

He nodded. "Adrienne's a great kid, too, but it's funny. We've never really been friends until this year."

Michael must have known the record was almost finished but he skated her through the snow out to the far edge of the ice anyway. As they stopped at the change of the music, he grinned at her. "It would be silly to go clear back there wouldn't it? Some other guy might want to skate with you. He might not appreciate this snow like we do." Before she could answer, he added, "Hey, we're in luck. It's a good old waltz." He lifted his arms to her as the strains of the music began.

When she had danced away the evening with Michael the year before at the Willoughby's, Luke had accused her of having amnesia. Whatever gave her that wonderful recklessness struck again, and she didn't even care. She felt weightless, suspended on air and joy as she waltzed and spun and turned in and out of Michael's arms.

They even quit talking and only smiled as they worked through the intricate patterns of the dance. There wasn't any time, only one glowing moment after another. There wasn't anyone else in the world, only Michael, and the music, and the reality of his eyes on hers, his hand warm against her back.

From the waltz, the music went straight into "Auld Lang Syne."

"Hey," Michael said, looking down at her with

surprise. "Is Mr. Ingram trying to tell us something?"

She nodded. "That always means that the party is over."

An aching began in her chest as they moved toward the shore with the dying strains of the song. It couldn't be over. It couldn't be over because she wanted to stay close to Michael forever and ever and ever. It couldn't be over because now she would have to face Hank's cold fury. She wanted to cling to Michael and cry, "Help me!" but that would be ridiculous.

But the music did stop and the laughter and voices of the crowd rose to fill in the silence. "Thanks, Ellen," Michael said, still holding her hand. "I almost didn't come because Dad and I ran so late with dinner. You're a good skater. Isn't there anything you don't do well?"

Then he grinned at Hank and wished them both a Merry Christmas. She watched him walk away. There were lots of things she didn't do well. One was to feel his hand release hers and know that her time with him was over. Another was to get through her farewells to Luke and his parents and face Hank alone.

Adrienne approached Ellen and Hank, jiggling her car keys nervously on her glove. "Whistle when you're ready to go," she told them. Then she flushed. "Tony Harrel is going to drop Maggie off at her place."

"We're ready now," Hank said without even

glancing at Ellen. "I hate to put you to the trouble just for us."

She grinned at him. "Hey! This helps to get me out of cleaning up some of this mess."

At Ellen's house, Adrienne offered to drive Hank on home. "Thanks anyway," he said. "And thanks for the great party, you and Luke." Ellen shivered with dread as they walked silently toward the porch. Hank's face was a mask.

"I guess I'll take the bracelet now," he said, holding out his hand.

She slid it from her wrist silently and dropped it in his hand. She couldn't have said anything for her life. He flipped the bracelet a couple of times, a slim silver coil flying through the falling snowflakes under the light of the porch lamp. "And thanks for two things, Ellen. For the evening and the education. It was a hard way to learn but I now get the message. You knew I'd be watching you out there with your precious Michael but you didn't care. You forgot that I was alive."

He caught his breath and looked at her, his face close to hers. "Not once have you ever had that shining look on your face for me like you did for him. In all this time, I've never seen you smile at anyone like that before."

"Hank, please," she said.

He shook his head. "Don't give me that. Talk about making a fool of myself! But that S in my name stands for stubborn, not stupid." He turned and started down the walk.

As she opened the door, he turned back. "And I hope you have a rotten Christmas, Ellen. You deserve it."

She closed the door behind her, knowing that this time Hank's good-bye was forever. Somehow she got upstairs and into bed but she couldn't get warm even with Tawny settled against her.

Why did she keep on making one big ugly mess of her life after another? She had worked so hard and come so far in breaking Michael's hold over her, only to throw it away for an hour in his arms. How could she have let herself down like that? How could she have been so cruel to Hank without even meaning to?

For the first time not even the memory of Michael's smile and his arms around her could help. She buried her face in her pillow, too heavy with guilt and grief even to cry.

Chapter 27

Maggie Martin called the morning of the day after Christmas. Ellen was too astonished by the brusqueness of her tone even to wish her a Merry Christmas.

"I've got to see you," Maggie said. "How about this morning, like right away?"

"Oh, okay," Ellen said. "Want to come over here?"

Maggie hesitated. "Let's meet somewhere. Any place you say."

Ellen's mother was still in her robe, drinking coffee and reading the paper to celebrate her day off. She would be there with Robin so getting away wasn't a problem.

"You name it," Ellen said, feeling her stomach tighten at the urgency in Maggie's voice.

"Some place dark," Maggie said, obviously thinking out loud to herself. "I could even bawl."

Ellen's stomach did a flip. She really needed this! Hadn't there been enough big emotional scenes this Christmas already? And how could she watch Maggie cry when it was Luke who had been hurt the worst. Inwardly she sighed. "How about a booth at Hemingway's? Half an hour?"

When Maggie mumbled agreement, Ellen put the phone down and stared at it, feeling miserable already.

"Trouble?" her mother asked, looking up from the paper.

Ellen nodded, and slid onto the bench across from her. "That was Maggie," she said.

Her mother looked surprised. "Oh, I don't know why I thought it might be Hank. Maybe because he hasn't been around. But neither has Maggie, now that I think of it," she added, smiling at Ellen.

There was no way Ellen could smile back. She had meant to tell her mother about breaking up with Hank right away but there hadn't really been a chance, not with Christmas Day, and Brad home, and Robin hysterical, the way she always was at Christmas.

"That skating party of Luke's turned into a killer," Ellen said, not wanting to meet her mother's eyes but making herself do it anyway. "Everything that could go wrong did." She didn't mean to stop talking but her voice just quit. Mostly she dreaded having to admit to her mother that all those good intentions and sincere efforts had come to nothing in a single evening.

"So what happened?" her mother asked quietly.

"Hank got mad when I skated with Michael Tyler," she said in a quick rush of embarrassed words.

"But you must have skated with a lot of people," her mother said, looking puzzled. "You always do. You're a good skater."

"Hank's not stupid," Ellen reminded her. "He didn't like the way I looked while I was skating with Michael."

Her mother sighed. "Like that, was it? Maybe Hank was just being overly sensitive." If her mother had looked cross or even disappointed, Ellen could have dealt with it. Instead, she looked sympathetic. That brought sudden hot tears behind Ellen's eyes.

"He had every right to be jealous," Ellen admitted. "I forgot he was even there while I was with Michael. Mom, I hate it that I'm such a failure. I've tried so hard for so long. And I've really been doing great. Then everything flew out the window the minute I was with him."

Her mother reached over and patted her hand. "Anybody can slip a little, honey. You only fail when you give up. It doesn't sound to me like you've done that. But what does all this have to do with Maggie?"

"That was the other ugly thing that happened. I not only made Hank mad enough to split up with me, but Maggie flipped out over a guy she'd never seen before. She skated with him all evening, then just plain walked out on Luke. She even let this other guy, this Tony Harrel, take her home."

Her mother sighed softly. "Killer party, indeed. Mostly I'm sorry to hear that about Luke. But it could be worse. At least he's discovered that he can care about somebody."

Ellen would have smiled if she could have managed it. "I learned that I could care about somebody, too," she reminded her mother. "Look what a big fat mess that's made of my life."

Her mother's dark eyes were soft with sympathy but she said nothing. Ellen rose. "I've got to change. You know I'd rather have a tooth pulled than go talk to Maggie right now."

"I'm pretty sure Maggie feels the same way," her mother said. "But be glad she feels like she can talk to you. She's got to be feeling perfectly rotten."

Maggie got there first. She was waiting in a back booth, staring at a napkin full of silverware that she was turning over and over in her hands. She started talking before Ellen was all the way into her seat. "I guess you know why I called you," she said defensively.

"Luke?" Ellen asked, sliding in across from her.

Maggie nodded and leaned toward her. "The last thing I ever meant to do in this world was hurt Luke," she said in a strange heavy tone. "You always said he was the greatest and he is, Ellen. I still think he is, but something came over me. It was like — I don't know what it was like." She dumped the silverware on the table and sniffled into the napkin. "See? I knew I couldn't talk about Luke without bawling."

"Amnesia," Ellen said quietly.

Maggie looked up at her but Ellen didn't explain. All the way to the restaurant she had only thought about Luke, how hurt he was, how unfair Maggie had been to him, how he didn't deserve to be treated like that in front of everybody — his family, his friends, everybody. But here was Maggie, hurting as much as Luke must be, and Ellen knowing exactly how she felt.

Maggie's eyes were streaming as the waitress approached. "Order for me," she croaked. "A cola and fries."

When the woman was gone, Maggie shook her head in a distracted way. "I don't even know why I'm talking to you," she said, her tone suddenly sounding cross. "There's no way you'd ever understand anybody messing stuff up the way I have. But I haven't even been able to sleep. I just can't stand it. I can't even stand myself. Every time I even *think* of Luke I cry."

"Hank and I broke up that night, too," Ellen said quietly.

Maggie stared at her with red-rimmed eyes. "Again?"

Ellen nodded. "This time I know it's for good. I had a little amnesia, too, as Luke calls it. I skated with somebody else in a way he didn't like."

Maggie frowned, her eyes narrowing as she tried to reconstruct that evening. When she remembered, she stared at Ellen in disbelief. "Michael Tyler? Hank blew because of him? But that's crazy.

You two have always just been friends. Since way back last year."

Ellen nodded. "That's the way Michael and everybody else sees it. Hank knows better."

"Knows better," Maggie whispered, leaning close. "Ellen, you can't be saying what I think you are. You can't be in love with that guy!"

Ellen managed a weak sort of smile. "I can be and I am, right along with about a hundred other girls. For a whole year and a half." She reached over to touch Maggie's hand. "I'm only telling you this so you'll know that I do understand how something like this can hit you. That doesn't make it any easier for Luke, or for you, but I do understand. It's none of my business, but do you really like this Tony Harrel or is he just a super skater?"

Maggie tightened her lips, then sighed. "I don't know about like yet. I only know I can't think about anything but him. When he calls me up I can hardly speak. The very first time he kissed me, I felt as if I'd never been kissed before, which is stupid on the face of it. I have to be in love with him. I can't explain how I feel any other way. And, Ellen, I hardly know him. It's terrible and wonderful all at once."

Ellen nodded. "Anyway, he *does* call you."

Maggie nodded, suddenly dimpling. "And, oh, Ellen, he says the greatest things. He could be handing me a line for all I know, but I just swallow it and love it. We've been out twice already since that night. He's going to get his folks to talk to my coach. He wants us to do skating tryouts as a couple. But it's not just skating, Ellen, it's him. I adore him."

"And that leaves Luke," Ellen reminded her.

"The awful part is that I love Luke, too," Maggie said, her voice beginning to choke up again. "Boy, does that make me sound shallow! But I do love Luke, only not the same way." She paused and took a deep breath. "For gosh' sakes, Ellen, say something. I hate it when I bawl like this."

"It's going to take time for Luke to get over this," Ellen said. "You know he never looked twice at a girl before."

"I'm really desperate," Maggie wailed. "But I don't want to lose him as a friend. And I don't know what to do."

"I don't think you'll lose him as a friend forever," Ellen said thoughtfully. "But it's going to take him some time."

"Like you and Hank?"

Ellen shook her head. "I don't think we can ever be friends again. Hank really hates me. He hates me so much that I'm even afraid of him. He gets crazy when he's jealous like that."

"All this over Michael when you don't even go out with him?"

Ellen nodded. "It's the loving that matters, not what you do about it."

Maggie stared at her thoughtfully a long moment, then leaned across the table. "Ellen," she whispered. "Will you talk to Luke for me? Try to explain what happened to me and how much I care about him?"

Ellen looked down at her plate. This was it, then. This was why Maggie had called her.

"You're the only one who could ever make him understand," Maggie went on. "I can't even explain how important he is to me. He's just such a super guy."

"I'll try," Ellen said. "But in the end it's your problem." That was what Luke had told her when she needed advice about talking to Hank. Luke was not only super, he was wise, too.

As the restaurant filled up with lunch traffic, the waitress had begun to stare at them. When she came by to look down again, Ellen picked up the check and put down a tip.

"Does Cricket know about you and Michael Tyler?" Maggie asked as she handed Ellen her share of the money.

"And Luke, too?" Maggie asked when Ellen nodded.

"I should be mad that you never told *me*," she said, "but maybe I can figure that out. What I don't get is how come you decided to trust me now when you didn't then," Maggie said.

Ellen laughed. "If you don't know, I can't explain it."

Maggie grinned and squeezed Ellen's arm. "Thanks," she whispered.

* * *

Ellen invited Luke on New Year's Eve while she baby-sat Robin. He jumped at her invitation. "I almost called and asked myself over," he told her as he took off his jacket in her front hall. "I'm sick of that place. Adrienne has a new boyfriend. They sit and stare at each other until I want to set off a bomb under them. Lovebirds make me barf."

Ellen asked herself if all guys had bad memories.

After Luke and Robin had eaten everything in the house and played a bunch of board games, Robin wandered off to watch TV. The minute she was gone, Ellen leaned toward Luke and said, "Okay, we have two things to talk about."

"If one of them is Maggie, forget it," he said, his eyes darkening with anger.

"I will after I say it," she told him. "She's sorry but she couldn't help herself."

"Where have I heard that before?" Luke asked, sneering.

"Get off that!" Ellen told him. "You've heard it from me, and I've heard it from Hank, and now you've heard it from Maggie."

"That's it?" he asked.

Ellen nodded. "She can't even say your name without bawling. All she really wants is for you two to be friends again."

"Oh," he said, his voice rising with sarcasm. "Is she having trouble with math again?"

"Luke," Ellen warned him.

"Okay. Let's just say that Maggie Martin and I will be friends again when pigs fly." He looked up.

"Now, can we get on to your second thing?"

"Let me tell you what I'm going to do this year."

Luke stared at her as she began to reel off her plans. She was going back to running camp with Christy. She was going to Wyoming with Cricket to meet her new stepmother and brother. And she was going to run the Chicago marathon with her friend Scott from camp if she could get her endurance up.

"Then I'm signing up for driver's training."

"Hey, hey," he interrupted her. "Don't get carried away. Have you forgotten how hard you have to study to catch up?"

She shrugged. "This semester's over in three weeks. I'm talking about the new semester in which I mean to make dean's list. That's what I'm going to do. You need the same kind of plans."

"Me? Run?" he squeaked.

"Don't be silly," she told him. "But you need to get busy. The school has stuff you'd like, science and math clubs. You've always killed me at chess. How about the chess club?"

He shrugged and made a face.

"Come on, Luke," she coaxed him. "Nobody's going to save our lives but us. We need to be so busy that we don't even remember that the two big M's even exist on this planet."

"Well, I guess I could always drop out of chess club if I didn't like it," he said lamely.

She glared at him. "Listen to you. Is this the same guy who gave me the big lecture about staying in drama group after Hank and I split? The guy who bullied me into turning into the walking happy face instead of drooping around like a wet rag?"

"That's different. You're a girl."

"You really burn me up when you make cracks like that," Ellen said hotly. "What makes you think that boys can't be dumped just as hard as girls are? Where's your pride? You want the whole school to think that Maggie dumped you?"

"Well, she did."

"That doesn't mean you have to broadcast it. Come on, Luke, quit being bullheaded. And while you're at it, give me a break. Admit it's a good idea. It's my turn to be right about *something*. You were sure right with your advice to me."

"Okay," he said grudgingly. "But I don't think you've gone far enough. You ought to try acting instead of just mucking around with costumes and sets. And what about your artwork? The stuff you've done since last summer is good. How about working on the school paper, or even the yearbook?"

She looked at him thoughtfully. "Actually, that is a neat idea. Maybe in the fall," she said. "But I think only juniors work on the yearbook. But maybe Quigley will let me design the play programs. I'd like that." Then she grinned at him. "This will be fun because it's our secret. And would you believe that you look less like a drowned rat already?"

"The word you're groping for is *discarded*," he told her.

Robin appeared at the kitchen door in her pajamas and robe. "You two are talking so loud that I can't understand the movie," she said, yawning. "You want to tuck me in, Ellen?"

When Ellen got back downstairs, Luke had fished the chessboard and pieces out of the hall closet and had it set up on the kitchen table. Ellen groaned. "You always beat me," she complained.

"If I'm going to join that club I'll have to beat everybody," he replied. "You get the whites and the first move. But that's the last favor I ever do anybody in a chess game."

Chapter 28

Ellen decided to take charge of her own life (and Luke's) the day the Christmas tree came down. She was curled in the corner of the sofa with Tawny, watching Robin shake each one of Ellen's snow-filled Christmas paperweights before carefully packing it into its box. She sat up so suddenly that Tawny glared at her and left.

This was spooky! She had sat in the same place, in the same room, watching Robin do the same thing exactly one year before. But with what a huge difference!

Back then she had been wearing her ears out listening for Michael to call after that "night she would remember forever" at the Willoughby party.

She had almost drowned herself crying when he left without a word. Then she had drooped into the New Year counting the days until she saw this guy who only remembered she was alive when he tripped over her or saw her name in the school paper.

Well, she was older and wiser now.

Michael Tyler wasn't going to call this year either. She knew that. Even if he realized that skating with him at Luke's party had left her life in shambles, he probably wouldn't care.

She had spent a year and a half being heartsick over a boy who not only didn't have a heart, but had a lousy memory, too.

But she was through, and that was that!

But it wasn't going to happen unless she made it happen herself. She even told her mother her plans. "They're not resolutions because I always break those," Ellen told her. "I'm just plain going to be a whole new person. You are hardly going to know me."

"Oh, please," her mother cried, only half-smiling. "Don't tell me we're back to purple eyelids and fake fingernails again."

"Think whirlwind," Ellen said, shaking her head. "I'm going to keep myself so busy, win so many races, and have so much fun that I probably won't even recognize that boy if he runs over me in the halls."

Her mother hugged her. "More power to you! This should be worth watching!"

At least part of Ellen's plan worked just the way she had hoped. She made it through her finals with flying colors and even managed to squeak onto the honor roll.

After that nothing worked the way she'd planned.

Hank was clearly out to drive her crazy if he could. Ellen wished he would go back to his old silent treatment of the year before. Instead, he seemed determined to make her miserable.

When she brought the cast costume sketches in for Quigley to look over, Hank glanced at them, made a rude sound and turned away. Quigley glanced at him but said nothing. Instead he approved them all except for suggesting some color changes that might take fuller advantage of the lighting.

When she filled in as a prompter at one of the January practices, Hank dropped his script with a disgusted look and glared over at her. "Can't we get someone who can at least read English sensibly?" he asked, his words heavy with loathing.

Ellen just caught her breath hard, but Ollie Samsom turned to glare at Hank and mutter something threatening.

Quigley rapped on the back of a seat and called out, "All right, clowns. When you're good enough to be temperamental, I'll be the first one to tell you. In the meantime, cool it."

Then there was Michael Tyler. While Hank was driving her crazy on purpose, Michael was probably doing it accidentally.

Driver's training wasn't exactly fun, but at least things moved along briskly. After studying the handbook, passing the written test, and taking the eye exam, Ellen got her learner's permit. With Brad off to school and her mother and father working long hours, Ellen almost never got to practice her driving.

That is, until Ollie Samson figured out what was happening.

"Hey," he told her. "You can drive with anybody your parents approve who's been licensed for a year or longer. I'm willing to put my life in your hands."

Fortunately her parents knew Ollie from the plays, and fortunately they liked him. It was great. He was a lot less nervous than her parents, and it was fun to meet him after drama group and drive herself home in his car by a different route every time.

It was through her driving with Ollie that she was plunged back into that awful yearning for Michael Tyler. After Ellen finished her work with the drama group, she would study in the library until Ollie got through and could come get her.

Ellen had managed not even to see Michael until the day that he came into the library. Ellen was putting her books away to be ready to leave when Ollie got there. Michael walked over to her study table and grinned down at her.

"I saw you from the door," he said. "You've really turned into a bookworm the last few weeks!"

She looked at him thoughtfully. Her table wasn't visible from the door. And why had he happened to notice that she had been haunting the library late ever since the end of Christmas break?

He shrugged at her silence, then sat down across from her. "Having a good year?" he asked.

"So far," she said. Until that very moment, she thought, take away Hank's crazy carrying-on. She kept putting her things away to keep from having to look up into that smile. "How about you?"

"No complaints," he said. Then almost as if he were embarrassed, he laughed softly. "I bet you haven't looked outside this afternoon." He leaned toward her with his arms on the table as he spoke.

"I really haven't," she admitted, furious at herself that he always softened her resolve with that engaging smile. "Am I missing something?"

He nodded, looking threatening. "Scary weather out there," he said. "Ice and sleet and freezing rain," he said. "I just thought that if you'd like a ride home, I'd be glad to drop you off."

He had to be able to hear that thump in her chest. She pressed her hands flat on the table because he couldn't help noticing how her hands were trembling. This couldn't be happening. And if it was, she didn't trust it because she didn't trust him.

Not that she didn't know the script by heart already. He would drive her home, chatting like her best friend in the world, he would drop her at her door, smile good-bye, and then become the old remote Michael Tyler, waving from down the hall or saying something flip and quick when they passed. It was almost as if he knew what effect he had on her and was working at keeping her from getting over him.

She glanced at the door desperately. Ollie should be there. Why didn't he come? Drama group had been almost over when she finished her work and left to avoid Hank.

For the first time she was afraid, not of Michael, but of herself with him around. Because her life depended on it, that was why!

Before she had to answer, Ollie breezed in with that light tread that was so remarkable in such a big guy. He came up behind Ellen and put both hands on her shoulders. "Hi, Tyler," he said, looking over at Michael. "How's it going?"

"Super," Michael said, rising. "I was just offering Ellen a dry ride home in this weather."

Ollie laughed. "Sometimes I win one. I beat you to it."

"Just so she doesn't drown, or freeze, or end up in a ditch," Michael said, smiling at Ellen. "And hey, tell your brother hi for me, will you, Ellen?" he asked as he walked away.

"I hope I didn't break anything up," Ollie said, looking at Ellen intently as she got in behind the wheel of his car.

Ellen shook her head. "He's just a friend of my brother's," she said, hoping the words didn't sound as bitter as they felt in her mouth.

"And I am the king of Siam," he said brightly as he got in from the other side and grinned over at her.

Luckily for all of them, the third time Hank got out of hand, Quigley was at the back of the auditorium where he couldn't see what was happening.

Ellen and Val were in the wings looking at the sketches for Val's third-act change. Hank came from the stage and walked briskly past Ellen, knocking her shoulder so hard as he passed that she was thrown off balance.

"Hank!" Val said, staring at him. "Take it easy."

He shrugged. "What's the big deal? There's barely enough room back here for actors. We don't need any stagehands mucking around filling up space."

Hank's back was to the curtains he'd just come through. He couldn't have realized that Ollie Samson had seen what he had done. Ollie instantly stepped into the wings and caught Hank from the back, gripping both his arms.

"Hey," Hank called out, fighting against Ollie's hold on him. "What do you think you're doing? Let go of me."

"First apologize to Ellen," Ollie said quietly.

Hank tried to jerk loose, but Ollie had his arms pinned too far backward for him to get them free.

"Look, guys," Val whispered fiercely. "Fighting will only get both of you suspended. Break it up."

"Knocking Ellen around is going to get him a lot worse punishment than that," Ollie said. "You want it here, Ober?"

Quigley's call sounded from back in the auditorium, "Cast onstage. Hurry it up."

Ellen held her breath against the fury in Hank's face as he muttered sorry without dropping his eyes from hers.

Ollie released Hank and put his arm around Ellen, grinning down at her. "Knight in armor on call. Have lance, will travel."

Hank glared at them both, his hands in fists at his side.

Later when Val and Ellen were in the restroom together, Val looked at Ellen curiously. "Maybe you should give lessons. Whatever you do to guys, it lasts," she said.

Ellen shivered, not liking the thought of living with Hank's fury indefinitely. "Hank'll get over it in time."

Val laughed softly. "Think so?"

Ellen stared after her as she walked away.

The spring play went on tour with really great reviews. Ellen was fascinated to watch Ollie and Hank onstage. Although they couldn't exchange anything but insults offstage, they managed to play their parts as first and second male leads with apparent ease. They smiled and bantered on stage as if they were blood brothers.

"That's acting," Val said, when Ellen mentioned it to her. "People become their roles onstage. Don't tell me you don't understand that."

"I don't know what you mean," Ellen replied, thinking guiltily of how careful she had been to act unconcerned every time she saw Michael in the halls with a new and different girl on his arm.

Val turned and hugged Ellen. "Come on, we're friends. Either you've managed to quit longing for that special guy or you are putting on a prizewinning performance. As I said, that's acting!"

When Ellen only shrugged, Val laughed softly. "I'm sorry you can't see a mirror. That blush is a dead giveaway."

Ellen's running got easier with the coming of spring but the schoolwork didn't. Neither did it get any easier to see the weeks pass and know that Michael's days in Jefferson High were steadily dwindling down to nothing. Sometimes when they passed in the hall he fell into step beside her, asking how things were, and about Brad, of course.

She had to be imagining that these meetings were not accidental. He couldn't have known to space their talks to fall only when she thought she had her feelings completely under control. But as sure as she thought she was immune to him, he was there, friendly and smiling beside her.

One day he started talking about college. She only nodded, as if she needed to be reminded that he would be gone in June. "It's a tough decision," he said. "It's hard to turn down a good swimming scholarship, but Dad really wants me at Princeton where he and my mother went." He had paused. "You must be looking ahead to that to. Are you figuring on following Brad down to Champaign?"

Ellen shook her head. "First I have to figure out what I really want to do later."

"Something in the arts?" he asked. "You did such a knockout job on those play programs."

She looked at him, startled. How could he always know everything she was doing without seeming to be paying much attention at all?

Even though she sometimes thought she saw Michael too much, Ellen felt out of touch with her old crowd. Her mother missed them, too. Although Cricket was in and out of the Marlowe house on the weekends, Ellen's mother complained about missing the other kids. "How's Luke?" she asked. "Why haven't I seen him lately?"

"Why haven't I seen him lately?" Ellen echoed. "First off, he joined the chess club and promptly made the interscholastic chess team. Since his birthday falls before June and mine after, we're even in different driver's education classes. I'm lucky if I get to watch him wolf down double lunches in the cafeteria."

Her mother laughed. "At least that sounds like he's the same good old hungry Luke."

Ellen nodded. "Everybody's too busy. Maggie shoots out of school to skating classes and spends her weekends skating with Tony Harrel. I only see Cricket when you do, on weekends. She went out for track and field in February and works as hard at it as I do at running. I miss them, too."

"What ever happened to Barb Sanchez?" her mother asked.

Ellen looked at her startled. "I must have forgotten to tell you. Her family moved away over Christmas. But she'd been going with a guy so long that I'd kind of lost track of her."

"That's too bad," her mother said. "But that's what happens when kids get involved too early." Ellen grinned. Good old Mom, never missing a chance for a little lecture on how to grow up all in one piece.

Ellen would have missed the other kids more if Ollie hadn't always been around, funny, flattering, and insistent. "Okay, Ellen," he finally said. "I have accepted that you have to baby-sit your kid sister every day after school. I have even been a good sport about your not going to the movies with me, even when you know you need night-driving practice. But there must be something we can do to revive the old American tradition of boy dates girl. I'm open to all suggestions and explanations except that you can't stand me."

Ellen laughed. "It's not that at all and you know it."

"Then how am I going to kiss you under the stars if you won't go out with me at night, answer me that?"

She laughed and touched his face with her hand. "Play that one back. You just answered your own question."

"Okay," he said. "I'll settle for having the best-looking chauffeur in town. For now, anyway."

"That's really great of you, Ollie," she told him.

"I'm a great date, too," he said. "You could check that out any time you weaken."

She only laughed and smiled at him. Every time

she began to weaken only a little bit, Hank made one of those low-level scenes that made her stomach ache. She wasn't ever going to get herself into a Hank kind of a situation again. Not as long as she lived.

Chapter 29

The last performance of the spring play was the night before the annual Saint Patrick's Day race.

"If you refuse to go to drama group pizza party with me, it's okay," Ollie told Ellen. "Just so we agree in advance that I get to take you home afterward."

When she hesitated, he groaned. "I can tell already. This excuse is going to be a humdinger."

She laughed. "Come on, Ollie, you know I'm a runner."

"Know it!" he interrupted her. "Haven't I been chasing you for at least a year?"

"What I meant was that I have a race the morning after the party. I'd be glad to have you take me home, but I can't stay out really late."

"I won one," he said, shaking his head crazily. "I'm going to see Ellen Marlowe under artificial light. Maybe even a moon!" Then he frowned. "You're really serious about this running business, aren't you?"

She nodded. "I'm training for the Chicago Marathon in October. In fact, I'm sorry you'll be gone. I have a friend coming in to run that race whom I think you'd really like."

"Does she look anything like you?" he asked.

Ellen broke up. "Not exactly. How about six foot two, dark blond hair, blue eyes, weight about one hundred and seventy?"

"A hundred and seventy!" he echoed bleakly "Wait a minute. What's this friend's name?" he asked, eying her suspiciously.

"Everybody at camp called him Scott from Scottsdale, but his real name is Scott Gilmour," she said, grinning.

He hit the side of his head with the flat of his hand. "Boy, the competition never ceases. And you even know how much this guy weighs!"

"That was just a guess, but I made a sketch of him running. When you draw a figure you get a pretty good idea of the model's weight," she explained. "He's my friend."

He linked his arm with hers and leaned over. "Far be it from me to educate somebody with your kind of brains, but somebody needs to wise you up. And how come you know he'll run this race anyway?"

"We write back and forth. He told me in a letter at Christmas. He'll go on from here to compete in the New York Marathon."

"A pen pal, and a friend," he said thoughtfully. "Then there's Luke Ingram. And Michael Tyler." He paused. "Correct me if I've missed anyone. For instance, do you consider Hank Ober your friend?"

She stared at him, startled. "Why do you ask?"

"Because that guy bothers me. I don't like the way he looks at you. I don't like the way he picks on you."

"I honestly don't know why Hank hates me so much," she said quietly.

Strangely, Ollie turned serious, too. "I don't understand it either," Ollie replied. "If I had you for my girlfriend and lost you, I'd take it out on the other guy — not you."

She stared at him, then dropped her eyes. She wasn't going to push that any further. His words were enough to make Michael Tyler fill her mind so completely that her breath came short.

Except for Hank's baleful glares, the pizza party was as much fun as usual. The senior actors were a little emotional at finishing their last play at Jefferson. When they started passing their programs around for everybody else to sign, even the underclassmen joined in. Some of the group wrote brief messages in the margin. Hank must have been watching his program make the rounds. When it reached Ellen, he leaned across the table and shoved it past her to the person sitting at her right.

At Ellen's door, she smiled up at Ollie. "I had fun," she told him. "Thank you."

"Thank you," he said. "And while my irresistible charm is fresh in your mind, how about you let me take you to the senior prom?" he looped his arms loosely around her as he spoke. In spite of his teasing smile, his eyes were intent and serious on hers.

"But I'm only a sophomore," she protested.

He laughed and hugged her. "Can you believe I noticed that? And can you believe I even checked it out? Fortunately Jefferson High doesn't have any silly rules about who a senior brings to his prom."

"Do you mind if I think about it?" she asked after a minute.

"All you want," he said. "But just remember that I was the first customer to take a number."

He kissed her gently, then smiled and touched both of her cheeks with his lips. "For luck tomorrow," he whispered before opening the door for her.

The morning of the Saint Patrick's Day race was clear and sunny with sailboats dotting Lake Michigan's silken surface. A perfect running day! Ellen knew she was beating her own time when she passed the third-mile marker. She wanted to laugh as she ran into the chute and handed her badge over. All those chilly mornings were paying off. She was streaming sweat but not a single muscle tingled or burned. And running, with the damp air from the lake cool against her face, made her giddy with the joy of her own strength.

"Look who gets congratulations again. You're second in your class," one of the older men from her club pointed out, pumping her hand. "Next year the trophy!"

Why did she have to spoil it for herself by remembering that on the next Saint Patrick's Day Michael would be gone from her life forever?

Everybody was loaded down with work right before midterm. You could walk the length of the hall and not see a smiling student. Then the school's schedule made spring vacation a joke that the administration was playing on all of them. With the third quarter beginning only a week after the break ended, nobody was going to have much fun. Ellen herself had three separate papers to do, one with tons of research. This didn't count having to finish a set of illustrations for her advanced drawing class.

She and Luke were eating lunch together that last week before spring vacation. Luke kept looking up at her so strangely that she finally leaned close to glare at him. "If I have managed to grow a third nose or turn green, please tell me," she said. "Then I would at least understand why you're staring at me."

Luke swallowed hard and looked down at his plate. "I was wondering about something," he said. "Mom's itching to have a party over vacation. Do you want to bring Oliver Samson?"

She stared at him. "You mean I have to have a date?"

"Well, you hang out around school with him, and drive his car all the time," he said defensively. "I just figured you might want to ask him."

"We're just good friends," she told him.

"Is that his idea or yours?"

It wasn't fair the way she still blushed at personal questions. "Mine," she admitted in almost a whisper.

"You're never going to get over you-know-who unless you give other guys a chance," he said crossly.

"I gave Hank Ober a chance," she reminded him. "You saw how that worked out." But Luke wasn't around during drama group. He couldn't know how rough Hank continued to make it for her.

"Second fiddle is not a chance."

She stared at him. Where was this all coming from? "Who are you to be talking to me about getting over things?" she challenged him.

Luke only stared down at his empty plate. Ellen realized that he didn't look like he felt very well. "You okay?" she asked. "You're a funny color."

He looked up at her crossly. "When you blush like a ten-year-old, I don't accuse you of looking funny. It's just that I have a favor to ask of you and I don't know how to start."

"You aren't thinking about asking Maggie as a date to your party!" Ellen asked, horrified at the idea.

He looked astonished. "Why would I do that?" he asked.

"Okay. Okay." Ellen said. "What's the favor?"

"I have a friend whose parents think she's too young to go on single dates. I thought maybe you and Ollie and my friend and I could double. Then her folks might let her come to my party."

"A girl!" Ellen said without meaning to raise her voice.

"Cool it, Ellen," he said, his face turning an even sicker color.

"I'm sorry, Luke. I just didn't know," Ellen said, practically bouncing with delight. "Why isn't she around? Why doesn't she eat lunch with us? Where are you hiding her?"

"She's shy," Luke said, looking up at her with his eyes suddenly shining. But his voice held that old excitement it used to have back when he dated Maggie. "She's quiet and shy but hilarious when you get her going. And I mean, is she ever smart. A whip, that's what."

"So what's her name? Where did you get to know her?"

"You probably don't even know her. Her name is Linda Perkins," he said. "She's captain of the chess team. I think, well, I hope her parents will let her come if there are four of us. It's too late for skating and too early for swimming but we could do a cookout with music and maybe dance."

Ellen stared at him, still trying to absorb the Luke Ingram-Linda Perkins combination. Of course she knew Linda Perkins — not well, but she didn't think anybody did. What a natural combination Linda and Luke made. Slim, little, redheaded, straight-A Linda Perkins and Luke falling in love over a bunch of plastic knights and pawns. Ellen wanted to hug him. How neat!

"Of course I'll double-date with you if Ollie wants

to come. But you have to ask him yourself," she told him. "Otherwise he'll take it wrong."

"How do you mean wrong?" Luke asked, frowning.

"I've worked real hard to keep from getting into the old Hank routine," she said, not meeting his eyes.

"That's not fair," Luke said, his strange eyes puzzled on her face. "You were the one who came up with all the bright ideas on how to break us out of our double M obsessions. Now I'm the only one who's following through."

When she dropped her eyes, he leaned toward her. "Come on, Ellen," he said quietly. "It's got to be getting better with you and Michael after all this time."

Why were her eyes suddenly hot with tears? "Let's say it's getting closer to the time I won't ever see him again," she said.

The warning bell rang and Ellen picked up her books. "I've got to run," she told him. "Fill me in on the party later. But you have to ask Ollie."

But she couldn't wait to fill her mother in on why neither of them had seen Luke lately.

Ollie caught her arm on the way into drama group. "Why didn't you tell me what a great guy that Luke Ingram was?"

"You probably didn't have time to listen," Ellen told him, smiling as he nudged her shoulder. "I could go on for hours."

"I give you that. Any guy who gets me out under the stars with you is the greatest in my book, too." He caught her other hand and waltzed into the auditorium and down the aisle, humming some wild tune that didn't match his steps at all. If only Hank wouldn't glare at them in that way that made Ellen shiver.

Cricket and Ellen were taking stuff out of their lockers when Luke came up to ask Cricket to his party.

"Thanks a lot, Luke," she said. "But I can't."

"What do you mean you can't?" he asked. "You're going to be in town, aren't you? You never go to Wyoming over spring break."

Cricket nodded but repeated she couldn't go.

"Are you mad at me for something?" Luke asked.

"Don't be silly," she said. "Nowadays parties are all couples. I'm only half a couple and don't qualify. Thanks, anyway."

"Come on, Cricket," Luke coaxed her. "You know how our parties are. Lots of kids are coming as singles. Any number of Adrienne's friends will come by themselves, too."

"Adrienne's friends?" Ellen asked, her heart sinking.

He shrugged, and looked over at her. "Sure. You know how my folks always give parties for both of our crowds. And this is her last year. She wouldn't miss it for anything."

At that moment Ellen began to dread Luke's party.

Even though she had stayed as busy as she knew how, even though she had more things going on than ever before, she still hadn't been able to push Michael Tyler all the way out of her consciousness. It took days for her to get over every one of their brief meetings. But Michael and Adrienne were friends. She knew with a deadly certainty that Adrienne would invite him.

But there was no way that she could back out. She couldn't even get deathly sick without letting Luke down. And it wouldn't be fair to Ollie either.

Already she knew that evening was going to be what Brad called a "no win situation." Michael would either come with another girl and break Ellen's heart, or he would come alone and break it.

Chapter 30

When Ollie came to pick Ellen up for Luke's party, Luke came to the door with him.

"Two boyfriends," Robin breathed, watching from the window. "Wait'll I tell the kids at school about this."

"Get lost," Ellen told her, swatting her on the behind.

"How can I learn about dating if you won't let me watch?" Robin wailed, retreating to the kitchen as Ellen opened the door.

"Eeny, meeny, miney, mo," Ellen said, pointing first to one of the guys and then the other.

Ollie caught her finger and laughed. "Lay off that! You're stuck with me tonight whether you like it or not."

"I wanted Ollie to see your artwork," Luke explained.

"He's seen all the stuff I did for drama group," Ellen said.

"I mean your figure drawing. That sketch in your bedroom."

"No!" Ellen cried as her mother and Robin joined them.

"Hi, guys!" her mother said. "Why the anguished wail, Ellen?"

"Luke wants to drag Ollie up to my bedroom," Ellen said, glaring at Luke.

"Just to see that sketch of her runner friend," Ollie said. "And I'm coming willingly. Nobody's even coaxed me."

Ellen's mother laughed. "I sense my daughter's vanity at risk. Do you want to check your room so we can come up, Ellen?"

"I do not," Ellen said, remembering with relief that she'd left it neat. "I just think it's weird to have a guy in my room."

"I've been there lots," Luke told her. "I never felt weird."

Ellen's mother motioned Ollie to follow her. "Let those two fight it out," she said. "They've had lots of practice. I love showing off Ellen's work. I think she's spectacular."

Ellen and Luke reached the door as Ollie and her mother were studying Scott's sketch. "It's fantastic," Ollie said quietly.

"I have never been informed that you were an art expert," Ellen said, cross enough at herself to take it out on him.

He laughed and stepped back beside her. "I'm not really," he said. "But I know what's good when I see it. I was raised on the stuff. My sister is a painter, exhibits in galleries all over."

Ellen stared at him. "I didn't know you even had a sister!"

He laughed. "A man of mystery. Thanks a lot, Mrs. Marlowe. Come on, Luke, we need to go inspect your girlfriend's bedroom now."

Luke wailed a protest as he followed him down the stairs. Ellen's mother was helpless with laughter. "That Ollie breaks me up," she told Ellen. "But I've forgotten who Luke's new girl is."

"Linda Perkins," Ellen called back to her from the hall where Ollie was holding her coat. For some reason Ellen didn't understand, her mother started laughing all over again.

Ellen had seen the Perkins' house when she was running but never knew who lived there. It looked more like a private school than a house anyway, a huge, sprawling, brick, three-story place half concealed behind a circle drive and a forest of fir trees.

Ollie whistled softly as Luke got out and went to the door. "What do you know about these people?" he asked.

"Only what Luke told me," Ellen said. "Linda's an only child, and her folks treat her like solid platinum. I'm pretty sure this is her first date. But Luke is really gone on her."

Ollie chuckled. "No wonder your mother lost it when I made that crack about the bedroom. What do you bet we have to bring her home by ten?" he asked, watching Linda and Luke come down the walk with her father standing stiff and watchful in the half-open door.

By the time they reached the Ingrams, it was clear what Luke saw in Linda. She was dressed in sea green slacks with a brief jacket showing off a ten-inch waist. At school her hair was always pulled back. That night it was a tumbled mass of glowing red curls around a heart-shaped face. Glasses. That was something else different. She'd only seen Linda in horn-rimmed glasses.

Ellen twisted around in the seat. "You know I've never beaten Luke at chess in a thousand years," she told Linda.

Linda laughed softly. Her voice was low and she spoke with a slight lisp. "I only beat him when I cheat," she told Ellen quietly. At Luke's astonished look, she winked at Ellen. "I consider flirting during a chess game cheating, don't you?"

At that precise moment Linda won Ollie's heart, too.

The Ingrams had lit the entire patio area with colored Japanese lanterns and the music had already begun when they arrived. Ollie held Ellen's hand as she got out of the car. "What a neat place. I feel a great evening coming on."

Ellen only smiled at him, wondering what he'd think if she asked him not to let anyone dance with her but him. Especially not Michael Tyler. But of course she wouldn't dare add that.

Later she was glad she hadn't said anything. Michael didn't show and Ellen danced with some of her favorite people as well as Ollie. But she still couldn't relax. She had seen Michael come in late to parties before.

Ellen had been dancing with one of Adrienne's friends when the music stopped between sets. She was looking around for Ollie when a tall, slender boy stepped in front of her and smiled. "You're Ellen Marlowe, Maggie's friend, aren't you?"

Startled, it took her a moment to place his face. "Oh," she said. "I didn't recognize you without your skates."

He had a nice laugh and took her hand warmly. "That's great. Yeah, I'm Tony Harrel. I wanted to meet the girl that Maggie says is her best friend." Then he paused. "Okay if we dance?"

Ellen told him as he took her hand, "We've been friends forever. She's the greatest."

"Yeah," he said with relish and turned to look to their left. It was pure luck that Ellen didn't simply collapse in his arms. Maggie, her dark eyes shining, was dancing with Luke and they were both laughing just like old times.

Tony Harrel was openly watching Ellen's face and smiling. "I've never seen Mag happier than she was when Luke called and invited us. He's as great a guy as Adrienne is a girl. And that says a lot!"

When Maggie and Luke approached at the end of the dance, Luke handed Maggie to Harrel and took Ellen's hand.

"Let's not dance," she told him solemnly. "Let's just go over by the lake and watch for the flying pigs."

He frowned a moment before he remembered. "Get off it, Marlowe," he said, grinning. "You're supposed to thank me."

She pulled away. "For the party? I do, of course."

"More," Luke said. "More gratitude, more appreciation."

"*What* are you talking about?" she asked.

He took her hand and walked her over to the side of the lake. "Adrienne and I made a deal. I would agree to her inviting her friend Harrel and his date if she promised *not* to invite Michael Tyler."

"Luke Ingram," she cried. "I don't believe you! I can't thank you enough. But, Luke, you had to tell her about me."

He shook his head. "She'd already guessed. But she's a closed mouth."

She grinned at him. "Luke, I could kiss your face. That's fabulous."

He shook his head modestly. "Sorry, lady, no kisses. This dude is taken." He paused and looked seriously at her. "Anyway Ellen, I saw your face when you realized that Michael Tyler could be here tonight. It was the least I could do and Adrienne didn't care anyway. Matter-of-fact, I figured I owed Harrel one. If he hadn't whisked Maggie off, I'd never ever have gotten to know Linda like I do. Isn't she fabulous? And beautiful, too."

Ollie was right about Linda having an early curfew. They drove her home and then took Luke back to the party, listening to him babble on about Linda the whole way. "Care if we check out early, too?"

Ollie asked Luke. "This evening has been the greatest."

As Luke walked away, Ellen called out of the window. "And I just loved the flying pigs, Luke." He made a face at her and waved.

"What's the flying pig routine?" Ollie asked over colas and potato skins at Bennigan's. He smiled as he listened to her explain the safe half of the story.

Then she looked up at him. "I hate having enemies," she told him. "I wish I had the nerve to make peace with Hank the way Maggie and Luke have."

"Why are you afraid of him?" he asked, taking her hand.

She sighed. "He gets crazy when he's jealous."

"Okay, Ellen," Ollie said, holding her hand in both of his. "I really like you. You know that. But I'm off in June and you're left. Answer me straight-out. Has Ober ever roughed you up?"

She hesitated. "Well, not really."

"Even a little? Now be square with me."

When she nodded, he lifted her chin with his finger. "Listen to me, Ellen. Forget making friends. Hank probably doesn't mean to be like that, but he can't help it. Stay away from any guy who even once lays a finger on you. Hear me?"

She nodded. "Ollie, I'm not stupid! I know how to look after myself."

He picked up the check as she reached for her coat. As she slid it on, she looked up at him. "I decided about the senior prom."

His eyes turned watchful. "So?"

"So I'm looking forward to going to it with you, okay?"

He hugged her tight. "I felt a great night coming on," he reminded her.

That second half of the last semester flew by. Scott called her from Boston after the marathon on Patriot's Day. He had bested his own personal time and was getting ready for the Chicago race in the fall. She was, and his call only made the sweet spring morning runs more important to her.

She and Ollie dated a lot after Luke's party. When the last play of the season was over, she rarely saw Hank except in the halls. It would have been a perfect spring if the days and weeks weren't taking Michael away as well as Ollie.

The yearbooks came out on the first of June. She was glad she had chosen the book rather than a videotape, which the school had offered for the first time. How could you get anybody's signature on a videotape? And anyway, she liked looking at the pictures and remembering.

She was in the library waiting for Ollie to finish some senior stuff when she realized someone was standing across the table looking down at her. For an awful moment she was afraid it would be Michael. It was too close to the end of school for her to have the strength to face him.

She looked up, totally startled to see a strange boy blushing down at her. "Ellen Marlowe?" he asked.

She nodded and smiled. Sure, she had seen his face around school but she didn't have any idea of who he was. He was tall and lanky with that kind of bushy hair that nobody could control. But he had a nice face, tanned and open, with a spatter of light freckles under his eyes and over the bridge of his nose. His mouth was wide and warm.

He scraped into the chair across from her and laid his yearbook on the table. "You don't know me, but we've run a lot of the same races," he said all in a rush. He thrust a broad freckled hand at her. "I'm Alec Zimmer, and I'd really appreciate it if you'd sign my book."

She smiled and took the pen he held out. "Of course," she said. "Alec Zimmer. What races?"

He grinned the way Cricket did. "Oh, boy," he said. "Where do I start? The Brookfield Zoo Run, the Turkey Trot, the Saint Patrick's Day for two years now."

"Me, too," she said. "How about the Jingle Bells Race?"

He nodded and kept reeling off the same races she had run for the past two years. "How come we've never met?" she asked.

He laughed. "What can I say? I'm shy. It's taken me since Tuesday to get up the nerve to hand you my yearbook."

She pulled her yearbook from her book bag. "Here, you sign mine, too. You mentioned a couple of ten-kilometer races. Have you thought about the marathon?"

Before she could answer, he looked up and started to rise. She felt Ollie's hands light on her shoulder and turned, smiling. "Ollie, I'd like you to meet . . ."

She didn't have to finish. "Alec Zimmer," Ollie said, shaking hands with him. "Alec and I went to the same junior high. I understand you're doing distance now instead of field events."

Alec nodded. "Ellen and I were just talking about that."

Ollie glanced at his watch. "Ellen's on a deadline so we have to shove. Can we drop you some place?"

Alec grinned and glanced at Ellen. "Thanks, but most places I get to, I run."

As they walked out together, Ollie turned to him. "You and Ellen ought to do those training runs together. It's bound to be more fun and it's probably safer."

Ellen was silent most of the way home. "I guess I never thought about doing training runs with anyone," she said.

"You did it at camp with that Scott Gilmour, didn't you?"

"That was different. There were about a hundred of us there." She hesitated. "Alec seems like a nice kid."

"He'd love that," Ollie said, laughing. "He's a junior this year but he's just so shy you'd never guess it. He was the hottest track and field man in my junior high and they had to drag him up in assembly to give him trophies. He's gotten a lot taller and a little heavier. What do you guess he weighs, Ellen?"

She stared at him. "How would I know?"

"Oh," he said. "That's right. You don't weigh guys until you draw pictures of them."

"You *are* a nut!" she said.

"I am a wise one," he corrected her. "Alec isn't going to wake up and smell the coffee until he's about twenty-five. But he's a solid guy and would be a good friend to you."

Ellen drew the car to a stop in front of her house and looked over at him. "Do I understand that you're setting me up, so to speak, with this guy friend of yours?"

He shrugged and wriggled his face strangely. "That's the best I can do at an innocent look," he said. "Yeah, I'm trying to set you up, Ellen. With a real straight-arrow guy. He'll be a good friend to you and you already have running in common."

He leaned over and touched his lips lightly to hers. "I am going to miss you, Ellen."

"Stop that," she said, getting a lump in her throat at the thought of missing him.

Relenting, she tossed him a kiss from her fingertip as he slid over under the wheel. He gunned his motor and left.

Since she had beaten Robin home, she started making toast. Robin loved cinnamon toast caramelized under the broiler but was too hungry to wait while Ellen made it. She buttered the toast and sprinkled on the cinnamon and sugar to pop in the oven when Robin came roaring in.

Ollie had called this shy guy, Alec Zimmer, a "straight-arrow." That's what Brad had called Michael Tyler, too. The two boys couldn't possibly be more different, but she knew what Ollie and Brad meant. And it would be fun to have somebody like Alec to train with. Then she remembered that Alec had written in her book. She opened it and grinned at his childish scrawl.

For Ellen Marlowe, he had written. *And her first six-minute mile.* What a nice guy!

Chapter 31

It wasn't fair to say that the prom and graduation sneaked up on Ellen. It was just that she was trying so hard not to let herself remember what the coming of spring really meant. She and Alec trained together through mornings that came steadily earlier and brighter. When the trees along their route bloomed and came into full leaf, she pretended it wasn't happening. If spring really turned into summer, Michael would graduate and be gone forever.

Then the end of May was there, and she wasn't ready.

She didn't like to dump things on her mother the minute she got in the door but that day she had to.

"Hi, love," her mother said that night. "How's my girl?"

"Desperate," Ellen told her. "I have three urgent problems and I need help."

"Three urgent problems!" Her mother laughed. "You sound like Cricket." She put her purse down and waited. "Let's hear."

Ellen counted them on her fingers. "What to wear

to the prom and two graduation gifts — one for Val and one for Ollie."

Her mother glanced at the school calendar on the front of the fridge. "You have cut it a little close on time, you have less than a week until the prom. If I remember rightly from Brad, that dance is all-out formal."

Ellen nodded, "Big hotel, band, flowers, the whole bit."

"What are the other girls wearing?"

Ellen shrugged. "None of my friends are going unless Val is. She hasn't said anything about it but I'm sure somebody's asked her. And you know Val, if she goes, she'll do her own thing. But I can't imagine her doing the bare shoulders, puffy skirt, and bangles bit, any more than I can see me doing it."

"In other words, you have an idea?"

Ellen nodded. "I want to wear that silk dress we bought for the Willoughby Party two years ago."

"Are you sure?" her mother asked, frowning. "Believe me, honey, I'd happily buy a new dress for you."

Ellen shook her head. "I tried it on last night," Ellen told her. "It's still the prettiest dress I've ever seen. It looks like me and I feel right in it. And I have the matching satin shoes. Then when I go to my own prom, we can really blow it."

Her mother grinned. "Well, clever Mom. I solved that problem pretty fast, didn't I? How about the others?"

"Val isn't really a problem," Ellen admitted. "I thought of a gold chain. She's in honor society and thespians. She'll need something to hang the charms on."

"That's wonderful," her mother said. Then she looked thoughtful. "You didn't have three problems at all as I see it. It must just be Ollie you're desperate about."

Ellen nodded. "I really am, and it's spooky. You see, I have the perfect gift for him, but I bought it for somebody else. I've tried and tried but can't think of anything else half as good."

"There you really lost me," her mother admitted. "What is this present you're talking about?"

"You remember ordering the recordings of the Shakespearian plays for me from the Smithsonian?"

"But that was way last fall. How can you still have those?" Ellen nodded. "They're still wrapped in Christmas paper in the back of my closet. I bought them for Hank."

Her mother looked at her thoughtfully. "Oh," she said. "That is hard, isn't it?" Her mother obviously started to say something else, then decided against it. Instead she only smiled. "You do specialize in actors, don't you?"

Ellen made a face at her but nodded. "Ollie would love those same records. He's going on to major in theater arts in college."

"I agree that they're perfect for him." Her mother rose. "Your own feelings are the only problem there," her mother said. "Why you bought them isn't going to lessen the artistry of John Gielgud and Richard Burton."

"I just don't want to feel cheap when Ollie has been such a good friend to me," Ellen said. "I even thought of giving him something else, too."

Her mother looked doubtful. "How much of a something else?"

Ellen was almost embarrassed to tell her. "Remember the fuss Ollie made about that sketch I did of Scott? I have one of him in the Henry VIII costume I designed. I could get a frame for it."

Her mother beamed. "Now that's a really great idea. And you need to concentrate on how much Ollie will enjoy those records."

She picked up her purse to go upstairs and change, then turned in the doorway. "I hadn't thought about it before but you're really losing some important people in this graduating class, aren't you?"

The moment her mother said it, Ellen knew she was sorry.

How many times had she and her mother thought Michael Tyler at the same moment without either of them mentioning the name aloud? It was almost as if his name hung invisibly in the air between them, the same way it stayed in her mind and heart.

Ellen had about five minutes with Val those last days before the prom. And Val did all the talking. She was radiant that her Eric had been accepted at Stanford University, too. "Can you believe it, El len? We survived this year," she grinned and hugged Ellen. "If anything, we love each other even more than we did before we spent this year apart."

When Ollie first asked her, Ellen hadn't really wanted to go to his senior prom with him. She had worked too hard at keeping him at a friendly distance. But in the two months since he asked her, she had gotten to know him so much better.

Was she ever going to stop comparing other guys to Michael? But Ollie was fun in the same teasing way that Michael sometimes was. And she trusted Ollie more than she would ever be able to trust Michael Tyler after the heartbreak he had caused her. Maybe the nicest thing was that he was as sensitive to her feelings and moods as Hank had been without that shadowy fear spoiling it.

She dressed with a bubble of excitement rising in her chest. She and Ollie would dance a lot together because she wouldn't know very many of the other guys well enough for them to ask her. While they might not stay out until dawn the way Brad had, she would come in later than she had ever been allowed before.

Since it couldn't be Michael and would never be Michael that she would go to a prom with, she'd rather be going with Ollie than anyone she could think of in the whole world.

Robin nearly wore out Ellen's wrist corsage of tiny pale yellow tea roses between the time the florist brought it and Ollie picked her up. She begged Ellen to let her pin Ollie's lapel flower on when he came.

"You better let Ellen pin on Ollie's flower," her mother said. "That's the way you are supposed to do it on dates."

Robin sighed and put it back. "Okay, but my turn's coming."

Then Ollie was there, so darkly handsome in his tuxedo that Ellen was almost wordless. Robin was. She only stared at him.

"What's the matter?" Ollie asked her seriously. "Don't you like penguins? Say the word. I'll change into my gorilla suit."

Robin giggled wildly and told him he was holding his feet wrong for a penguin. He was supposed to walk with them sticking straight out at the sides. Ellen could still hear her mother's laughter when Ollie walked out of the door with her, slapping his feet down penguin style.

Once out on the walk he stopped and put his arms around her. When she glanced up, she was startled at his serious expression.

"I'm sorry, Ellen," he said, his voice deep and vibrant with emotion. "I can't take you to this prom." His face had changed so swiftly from laughter to that somber Heathcliff look that she felt her heart tumble.

"Ollie," she cried, lifting her hands to his shoulders. "What's happened? What's wrong?"

Then she saw his eyes dancing as he grabbed her

close. "It's not what has happened, it's what will happen when I walk you in looking like that. Men have killed for women like you. I'm far too young and talented to die in a penguin suit."

She melted with relief and laughter, then pulled free to walk away with her head high. "It will be a loss to the world, no doubt," she said in the loftiest tone she could. "But I do ask that you take care not to bleed on my dress when it happens."

He caught her, laughing. "Ellen, you really should act."

"I'll settle for an audience of one," she told him.

Ellen wasn't really prepared for the beauty of the ballroom, the air scented with massed flowers and the music swelling like a promise even before they got through the doorway.

They had danced and drunk punch and talked with Ollie's friends and done it all over again before Ellen saw Michael across the room. He was standing near the band with his arm loosely around Val Frederick's waist. His expression was serious and he seemed to be listening intently to what Val was saying. Before Ellen could look away, Michael glanced up and their eyes met.

She caught her breath hard. He had looked at her and seen her without acknowledging that he even knew her. She felt his look like a blow as he turned back to Val, took her in his arms, and moved onto the dance floor.

Suddenly the room was cold and she shivered in

the sheer silk dress. "Hey," Ollie said, looking down. "What's wrong?"

"Nothing," she whispered. "Just a chill."

"I can fix that," he said, tightening his arms around her. "Want my coat?"

When she laughed softly, he protested. "Listen," he said, "I'd be happy to give it to you. How else can these people appreciate my truly fancy cummerbund? On second thought, I'll give you the shirt off my back, too, so they can see my manly chest. But I do draw the line at sharing my penguin feet."

She clung to him, laughing in spite of herself, but her head whirled with questions. She tried to remember the last time she and Michael had talked. What had she said? What had she done to turn him against her? Had he noticed her avoiding him and not understood? Of course, he hadn't understood. How could he, when she didn't understand her own crazy mixed-up feelings toward him. "There's more than one way to warm an ice maiden," Ollie said. "We could dance double-time to this number." As he spoke, he caught her and began to whirl her around and around the outside of the dancing crowd. She clung to him, laughing at first, then hopelessly dizzy.

"Help!" she finally cried. "Enough! Enough!"

A bunch of the dancers had stopped to watch them and clap at Ollie's private show. He stopped, braced Ellen with one arm and bowed from the waist smiling.

"Ham," she whispered, clinging to him as the room spun.

"I may copyright that strategy," he said, holding her close. "This feels wonderful. Every guy in the room is jealous."

Somehow Ellen got through the rest of the evening without meeting either Michael's eyes or Val's.

At her door, Ollie, his face half in shadow from the dim porch light, kissed her gently a long time. "Every guy wants a prom night like that one, Ellen," he said. "One week of exams and I'm over and out, but this should see me throught it."

"I'm going to miss you a whole lot more than you can possibly know," she whispered against his chest.

"I hope so," he said, holding her. "I really hope so."

Ellen made it through the next two weeks only by sheer force of will. The sense of shock that had come when Michael turned away from her never really left. She was even grateful that the mixed-up schedule of the two exam weeks that followed prevented her from seeing anyone at all but Ollie.

He was struck dumb by her graduation gifts. "How could you know?" he asked her over and over, his eyes suspiciously shiny. She would have died inside except that it was her sketch that he kept looking at when he said it.

Val told her good-bye, openly tearful. "My first

friend and my lasting one," she said in a broken kind of way. Then she hesitated. "I know you were surprised to see Michael and me together at the prom. We decided it made sense because both of us knew where the other one stood."

She didn't see Michael even once after the night of the prom.

Ellen could remember clear back to when summers had been long and lazy and idle. She was glad this summer promised to be as hectic as the last one had been. That way she would have less time to mourn. And it really felt as if something had died in her. Hope. Maybe that was what was over for good.

But it was fun to go back to camp as an "old-timer." She and Christy started out spending all their free time together. But this year it was Christy who charmed one of the guys into the kind of summer friendship Ellen had with Scott the year before.

Another good-bye, another part of her life over.

Spending that month in Wyoming with Cricket was the best idea anyone ever had. It was a world so different from the one she had left, that Chicago seemed the strange place.

Ellen tried, without success, to make Wyoming and Cricket's father's ranch come alive in her letters home. She knew she failed because you couldn't put those broad skies and endless sunsets down onto paper. "You'll have to wait to see my sketches," she told her mother. "But none of them does Zach or the horses justice."

She didn't even try to explain the new Cricket she saw out there with her dad and Lynn and the baby. This was a softer, less angry Cricket whose cowgirl clothes failed to disguise her developing figure and the new gentleness in her smile.

That last day Ellen sat on the corral fence with Cricket watching Lynn train a young foal to the halter.

"You haven't mentioned your old flame even once," Cricket reminded Ellen. "Does that mean what I hope it does?"

Ellen grinned at her. "It means that Michael's gone and I probably won't ever even see him again."

Cricket chewed on her strand of hay and nodded. "Boy, I hope I never get hit by that lightning," she said.

Ellen looked at that cute tanned face and agile slim body and grinned. "That is what I call a fat chance," she said, then jumped off the fence before Cricket could shove her off.

Chapter 32

Ellen came home the week of her sixteenth birthday to discover her family had made some new plans.

"You'd think this was your birthday instead of mine," Ellen teased Robin. "Do you know something I don't know?"

"Yes," Robin agreed.

"I hope you don't mind this, Ellen," her mother said. "Instead of a horse for her birthday, we gave Robin a gift certificate to the riding stables for the next six months. That is, if you'll haul her around after you get your driver's license." her mother added.

Ellen grinned at Robin. "Come on," she said. "Let's see how long you can hold your breath until I agree."

Then, as Robin's face turned scarlet, Ellen hugged her. "Of course I'll haul you back and forth to the horses. Just don't make me ride with you. And cross your fingers that I pass the driving test."

* * *

Brad took a day off from work to go with Ellen to get her license. "Sixteen," he said, shaking his head. "I can remember taking off the training wheels on your bicycle."

She grinned at him, a little nervous in spite of herself.

When they got to the motor vehicle bureau, she could barely stammer good afternoon to the unsmiling examiner who motioned her to get behind the wheel and settled himself in the seat beside her. It'll be *okay*, she reassured herself, fastening the seat belt and, at the examiner's command, turning on the ignition switch. Out of the window she saw Brad signal with a reassuring thumbs-up.

She remembered to signal before every turn, bit her tongue but made a perfect U-turn, and didn't go back and forth too often when finally she parked at the curb in front of the motor vehicle bureau. She was weak with relief when the straight-faced man beside her broke into a broad grin and congratulated her on her successful driving test.

"Your license will be in the mail in a week," he said. He got out of the car, tipped his baseball cap at her, and vanished. Ten days later, Ellen drove Robin to the stables as a full-fledged, fully licensed driver.

During the first few days of school in her junior year, Ellen found herself startled by three separate things.

Number one was the freshman class. They seemed so young to her.

The second surprise was that early in the week she had been called into the assistant principal's office. When he asked Ellen to be one of the orientation monitors for incoming transfer freshmen, she looked so astonished he laughed out loud.

"What's the matter, Ellen? Not used to being an upperclassman yet?" he said.

"I guess not," she admitted. "I thought monitors were always seniors, and honor society."

"The seniors we ask to monitor do have to be honor society," he said. "But juniors, like you, are handpicked." He frowned. "I seem to remember that you had late orientation when you came here. Do you remember who your monitor was?"

Ellen had felt a shock run all the way through her. It turned into the familiar tightening in her stomach as she almost laughed. Did she remember? "Michael Tyler," she said.

The assistant principal nodded. "There you are. He was another handpicked junior."

Alec had been impressed when Ellen told him about being tapped for orientation. As soon as she told him, he said, "You're going to have to be careful you don't get a swelled head, Ellen," he said earnestly. "Monitors are idols. For a whole year the guy who was my monitor was the only upperclassman who treated me like a human. I worshiped the guy."

With that, Alec went into his classroom, leaving Ellen staring after him. Why did he have to say that? He had completely surprised her. So Alec had been bowled over by his orientation monitor almost the same way she had been bowled over by Michael.

The rest of the week Ellen watched the freshmen with different eyes. Had she seemed that young and unfinished to Michael? Had she appeared wide-eyed with fear when she looked at him, the way some of the freshmen girls did when they looked at her? Had she seemed worshipful? Well, one thing for sure. She wasn't going to pull rank on her orientation freshman the way Michael had on her. She wasn't going to make anybody feel like a second-class citizen straight out of the cradle. Ellen shivered for a second, she wasn't sure why, and took out her instruction sheet to reread it. Her transfer freshman's name was Sarabeth.

In the assembly room, second period Friday, when the principal called out Sarabeth Laramie, Ellen saw a small black-haired girl in a long blue bulky sweater and black tights stand up and remain very still, too nervous even to look around for the upper-class monitor who would claim her. Ninety pounds, no more, Ellen thought. She felt an unexpected surge of compassion for the girl and quickly went over to introduce herself.

"Let's go out into the hall and get acquainted before we make the grand tour," she said with a smile. "There's nothing to be scared of, but I bet you've already discovered that this is a bigger school than our junior high."

"I didn't go to junior high here," Sarabeth said softly. "We just moved from Nashville, Tennessee."

"Oh, that's super heavy," Ellen said. "You have to get used to a whole new hometown as well as a new high school, don't you? But, listen, I'll let you in on a secret, Sarabeth. All the other freshmen feel the same way you do, even if they've lived here all their lives."

Her reward was a tremulous smile.

"We'll just take it slow and easy, top to bottom, how about that?" Ellen said, unfolding the school map.

"That'll be fine," Sarabeth said, sounding doubtful.

Ellen conducted the standard tour, following the guidelines on the instruction sheet but, remembering how Michael had irritated her by talking down to Brad's "little sister," tried to make it nonfrightening. She had a little anecdote, a little word of advice, a little quip to share at almost every room — the same classrooms and art rooms and science rooms and sports areas that Michael had shown her so long ago. They were rooms that now were as comfortable and familiar to her as rooms at home. At almost every area, people called greetings to her, as they had to Michael when he was showing her around. She remembered how awed she had been by his obvious popularity in this grown-up place, her new high school. Through it all Sarabeth, alternating between looking awed, admiring, and excited, juggled books and notebooks from one hip to another and marked her map with red and blue pencils.

"I need to remember where the music room is particularly because I sing," Sarabeth said hesitantly when they were walking down a staircase. "I mean, I hope there's a glee club or a music club or something."

"There certainly is. You go to the school office to find out when and where they hold auditions. They put the notices up on the bulletin board. It's just on the right as you go in."

"Thanks. I'm a second soprano," Sarabeth said.

"You're lucky," Ellen said, smiling. "I'm a low monotone."

By the time they got back to the main hall, Sarabeth seemed to have gathered strength and assurance.

"Ellen, I have a problem I'd like to ask you about if you have an extra minute," she said.

"Sure," Ellen said.

"Please, could you tell me how to work my combination lock? I just haven't been able to figure it out, even with the instructions."

"Poor you," Ellen said. "It's really sort of easy but I know what you mean. I had a hard time, too, at first."

It only took a minute to show Sarabeth how to

set and use the combination. "But what have you been doing about leaving things in your locker if it was unlocked?" she asked.

"I've just been carrying everything home every night and bringing it all back in the morning."

Ellen didn't laugh, and she didn't give the girl a hug, either, but her impulse was to do both. How naive Sarabeth seemed. The colored pencils, the earnest writing down of every word that dropped from Ellen's lips, the wide-eyed amazement. Had she, Ellen, ever been that young? Is that how Michael had seen her?

And that was the third thing that startled Ellen at the beginning of school. When she and Sarabeth parted, the freshman so clearly impressed by her, Ellen told herself that she finally understood how she felt about Michael: that powerful feeling she had had since the moment she met him was no more than the typical hero worship all underclassmen feel for upperclassmen. It was not a real crush at all. That's what she told herself.

In early October, as he'd promised, Scott arrived to run the Chicago Marathon. He was as funny and bright as he had been the summer they met, but much taller and stronger-looking than Ellen remembered, and older than he appeared in her sketch.

Her exhilaration at training for the marathon increased with Scott's arrival. Alec and he took to each other like long-lost brothers. When Scott came to her home on Saturday, the three of them drove Robin out to the stables and then took off for an easy, short-distance practice as though they'd been running together for years. When they got back to the stables, Alec went on to do a few more miles and Scott and Ellen toweled off and got into their sweats. They sat up on the railing of the ring where Robin was happily trotting around and around on a big brown horse. Scott put his arm around Ellen and gave her a quick hug. She felt comfort in the touch of his lean runner's body but he heard the little sigh that escaped her lips.

"You still living in wish land with that Big Man on Campus?" he asked.

"I'm trying not to," she admitted.

"There's definitely something wrong with that guy — but tell me."

"Oh, there isn't anything to tell, Scott." Ellen said. "He's away at college this year but when he comes home, if he sees me at all, he still only sees me as my brother's little sister. I wish I could be casual friends with him, but I can't manage that. I feel . . . I just feel too strongly. I miss him so much."

"I'm really sorry, Ellen, and I'm going to write you the funniest, cheeriest letters you ever got until you start smiling again."

Ellen squeezed his arm.

"I smile, Scott. I really do. It's just that . . . oh, well, I've always got the marathon to think about and enjoy."

Scott sat very still on the railing. Then he turned

and put his hand under her chin. "No, Ellen."

"What do you mean, no?"

"I watched you. You're really running great. Very impressive." He took a moment to wrap his towel tighter around his neck. "You're probably going to knock out records right and left when you get to run a marathon. But it can't be this one."

"Of course it can. Is that a joke, Scott, or is that a joke?"

Of course she was going to do the marathon. She found herself remembering the Saint Patrick's Day race the year before, that clear, sunny day, that perfect day when she had beat her own time; when she had been streaming sweat but every muscle felt in top form; when she had exulted in her runner's strength. She couldn't give up trying for the same kind of runners' high in the marathon.

"You're too young, Ellen. Your body is just not ready for marathon running."

"But I've been training so well. I hate to start things I don't finish, Scott."

"Sure you do, but that's not the point. It's a question of age," Scott said. "Nobody under eighteen, male or female, is even *allowed* to enter the New York Marathon. The same ought to be true in Chicago. Your body's just not strong enough yet."

"You're not so much older," Ellen said indignantly.

"I'm a couple of months away from eighteen, Ellen. So's Alec, and we're on the young side, too. But not as young as you are."

"I've trained hard and well," Ellen insisted. "I'm really strong. I know I could do the distance."

"Be sensible, Ellen, You've got plenty of time. Stay with five- and ten-kilometer races for a couple of years more and we'll run the Chicago Marathon together for years to come. That's a promise."

In the end, Ellen grudgingly and sadly agreed.

On the day of the marathon, she was on the sidelines, a volunteer for the Chicago Area Running Association, handing out water at the twenty-mile point and then hurrying to be at the finish line to see marathon medals presented to Scott and Alec. But she couldn't help the despair that washed over her. She was too young for everything she wanted in life. She wanted to be among those exhausted runners finishing the race. She wanted to be with Michael.

"I knew you a long time ago, from being in the frame upstairs," Robin announced to Scott as soon as he arrived at Ellen's house for a farewell dinner with Ellen's family and Alec before he left for the New York Marathon.

"Could you please play that back?" Scott asked with a puzzled smile.

Robin giggled, glancing over to Ellen. "It's Ellen's secret," she said.

"It's not a secret, Scott. Robin's a big tease," Ellen said. "Remember I did some sketches of you at camp? I finished one of them and framed it, that's all."

"No kidding. I'm flattered. Is it around somewhere? Can I see it?"

"It's in Ellen's room. I'll show you," Robin said, jumping up and holding out her hand.

They trooped upstairs, Robin leading Scott, Ellen following and trying to remember if there was much lying around that she should have hung up or put away. But it didn't matter. Scott didn't see anything but the drawing. He actually gasped when he saw it.

"Ellen! This is great!" he said. "Not because it's me," he hurried to add. "It's just a great drawing. You're good at *everything* you do."

Ellen heard an echo. Michael had said something like that at Luke's skating party last year. But it wasn't true. Not everything, Ellen thought. I can't make Michael think of me as anyone but Brad's little sister, if he thinks of me at all. Out of sight, out of mind. She shook her head vigorously, as much to shake away old yearnings as to answer Scott.

"It was just fun to do," she said.

"My mom would kill for that picture," Scott said. "I'm a long way from home all the time now and she's not adjusting to that too well."

Everybody misses somebody, Ellen thought suddenly and surprisingly. She was with her special friend Scott of Scottsdale, and he was as terrific as she remembered, yet she was missing Michael, finding that everything reminded her of Michael. If she was still doing a freshman-idolizing number, when would she grow up?

Chapter 33

October isn't a good month, Ellen definitely decided one early morning as she ended a long practice run. She felt the chill in the air and when she saw the trees getting bare, the last leaves made her feel gloomy.

The autumn leaves underfoot were a strong hint of the coming of winter, Ellen's favorite season. Winter meant sparkling snow, but she wouldn't be sharing any of it with Michael this year.

As always, running gave Ellen a lift but she still had to force herself to stop thinking about Michael.

"I will not be gloomy, I will *not* be gloomy," Ellen repeated to herself as she met Cricket in the hallway and they walked to their English class.

An altogether new Cricket had come back from Wyoming. Ellen had noticed a softer Cricket emerging from her tomboy friend during her month's visit at the ranch. Then, coming home in the plane, Cricket had sat next to a boy from Chicago named

Jason and lightning had struck. Now Cricket was intensely in love.

"I think he's my destiny," Cricket had confided earnestly to Ellen. "He's so cute. He has such crinkly eyes, and his ears stick out a little but I like that, and — promise not to laugh — his hair's exactly the same color as that little foal I was working with at the ranch when you were there. Isn't that extraordinary?"

That Cricket could be so intense — and so silly at the same time — occasionally made all her friends gasp with disbelief. It also sometimes made them collapse with the giggles.

"I think that's about the most terrific coincidence I've ever heard of," Ellen had said seriously. "I just can't *wait* to see the top of that boy's head."

Cricket had suddenly relaxed and grinned.

"You're going to have to help me, Ellen," she said now as they went into the classroom. "Jason's coming here on Saturday and his birthday's the following Wednesday. Do you think I should give him his present when I see him? Or do you think it would be better if I sent it to him in Chicago, so he got it on the actual day?"

Before Ellen could answer, Cricket went on desperately. "Do you know what I'm going to get him?" she asked earnestly.

"No, what?" Ellen answered.

"I don't *know*!" Cricket wailed.

"Girls! Class has begun!" their teacher reminded them.

The cafeteria was, as always, rocking with noise. Maggie had gotten there before Ellen and Cricket and held places for them at a table where the decibel level was somewhere below crash-level.

"Be honest, can either of you tell there's a patch on my cheek that I haven't washed?" Cricket asked after they had filled their trays and made the appropriate ugh noises. Both girls leaned over to look at Cricket.

"What are you talking about?" Ellen asked.

"Right there," Cricket said, pointing to but not touching a spot on her face. "It's the place Jason kissed me. Right here. I cover it with a waterproof Band-Aid when I shower."

Ellen and Maggie gazed at each other.

"I can't help myself," Cricket confessed awkwardly.

Just as they were finishing the last cookie, Lewis Albany, a short, pleasant boy with brown eyes and very blond hair, stopped by. Ellen knew him from grade school.

"Hey, Ellen, I was looking for you. Want to come with me this afternoon to see the new science show I was telling you about the other day? I can offer pizza and other good foods, some excellent scientific talk, and riding around in my brother's jazzy car that he said he'd lend me. All this, and the show, if you will."

"Ah, Lewis, thanks but I really can't. I drive my sister Robin to the stables this afternoon. Way out in the country."

"You're all invited," Lewis said, looking over at Maggie and Cricket. Maggie just smiled and shook her head while Cricket looked as though she were thinking hard about something else.

"Ellen isn't awfully interested in science. I guess it's catching," Lewis said to them ruefully and waved good-bye.

Cricket hurriedly gathered up her things. "Wait a minute, Lewis. I want to ask you a question about birthday presents for a boy who . . ." She rushed out after him.

After Cricket and Lewis disappeared, Maggie and Ellen walked out of the cafeteria.

"Lewis is nice," Maggie said.

Ellen shrugged. "Sure he is. Always has been. But need I tell you I'm not crazy about his favorite hangout, the chem lab?"

Maggie nodded, smiling. Ellen's antichemistry feelings were well-known to her friends.

"Lewis is going to be a professional chemist. That's what he's going to major in at college. Chemistry. He actually has fingers that are stained yellow from working in the smelly old chem lab. Lewis lives and breathes chemistry."

Maggie didn't answer Ellen's words. Instead, she answered what Ellen really was saying.

"You're still thinking about Michael Tyler," she

said. It was a statement, not a question.

"Dumb, isn't it," Ellen said.

As she looked at her friend, Ellen experienced a curious new feeling. Maggie had changed even more than Cricket since last year, since skating and then falling in love with Tony Harrel. Gone was Ellen's old boy-crazy chum of the purple hair and gold tights, the knife and fork earrings, the voice booming across a room. Walking up the staircase, she realized — something deeper than just seeing — that Maggie's slim athlete's body was sheathed in black tights and boots topped by a simple loose black-and-white striped top; that Maggie's heart-shaped face and dark eyes were enhanced by a series of very small gold hoop earrings; and that Maggie's different look was matched by a calm, sympathetic maturity in her face and her voice.

"I try not to think about him," Ellen said. Then, in the silence that followed, she smiled weakly.

"Enough, already, Ellen. He's not even in town. It's time you look at some of the great guys around here."

"You're right."

"There are plenty of guys. And we both know that all you've ever had to do is blink and they come around."

"Maggie, there's nothing you can say that I haven't told myself maybe a million times." She smiled. "Well, maybe I use different words," she said. "But nothing seems to help. It's a good thing I really love running."

"I know what you're talking about, Ellen, and I'm sorry."

They walked the rest of the way up the stairs in a congenial silence that finally Maggie broke.

"I never dreamed I'd be so lucky," she said softly but with her Maggie vitality. "I don't have any of my old miseries anymore. I mean, it's so different with Tony and me. It was terrible and wonderful when it began, but now? I can't even describe how I feel now. Wait. Not true. I *can* describe how I feel. I'm *comfortable* about Tony. Not just seeing him, and working with him the way we do — that's terrific in every direction." Her voice held so much happiness, Ellen could almost catch it in her hand. "But it's more than that. We talk about everything . . ."

Ellen suddenly thought of how freely she and Michael talked, even when it was just for the length of a dance at a party or for an hour together looking at winter snow.

"I'm not even sure my day could start without Tony's morning-hello telephone call." Maggie laughed. "It's a good thing he doesn't live in this town. I wouldn't have any grades at all if we went to the same school."

"Maggie and Tony are, I mean, *serious*," Ellen told her mother that night — while kneading bread dough.

Ellen had started to make homemade bread once in a while. After some disasters that tasted like glue, and others that turned into crumbs at the first slice, some of it turned out all right. It wasn't that she stopped other activities. She ran. She drove Robin to the stable. She was involved in the drama group as it began to rev up for the junior play and she was always on hand when Luke needed cheering for his chess tournaments. She was there when everybody got together at somebody's house with music but somehow, she recently had taken to the big kitchen at home, baking bread.

"You ought to see her, Mom. Maggie used to have the most roaming eyes in school and these days, well, she's completely faithful to Tony Harrel and their work together. They're hoping to qualify for the Olympics, you know. They go to the rink to practice even earlier than I go out to run. Maggie's simply a new person. Absolutely changed. It's as though . . ."

Why was her mother looking at her sadly?

Maggie was busy with skating, but one free afternoon, after school, she agreed to team up with Ellen to help Cricket pick out wool to knit Jason a sweater.

"Except Cricket, you don't know how to knit," Maggie said with a smile before they set out on the expedition.

"I can always learn," Cricket said, examining her strong horsewoman's hands apprehensively. "Can't I?"

"Probably not in time for Christmas," Maggie teased.

"I know."

Cricket sounded woebegone but Ellen didn't hear it. All she heard was the word *Christmas*. And that meant Michael . . . and misery.

"I have a great idea," she exclaimed. "Why don't we skip the knitting project — just for now, Cricket — and hop into my mom's car and drive to Smithville for a pizza supper at Busky's. Maybe even a movie. I'll get you back in plenty of time for homework."

"Oh, that's a terrific idea, Ellen, but I couldn't," Maggie said.

"But you told me you weren't skating today. You said you had a free day."

"I do, but I want to be home for Tony's call."

"And I want to get wool for Jason's sweater, the sooner the better," Cricket said.

Ellen felt outside. For almost the first time since she had started noticing boys as boys, she was the one among her close friends who was not involved with a boyfriend she liked who liked her.

"A dumb idea," she said. "Who needs pizza? Let's get to that knit shop. What color do you think, Maggie? Cricket, name a color!"

Chapter 34

"My life just doesn't have Michael in it," Ellen said to Luke as they sat together in a booth at Bennigan's, eating from an enormous platter of french fries swamped in ketchup. As a runner, Ellen always ate sensibly — except sometimes, like this time. Luke ate two, three or four potatoes to her every one; nothing could disturb his mammoth capacity for food.

"It's clear and simple," Ellen went on. She tried to smile at her misery, but did not succeed very well. The french fries didn't really help.

"Nobody measures up," she said. "I've got terrific friends who are boys — you first of all, of course, Luke, and Alec's the greatest, my best running friend next to Scott from Scottsdale. And you know I date Lewis Albany once in a while." She paused. "Lewis is something special. He's on a different planet." Again there was a pause. "Oh, Luke," she said. "None of them is ever Michael."

Luke gave her a long look. "Maybe nobody ever will be," he said.

"Don't even think that!" Ellen exclaimed. The idea was too awful. "You're saying it might be like this for the rest of my life!"

Luke shrugged but kindness and concern were on his face as he answered. "I think you ought to try to put Michael out of your mind for good, Ellen. Figure him for your big high school crush and move on. You can do it." Then, seeing Ellen's face grow even more unhappy, he leaned forward. "Come on, hey, where's Ellen?!" he said, in his old-friend way. "Is this the girl who's probably the best junior-class runner our high school's ever seen? The volunteer the Chicago Area Running Association asked to be in charge of all volunteers at the next senior runners race? The good-guy sister who drives Robin back and forth from the stables every week? Where's Ellen, the queen of the drama group?"

Ellen straightened her back slightly.

"Well," she said slowly. "I *am* thinking about trying out for the junior play. For an acting part."

"There's Ellen. I knew she was still in town," Luke said cheerfully and offered her a french fry.

Tryouts for the junior play took place late in the month. Ellen decided to take the big plunge and if, as Luke said, she was queen of the drama group, she would read for the queen part, the lead. When she came into the room they called the Green Room — because, as Hank once had said, the walls are painted yellow, *yuck!* — all the actors trying out were sitting around the big round table. Ellen quickly found a seat, smiling but suddenly feeling shy. As Mr. Quigley handed out the scripts, she wondered at herself. She was a proven artist who had designed sets and costumes for school plays. But what did she think she was doing, coming in like an actress and aiming for the most important part in the play. When she heard other girls reading, she was sure she had made a mistake; should never have entered the Green Room; should stick to what she knew best; should just pick up her books and leave quietly. She was so busy worrying that she didn't hear Mr. Quigley call on her — twice.

"Act two, scene one, top of page twenty-three. Will you please read Oswald, Tommy, and Ellen, you read Cora. Ellen? Ellen?"

"Oh, Mr. Quigley, I'm so sorry. What part?" she said.

"Cora, Ellen. Top of page twenty-three."

"Oh, yes, sure. I'm sorry." Ellen hurriedly riffled through the script, found the right page, took a deep breath, and dove in.

A week later, when she went to the Green Room to check the cast list Mr. Quigley just had tacked up on the bulletin board, she saw her name opposite the name *Cora*. She screeched and jumped up and down. She had got the lead. Reading down, she saw that Tommy Evans was cast as the male lead, which delighted her. They always had a great time together. Even Hank's name listed for a smaller part didn't bother her — too much. She never forgot Ollie's advice about Hank.

When rehearsals began, Ellen found herself thinking of something Val had told her about acting a long time ago: People become their roles on stage, Val had said. Ellen discovered how right that was during one early rehearsal, when something peculiar and interesting happened to her. She and Tommy were doing a scene together. Having already learned her lines, she felt completely in the part. She gazed at Tommy, made a gesture, spoke her line, and waited for his answer.

Before he spoke, Tommy was supposed to put down a suitcase and cross in front of the sofa, which, in rehearsal, was three folding chairs side by side. But he forgot he would be carrying a suitcase and pantomimed slipping a backpack off his shoulders before he remembered. After he said, "Whoops" and pantomimed putting down a real suitcase, he moved awkwardly toward the "sofa," tripped over the first of the three chairs, knocked down the chair next to it, and abruptly flopped into the last chair to keep it upright. Then he simply burst out laughing. So did everybody else. Except Ellen. Through all the laughter and wisecracks, Ellen found herself still Cora, so much *in* the character she was playing that she simply stood and waited until the laughter quieted down and Tommy was ready to do the scene again. Then she picked up as though there had never been an interruption.

It was a spooky feeling, she realized afterward, but sort of wonderful. She had really been acting, really been in another person's skin for those few moments. If only she could be another person forever. Cora had never even heard of Michael Tyler.

As the play date came nearer, Ellen found herself increasingly nervous. Acting involved her in the same camaraderie that drama club work always had, but this time the material she was working with was not inanimate plywood or canvas or paints or hammers and nails. The material was her own body.

When Brad arrived home to see the play, she was surprised and happy. "Just to see the play?" she asked him when he arrived.

"Just to see you," he answered, leaving her delighted and amazed.

Brad was almost ridiculously proud of her, and when the performance was over and the cast was taking curtain calls, Ellen saw him standing and applauding with a triumphant smile on his face. He was glancing around to make sure everyone else appreciated her, too. Ellen didn't care that she didn't have a date for the cast pizza party. Her brother happily escorted her into Donovan's, where the party took place.

As always, she hated to see him go back to college.

"Thanks for being the world's greatest older

brother," she said to him when she hugged him good-bye.

"Couldn't do it if you weren't the world's greatest kid sister," he said.

Having her drivers' license gave her wonderful new freedom.

She and Cricket, who was so true to Jason in Chicago that she never looked in the direction of another boy, sometimes rode out to the mall together after school, to shop around and stay to have supper at the Chinese restaurant. Sometimes, when a longing for what never would be — for Michael beside her, to laugh with, she felt overwhelmed. She would drive off alone, often to the village beyond the next village, far away, then stop and get out and run a little. When she drove back, she always felt almost restored, almost content.

The car, with Ellen at the wheel, served other, more practical purposes, too. Ellen regularly drove Robin out to the stables for riding lessons. Robin, at twelve, was still wild for horses and her Wednesday afternoons and Saturday mornings at the stable were the twin highlights of her week.

Ellen enjoyed them, too, and so did Cricket who often came along. Cricket's love for Jason did not diminish her love of horses. Even her mother's promise of a car of her own if she would only give up what her mother called her crazy obsession about horses couldn't change her. She would not even take driver's training. On the way to the stables, she and Robin carried on horse conversations Ellen could barely make sense of.

When they arrived, Ellen would run while Cricket hung around the ring the whole time to watch Robin take her class. Robin was learning to jump. She hoped desperately to qualify for the beginner's jumping events in the stable's annual Thanksgiving weekend students' horse show.

At the end of November, with her mother so occupied with work and her father, as always, coming home from one of his business trips just in time for the holiday, Ellen's family and Maggie's family decided to team up for Thanksgiving dinner. Ellen was in charge of cornbread stuffing — her specialty, for which she used crumbs she made from a spicy herb bread she had baked. She was so busy getting things organized, and fussing with Robin over the Saturday horse show, that she almost didn't have time to remember that as soon as Thanksgiving was over Christmas came. And Michael, like Brad, would be home for Christmas vacation.

She wouldn't think about it, she wouldn't think about him, she told herself, but she could hardly put her hands over her ears when she and her mother went to the mall on Wednesday before Thanksgiving Thursday to pick up last minute things. Every loudspeaker in the mall was blaring out Christmas music.

"Dumb malls," she said to her mother in exasperation. "It's still Thanksgiving."

"That reminds me," her mother said, distracted. "Didn't Robin say she needed something for the horse show?"

"Yes," Ellen said. "Yes, she said she needed new riding gloves."

"Where's that riding supply shop?"

"Over this way, Mom."

But no amount of distraction could keep Ellen from hearing the Christmas carols. The sound of them banged against her ears and made her miserable, even after they left the mall and were halfway home. She decided that this Christmas season her survival depended on never being where Michael was and not ever seeing him, not even once.

Cricket asked if she could come along when Ellen drove Robin to the stables an hour early in order to do whatever Robin, who was going to be in two events, had to do to before the students' horse show began. Ellen's parents would be along later to watch their daughter perform. Robin, who looked like a genuine riding star in a hard black velvet hat, gray turtleneck sweater, real riding breeches and boots, bounced up and down like a jack-in-the-box in the back of the car during the whole drive to the riding academy and vanished into the vast barn the instant they arrived. She seemed to come out again immediately.

"I told them you'd help," she said, racing over to the car.

"Help who? What?" Ellen asked.

"It's an emergency. One of the stablehands didn't show up and there are four horses that have to have their manes braided."

"You want *me* to braid a horse's mane?" Ellen exclaimed in astonishment.

"I said you would. It's not hard."

"How do you know?" Ellen demanded.

"Why would it be?"

"Lead on, Robin," Cricket said. "We'll be happy to do it."

Ellen gulped.

Robin raced back into the stable and soon Louis Radom, the owner and riding master, and a stable boy were leading out two horses each, bringing them right up to Ellen and Cricket. Robin followed after with two low ladders.

"I really appreciate this, Ellen," Lou Radom said. He had a no-nonsense quality that Ellen knew meant there was no chance to back off. "Now, stand up there and here's what you do."

Cricket laughed out loud at the expression on Ellen's face as she bravely stood on the ladder with an enormous horse's head inches away from her.

"Don't stare in his eyes," Cricket warned. "And pat him and talk softly to him every once in a while."

"I can't believe I'm doing this," Ellen muttered as she grasped thick clumps of harsh hair, divided them into three sections, and braided them tight over the horse's forehead. "Nice horse, nice horse," she said as gently as she could, trying not to respond to the gigantic eyes staring at her.

"You're doing it just right," Cricket called over.

Ellen knew she had never in her whole life been so close to anything as alive and enormous as that horse's head.

The senior horse show of Louis Radom's Oak Mill Riding Academy was always held in May in the outdoor ring. But the Thanksgiving show for the young student riders took place in the indoor ring, safely sequestered from the sometimes biting November winds. It was, as always, a friendly show, with parents and grandparents and friends of the riders and owners settling on the tiers of benches on one side of the ring. When Ellen's parents arrived, Ellen and Cricket joined them on a bench. Ellen caught a glimpse of Robin with several other girls, already mounted on their horses, watching the opening event from the L that separated the ring area from the stalls.

"Robin looks so small and her horse looks so big," Ellen's mother said with a smile when she looked over at them.

"You don't know *big*," Ellen said, exchanging glances with Cricket.

But she didn't have time to tell her mother or father about the extraordinary thing she had done less than an hour before.

First out were the littlest riders of all, children

six and seven years old who sat on ponies that were led around the ring to the acclaim of the audience. Then Robin was riding out, circling the ring, prodding her horse into a slow canter and taking one jump and another and another perfectly. Ellen was as proud of Robin when her sister received a blue ribbon for first place as Brad had been proud of Ellen in the junior play. But she could hardly believe the rest of her reaction to Robin's wide grin as she trotted back to the L and disappeared. Ellen wanted to share her delight and pride in Robin with the one person in particular she would never be able to. *Oh, Michael, please don't come home this Christmas.*

Suddenly, there was a flurry. A frightened young rider lost control of her horse and galloped straight across the area to where Robin was dismounting and rode right into her. Ellen, her parents, and Cricket rushed to the spot where Robin lay whimpering in the sawdust, one leg twisted awkwardly under her and her eyes wide with shock and pain. Louis Radom immediately called for an ambulance. Time seemed to stand still until it arrived and Ellen watched Robin being gently lifted onto a stretcher and into the ambulance. Her parents, both ashen-faced, climbed in after her.

"I'll tend to things at home, Mom. Don't worry," Ellen called into the ambulance right before the door closed and the ambulance started its trip to the hospital.

I'll have to help take care of Robin all through Christmas, Ellen thought as she and Cricket were driving home. Poor Robin. But because of her accident, Ellen wouldn't have time to be unhappy about Michael. She wouldn't be able to be anywhere he would be when he came home for the holidays. She wouldn't even have time to think about him.

Chapter 35

Ellen held the door for her father to carry Robin inside. She had to fight back tears when she saw the size of the cast on Robin's long, skinny leg. Robin's face looked pale and pinched, but she managed a tight-lipped smile when Ellen leaned to kiss her.

"I started a fire," Ellen told her father. "Maybe she could stay down here until after dinner."

"Better yet, let's just eat in here," her mother suggested as her father set Robin on the divan in front of the fireplace. "We're only having pizza anyway. We'll pretend it's a picnic."

They had just cleared the dishes away when Cricket came in with cupcakes she had baked herself. They looked like Christmas with green candy trees sticking straight up out of the white frosting. "They're chocolate inside," Cricket told Robin. "I just make them out of cake mix, but Jason likes them fine."

"I'd love coming by to help you with schoolwork,"

Cricket offered, plopping down on the floor beside Robin.

"Oh, but I can't stay away from school!" Robin cried, looking at her, horrified.

"It's only three weeks until Christmas vacation," her mother told her. "That's not a whole lot to make up when you're back up on your feet again."

"My feet are fine," Robin wailed. "It's only my leg I broke. You watch, I'll do great on crutches. And Ellen can drive me back and forth. Oh, Mom, please don't make me stay home and miss school!"

"I think Robin's right," Ellen's father said, nodding. "She would just be miserable around here at home. She'd have to have someone here with her and she'd miss the Christmas party and all that stuff she's so crazy about. And that doesn't count her schoolwork. Ellen, you wouldn't mind taking her to school and picking her up, would you?"

Ellen shook her head. "You know I'd be happy to drive her."

Cricket ran her fingers down the long white cast. "And I bet Ellen could really decorate that cast up fine for Christmas," she said. "You'd be the hit of your class."

Robin's eyes glistened. "Could you, Ellen? Would you? I need a Christmas tree painted on it. With balls. You only need to paint twenty-eight balls on it. No, twenty-nine, counting the teacher."

Ellen's mother rolled her eyes up and then laughed. "Come on, troops. Can't we think of more jobs to dump on Ellen? Maybe she could write all your classmates names on the ornaments?"

"Oh, no," Robin said, shaking her head. "Everybody gets to sign his own ornament. Don't you think that would be beautiful?"

"Different," her mother said. She looked at Ellen and sighed. "How do you always manage to get the short end of everything around here?"

Ellen laughed. "Just lucky, I guess. But I really don't mind. Anyway, it's only three weeks until vacation. Robin and I can manage without half trying."

"Thank goodness for that wonderful driver's license of yours," Ellen's mother said. "I hate always leaning on you, but it saves my life."

Within days Robin was buried in get-well cards. Although she looked like a waif swinging out on her Christmas tree crutches, she only missed one day of school.

"That's what I call game," her father said proudly.

Ellen was game, too, but she simply couldn't find enough hours in her days. By the time she drove Robin back and forth, did her own schoolwork, and got supper started every evening, she went to bed wiped out. It wasn't that nobody wanted to help her, it just wasn't possible. With her father traveling, her mother buried in year-end accounting, and Brad working every day in the Loop, Ellen was it. Alec grumbled a little when she checked out of the Christmas events at school, and said no to all the parties that came along, but he really understood.

Her mother kept worrying that Ellen wasn't having any fun.

"I get to decide what's fun for me," Ellen told her. "If it's okay, I want to give a little party for Cricket before she takes off for Wyoming."

"That's a great idea," her mother said.

"I get to come, too," Robin put in quickly.

Ellen nodded. "Sure you do. I thought maybe we'd do chili or pizza by the fire. I'd just ask Cricket and Jason, and Luke and Linda, too. And Robin and I, of course."

"What about Alec?" her mother asked.

Ellen shook her head. "It's not his kind of party. Anyway, it's mostly for Cricket before she leaves for Wyoming." She grinned at her mother. "This is the first time Cricket has ever gone off and left a boyfriend. They ought to be cute that night."

"You sound like somebody's grandmother," her mother said, laughing.

"Sometimes I feel that way," Ellen told her. She certainly felt a lot older than Cricket and Luke, that was for sure. For one thing, their feelings were out in the open while hers were a painful secret.

Michael Tyler's name hadn't been mentioned in her house since he left for Princeton in the fall. But that hadn't kept Ellen from thinking about him. When Brad came home for his college break, Ellen thought about Michael. He was either already here in town, or coming. The last thing she wanted was for her mother to realize how important it was for her to avoid being places where she would run into him or see him.

"Everything fades with time," Brad had said. She was the only one who knew how little the passing of all that time had faded her memories of Michael. Or how little it had changed her yearning to see him. The first snow had only strengthened her longing and deepened her memories.

The party was wonderful. Cricket looked beautiful. She had pulled her ponytail back with a little chain of sleigh bells that tinkled when she moved her head. Either she had been experimenting with makeup or the excitement of the party had brought a rosy blush to her cheeks.

Luke and Linda sat so close together that Ellen wondered how they could eat. As she refilled Luke's chili bowl, she leaned down to him and whispered, "Lovebirds make me barf." He stuck his tongue out at her. But he laughed.

Once Ellen's father's out-of-town travel was over, and school was out, she had no responsibilities in the evenings. The freedom was delicious. Driving out alone with no deadline for her return brought the same heady sense of belonging to herself that came when she was running well. She'd had plenty of time to make good shopping lists, complete with where she could probably find things. It was wonderful to prowl through the stores by herself until they closed for the night or she ran out of things to buy.

A fresh snow was predicted on one of Ellen's last possible nights for shopping. Ellen was waiting to leave when her mother got home from work. "I'll only be in Oakbrook," she told her mother. "And I'll come right home if a storm starts."

"But what about your supper?" her mother asked.

"I'll catch something at the mall or have a sandwich when I get home," Ellen told her. "I'm so close to being through, and shopping is really fun this year."

Oakbrook Shopping Center was glorious with Christmas. The music was muted and the greenery brilliant with lights. It was hard to pass the windows of a single store without stopping to look. She had found the book she wanted for Luke and a leather purse-sized photo album for her mother, when the snow began.

She left the bookstore as the first lazy flakes of the fresh snow began to drift past the roofs of the stores. She looked up, tasting the coolness on her face. When the snow began to fall more thickly, and the crowd grew thinner, she sighed. It wasn't that she didn't want to be at home, it was more that being almost alone there with the snow made Michael feel very close.

While she was sure in her heart that she was home free from what Luke called her "obsession" with Michael Tyler, she was equally certain that fresh snow would always remind her of him.

But she would just have to deal with that. As she maneuvered her car out of its parking space, she thought about college. There had to be a good art school somewhere that she would never have to see snow. Florida, maybe, or even the southwestern desert out where Scott had come from.

Snow piled up along the struggling windshield wipers. She had to squint a little to see her way through the steadily deepening whiteness between the indistinct streetlights.

By the time she reached her own street, she breathed a sigh of relief to have made it home at last. She had to concentrate to keep her foot off the brake pedal as she steered around the car parked across the street from their house. Once in the driveway, she sat a moment just catching her breath behind the wheel.

With her parka hood up, she got out to unload her packages from the trunk. The next problem was to get them past Robin's curious eyes until she had a chance to wrap them.

She had piled the last of the packages on the top of the car when she heard a familiar voice call her name softly. She turned and closed her eyes a moment before being able to breathe.

Michael.

Michael, with his hands in his jacket pockets was standing in the snowy driveway grinning at her. "I didn't startle you, did I?" Those were the exact words he had said to her, all those years ago when she met him for the very first time.

"When I called, your father said you were shopping," he went on with that veil of snow steadily falling between them. "I drove over to wait for you."

He reached for the bundles from the top of the car. "Here, let me help you with those." Then he smiled over the pile he was holding. "Brad came in while I was waiting out here. He looks great, just like always. He invited me in but I told him I'd just wait for you. I didn't want you to turn me down for a ride in the snow and dinner in front of your whole family." He grinned. "You know how much we men hate being publicly embarrassed."

She didn't realize she was shaking her head at him until he quit smiling. He was just looking at her, his expression strange, as if he were puzzled or maybe hurt. "Come on, Ellen," he said quietly. "Don't you think somebody needs to go out there and check on how the snow looks, falling into Salt Creek?"

Ellen was too stunned to protest. Anyway, he had taken her arm with his free hand and was leading her toward the front door.

Under the porch light he turned to her. "Should I ring or do we just go in?"

When she reached for the doorknob, he beat her to it, then stepped back as she entered the hall. In spite of all that had gone on in the past few weeks, the house was Christmas. The tree was up and decorated with bright packages piled under it. The hearth fire burned brightly under loops of greenery Ellen had draped along the mantel. The bayberry candles in the dining room bay window perfumed the air, and Tawny was curled on the round rug in front of the fire.

Ellen's father rose from the wing chair by the hearth, his hand out to Michael. "Well," he said. "Good evening. Michael, isn't it?"

Ellen couldn't look at her mother or Brad.

"I thought you were going to freeze out there before Ellen made it home," Brad said.

"It's not as cold as it is snowy," Michael said. Then he looked at Robin's leg, propped on the footstool in front of the divan. "What have we here?" he asked. "Your own private Christmas tree?"

Robin giggled and turned the cast so he could see it better.

"I can't believe that," he said, reading the names with a look of horror. "Don't tell me that Mrs. Bartlett is still teaching!"

Robin giggled again and nodded at him.

"But how did your leg get broken anyway?"

"A horse rode into me," Robin told him.

He stared at her, and whistled. "Boy, am I ever glad it was your leg instead of his!" he said very seriously. "They shoot horses, you know."

Robin was still giggling when Michael turned toward Ellen's mother. "I'm not absolutely sure," he said. "But I think I've talked Ellen into a drive and supper with me. I hope that's all right with you?"

Ellen watched her mother lift her chin, catch a

small breath, then nod the faintest bit. "You will be careful," she said in a defeated tone. "The weather report was really quite threatening."

"No way would I take any chances," he said, taking Ellen's arm.

At the door he paused and smiled back at the family. "Have a nice evening," he said and winked at Robin. Ellen could still hear her funny little giggle as Michael closed the door behind them.

Chapter 36

The air was warm inside the car and smelled of leather and some kind of Christmas greenery, maybe balsam. Ellen felt Michael turn to look at her in the dark. "Do you want to go for dinner first or shall we go look at the snow?"

What was she doing to herself? Did she have some kind of selective amnesia that when she was with him she couldn't remember the pain of *not* being with him? She should just tell him that she wasn't going, right out. She didn't have to do this to herself one more time. Instead she made the decision he was waiting for. "Snow," she said.

"Good," he said. "And we'll see at least a hundred Christmas cards on the way. You can't imagine how I miss this town when I'm off at school."

He drove slowly, his tires crunching and squeaking on the freshly packed snow. The limbs of the giant fir trees along the old brick streets were weighted down under deep blankets of snow. The oak trees, barren of leaves, wore frosting on every twig and branch.

The entrances of almost all the houses were outlined by colored lights. The fused brilliance of trimmed trees glowed behind downstairs windows. At the next corner he turned. "Aha," he said. "I was afraid these people would let me down."

He stopped in front of a huge three-story square house set back behind its circle drive. Tiny candlelights shone in every window and the twin juniper trees by the front door looked like traps for stars with their abundance of tiny clear lights.

"They've put candles in all those windows ever since I was a little kid carrying newspapers along this street," Michael told Ellen. "Aren't they something?"

When she nodded, he turned to her. "If you get cold, my hooded parka is in the backseat, but I have to roll the window down to show you this next house."

When delicate flakes of snow spun in through her window, Ellen reached in the back as he had suggested. He shifted into neutral and parked a moment to free his hands so he could drape the huge down parka around her.

He drove a half block and stopped again. "Now," he said with barely suppressed excitement. "Smell."

When she breathed deeply, the scent of fragrant wood smoke filled her head. It was almost like a perfume. She leaned to stare at the house whose chimney fed lazy whirls of smoke through the falling snow.

"Cedar," he said. "Did you ever smell anything

more like Christmas? I used to just about go crazy when I walked by here when I was a kid. I couldn't stand it until I found out why this house smelled better than any other place in town."

He smiled as she looked over at him.

"The answer is almost as good as the smell," he told her. "This family owns a Christmas tree farm up in Michigan. They collect the cedar trimmings for their fireplaces all year long."

There truly were a hundred Christmas cards glowing along the town's quiet streets. It even sounded like Christmas with scraps of carols drifting through the crisp air. When they crossed the arched wooden bridge above the railway tracks, the cold boards chattered under the car's wheels.

"Have we missed any of your favorites?" he asked, looking over at her.

"One," she admitted. "You need to turn right on Oak Street and go about three blocks."

"Why is it special?"

"You look and see if you can guess," she told him.

Whoever lived in the Georgian brick house was giving a party. Cars were lined up clear to the corners on both sides of the street. When Michael slowed down with the car windows still open, music came faintly from the brilliantly lit house.

Michael leaned over Ellen to stare at the house. When he was that close, she caught the faint smell of after-shave lotion and the scent of his skin. Then he let out a slow breath. "I don't believe it. Look at those icicles."

Ellen laughed softly. "Aren't they wonderful?"

Giant glistening pillars of smooth ice extended down along the entire length of the roof. They glistened from the lighted windows behind them. They looked more like crystal columns than icicles, glittering columns holding up the huge house under its snow-capped chimneys.

"Home-grown stalactites," Ellen said. "Or is it stalagmites?"

He shook his head. "That's fantastic. What causes that?"

"I'm not sure you want to know," she said. "The reason isn't as wonderful as your answer about the cedar-smelling smoke. Brad says it's only a badly insulated roof. Snow melts up there from the heat escaping through the attic. The melted snow water drips into those icicles. Trust an engineer to cut the fantasy down to size."

Michael laughed, then shook his head. "Never mind. If I owned that house, I'd think it was worth the monster fuel bills to look out at winter through that cage of icicles."

After the charm of those well-loved houses, the downtown decorations looked stupid and commercial as they passed through the business section. Only a mile or so further, Michael left the car on a safety pullout by the roadside. They walked onto the bridge silently. Ellen was warm inside his immense parka and he gripped her hand firmly as they slipped and slid along on the fresh snow.

They stopped at the center of the bridge to look

down. Salt Creek wound along lazily, it's black surface studded with small floes of ice. The trees along the banks were weighted down with white as they leaned into that flowing darkness. Snowflakes spun dizzily all around them, either piling the ice floes higher or diving into the water to lose their brightness and disappear.

Michael reached over and fitted Ellen's hand inside his glove with his own. "I want to tell you about a girl, Ellen," he said, his tone very hesitant and uncertain.

She felt her breath catch in her throat and sudden hot tears burn behind her eyes. He must have felt her flinch because he tightened his hand on hers. "No," he said, "Don't pull away. I *have* to tell you about this girl."

The warmth that had seemed to seep from the parka at his first words came back only slowly as he kept on talking.

"She was tall and really slender without looking breakable. Her hair was like a reddish blonde cloud around the most interesting face I had ever seen. Blue eyes, very dark, and a wide smiling mouth with no secrets in it."

As he kept talking, his tone lightened. She didn't look at him but could tell he was smiling anyway. "I told myself I was completely bonkers to think that way about a fourteen-year-old kid. A sane guy doesn't look at somebody's kid sister that way, wanting to know all about her, what her favorite colors were, how she liked to spend her time, even what she liked to eat. I had an hour with her. It wasn't even a whole hour actually, only fifty-five stinking minutes. Then she went off into being what she had to be, and I had to go, too."

Ellen had closed her eyes against the tears. What was he doing to her? Did he have any idea how much pain she'd gone through because of that — what was it — fifty-five minutes?

"So I made a deal with myself," he went on. "I intended to stay friends with that girl until we were both grown-up. Then I could talk to her all the hours I wanted to, know everything about her. I promised myself I wouldn't make any moves on her at all. I wasn't even going to let her know how I felt about her or how much it meant to me every time I even saw her from a distance. I was just going to stay friends with her and nothing more.

"And don't think I didn't try to break her spell over me. I dated other girls and tried to feel the same way about them. All this time I kept treating her like a friend and her brother's little sister. I slipped badly only a couple of times, once that night I kissed her after she and I had been here at the bridge. Then again when I gave it away to her in the library that I watched her and cared about what she was doing. But that kiss had stayed with me all the way back to Connecticut that semester that I had to leave Jefferson. And that afternoon in the library I felt that if I didn't get even a little bit of time with her, I would go nuts. Does this story ring any bells for you, Ellen?"

She nodded. She couldn't believe he was saying these things. She had dreamed of this, but now she felt a little anger, too. How could he have put her through these years of anguish and now just assume she would fall into his arms? But he didn't give her a chance to say anything. He just went on. His pale face almost broke her heart.

"I figured that when I got back, I would discover that she was just another pretty girl and I'd quit brooding about her. But what do you know? When I came back and realized that I hadn't regained my sanity, I told myself she couldn't possibly be the only girl for me.

"What kind of a hermit could I be for the rest of high school and all of college? Then I met a great girl who was as crazy about her as I was. She had the same kind of class and sometimes even reminded me of you. You wouldn't believe how long it took Valerie and me to realize that the big thing we had in common was you? We even laughed about it when she told me about her boyfriend back in California.

"Val swore she'd never give my secret away and she's enough like you that I trusted her. You'll never know how much I wanted to dance with you when you showed up at that prom with Ollie Samson. Val convinced me that it wouldn't be fair to either of us. But how could Val or anybody compete with the girl who had meant Christmas to me all those years that didn't have any other holidays in them because of her? I first danced with you on Christmas, Ellen. I first kissed you on Christmas.

I skated with you under the stars on Christmas. Then I waited all year for this Christmas."

She shook her head, not caring that hot tears burned her cheeks, "You should have told me sooner. I've loved you so long," she cried.

"Do you really?" he cried. "I thought so, I hoped so, but I couldn't risk finding out for sure.

"I've got to finish this while I still have guts for it, Ellen," he said, his voice suddenly a little hoarse. He pulled her into his arms.

"I'm still young and you're still younger, but we're gaining on it. I'm so far away off at college and in another year you will be, too. I just wanted to be sure you knew how I felt, even if I was still in the dark about your feelings for me."

She pulled away from him and took his face in both her hands. But she hadn't figured that standing on her tiptoes in boots in the snow was some kind of a gymnastic trick all by itself. She slipped a little and he caught her, holding her very close and warm for a long moment. When he released her, she found his mouth with hers. When they finally pulled apart, he hugged her so tight that for a minute she couldn't even breathe.

"We have so much time to make up," she said.

"Boy, I never mean to go through anything that tough again as long as I live," Michael said.

"I hope you don't have to," she whispered. "I'm not even sure I could take going through any three years of my life as painful as the last three."

"Then I wasn't just in this by myself?" he asked,

as if needing to be reassured over and over.

"Not for one moment," she whispered.

He laughed and hugged her. "Ellen, I love you with all my heart. I get to say it right out loud after all this time! I may even shout it!"

Then he did shout it at the top of his lungs so loudly that Ellen, laughing, covered her ears against the sound. That sudden blast of noise in the still air trembled the branches of the overloaded trees, sending clumps of snow plummeting into the dark spinning water.

They both laughed then, and he put his arm around her to walk back to the car. "Are you as hungry as I am?" he asked.

"Starving!" she told him.

"I know a place that makes great pasta," he said. "That's white food, you know."

Later she didn't remember all the things they talked about. What she did remember was how much laughter there was and how much feeling there was between them.

They were friends who loved each other, and they had all the time in the world to see what came of that. But for now, they had the rest of this Christmas season to spend together, to make memories for the next time.

Finally their waiter pointed out that the restaurant was empty and had been for twenty minutes because that was when the place was supposed to have closed down for the night.

"Can I just give her her Christmas present?"

Michael asked the waiter. "Then I promise we'll clear out."

The box was about six inches square, and heavy. The waiter craned his neck to watch as Ellen undid the ribbon.

What a crybaby she had gotten to be! She had to blink back tears as she pulled out the paperweight. The tiny snow maiden with the fur hat and muff almost disappeared when Ellen set the snow to whirling around her. "Michael, I love it," she whispered. "You remembered."

"Everything," he said, tightening his hand over hers. He rose and put a tip on the table. "Everything. Every word. Every minute." He smiled, pulling her to her feet. "And that, sweet Ellen, is only the beginning."

The waiter called out Merry Christmas as he locked the door behind them.

"Little does he know," Michael told Ellen as he tucked her into the car and plowed around to his side through the deepening snow.

About the Author

MARY FRANCIS SHURA was the author of sixty-nine books, including *The Josie Gambit*, an ALA Notable; *The Search for Grissi*, recipient of a Carl Sandburg Literary Arts Award for Children's Literature; and *Chester* and *Eleanor*, IRA-CBC Joint Committee Children's Choices.

Ms. Shura wrote several other novels including *Kate's Book*, *Kate's House*, *Jessica*, and *The Mystery at Wolf River*.